Praise

AIRTIGHT

"The tension is palpable, and the pages fly by in this riveting stand-alone thriller . . . The voice here is every bit as engaging as in the Carpenter novels, with enough humor to lighten the story without diminishing the suspense. And the ending is a real shocker. Sure to appeal to fans of Harlan Coben and Robert Crais." —*Booklist*

"As usual, there is plenty of irony, humor, suspense, and affection here . . . Rosenfelt is, indeed, one of a kind; you will burn through this novel—like all his others— non-stop and totally rapt. It's an airtight cinch."

—Examiner.com

"Perfectly controlled suspense." —*Kirkus Reviews*

"Keep[s] you on the edge of your seat."

—*Criminal Element*

HEART OF A KILLER

"A full-blown suspense chiller." —*Publishers Weekly*

"Rosenfelt has crafted another terrific thriller that will keep the reader up late at night." —*Huffington Post*

"Warmhearted, satisfyingly inventive, and almost too clever for its own good. Why isn't Rosenfelt a household name like Michael Connelly and Jeffery Deaver?"

—*Kirkus Reviews*

More . . .

ON BORROWED TIME

"An absolutely irresistible hook . . . No one who picks up this greased-lightning account will rest till it's finished." —*Kirkus Reviews* (starred review)

"Outstanding . . . Anyone who enjoyed Dennis Lehane's *Shutter Island* will love this thriller."
—*Library Journal* (starred review)

"Excellent. All will marvel at the way Rosenfelt builds suspense." —*Publishers Weekly* (starred review)

DOWN TO THE WIRE

"Dynamite . . . Sly humor, breathless pacing, and terrific plot twists keep the pages spinning toward the showdown." —*Publishers Weekly* (starred review)

"Rosenfelt's Andy Carpenter novels are known for their breezy storytelling and humor . . . This one eschews humor to focus on the actions of ordinary people faced with extraordinary trials. It also employs a whiplash plot turn . . . an engaging suspense tale." —*Booklist*

"A terrific plot and a gripping narrative." —*Toronto Sun*

"I am raving about this book . . . a page-turning thriller."
—*Deadly Pleasure*

DON'T TELL A SOUL

"Stellar . . . Rosenfelt keeps the plot hopping and popping as he reveals a complex frame-up of major proportions with profound political ramifications both terrifying and enlightening."   —*Publishers Weekly* (starred review)

"This fast-paced and brightly written tale spins along . . . *Don't Tell a Soul* is a humdinger."
                                               —*St. Louis Post-Dispatch*

"High-voltage entertainment from an author who plots and writes with verve and wit . . . Rosenfelt ratchets up tension with the precision of a skilled auto mechanic wielding a torque wrench."   —*Booklist* (starred review)

"Rosenfelt has earned his crime-novelist pedigree."
                                               —*Entertainment Weekly*

"He delivers a fast, inventive stand-alone thriller you'll never put down."   —*Kirkus Reviews*

"[Rosenfelt] has pulled together a cynical political thriller that rings true in this age of terrorism, media hype, and Washington scandals. . . . It's an enjoyable tale."   —*Minneapolis Star Tribune*

"Rosenfelt's first stand-alone novel is a riveting thriller that should boost him to bestseller status. . . . Compelling twists and turns, a lightning-fast pace, and breathtaking suspense make this a harrowing ride. . . . The book deserves a wide audience."

                                               —*Library Journal* (starred review)

ALSO BY DAVID ROSENFELT

AIRTIGHT

David Rosenfelt

St. Martin's Paperbacks

NOTE: If you purchased this book without a cover you should be aware that this book is stolen property. It was reported as "unsold and destroyed" to the publisher, and neither the author nor the publisher has received any payment for this "stripped book."

This is a work of fiction. All of the characters, organizations, and events portrayed in this novel are either products of the author's imagination or are used fictitiously.

AIRTIGHT

Copyright © 2013 by Tara Productions, Inc.
Excerpt from *Without Warning* copyright © 2013 by Tara Productions, Inc.

All rights reserved.

For information address St. Martin's Press, 175 Fifth Avenue, New York, NY 10010.

Library of Congress Catalog Card Number: 2012038714

ISBN: 978-1-250-04076-3

Printed in the United States of America

St. Martin's Press hardcover edition / February 2013
St. Martin's Paperbacks edition / November 2013

St. Martin's Paperbacks are published by St. Martin's Press, 175 Fifth Avenue, New York, NY 10010.

10 9 8 7 6 5 4 3 2

This book is dedicated to Pete Souza. Not just because he's a good friend, and not just because he and Darlene run the great Damariscotta Lake Farm Restaurant. Rather, it's because he is a true American hero.

The tabloids called it "The Judge-sicle Murder."

It was a ridiculous name for an event so horrific and tragic, but it sold newspapers, and generated web hits, so it stuck.

In the immediate aftermath, very little was known and reported in the media, so they compensated by detailing the same facts over and over. Judge Daniel Brennan had attended a charity dinner earlier that evening at the Woodcliff Lakes Hilton. Judge Brennan generally avoided those types of events whenever he could, but in this case felt an obligation.

The Guest of Honor was Judge Susan Dembeck, who was at that point a sitting judge on the bench of the Second Circuit Court of Appeals. Since Judge Brennan's nomination to that court was before the Senate and he was replacing the retiring Judge Dembeck, he made the obvious and proper decision to support his future predecessor by attending the event.

Others at the dinner estimated that Judge Brennan left at ten thirty, and that was confirmed by closed-circuit cameras in the lobby. He stopped at a 7-Eleven, five minutes from his Alpine, New Jersey, home, to buy a few minor items. The proprietor of the establishment, one Harold Murphy, said that Judge Brennan was a frequent patron of the store. He said it on the *Today* show the following morning, in what the network breathlessly promoted as an exclusive interview, which aired seven minutes before *Good Morning America*'s breathlessly promoted exclusive interview with Mr. Murphy.

Among the items that Murphy described Judge Brennan as buying was a Fudgsicle. It was, he said, one of the Judge's weaknesses, regardless of the season. As was the Judge's apparent custom, Murphy said that he started opening the Fudgsicle wrapper while walking to the door, such was his desire to eat it. Murphy seemed to cite this as evidence that the Judge was a "regular guy."

Murphy didn't mention, and wasn't asked, the time that Judge Brennan arrived at the store. It was eleven forty-five, meaning the ten-minute drive from hotel to store had apparently taken an hour and fifteen minutes.

It was ten minutes after midnight when Thomas Phillips, who lived four doors down from Judge Brennan, walked by the Judge's house with his black Lab, Duchess. In that affluent neighborhood, four doors down meant there was almost a quarter mile of separation between the two homes.

The Judge's garage door was open, and his car was sitting inside, with its lights on. This was certainly an unusual occurrence, and Phillips called out the Judge's name a few times. Getting no response, he walked towards the garage.

In the reflected light off the garage wall, he could see the Judge's body, covered in blood that was slowly making its way towards where Phillips was standing. The Fudgsicle, melting but with the wrapper around the stick, was just a few inches from the victim's mouth, a fact that Phillips related when he gave his own round of exclusive interviews.

The murder of a judge would be a very significant story in its own right, especially when the victim was up for a Court of Appeals appointment. But the fact that this particular judge was "Danny" Brennan elevated it to a media firestorm.

Brennan was forty-two years old and a rising star in the legal system. It was a comfortable role for him to play, as he had considerable experience as a rising star.

He was a phenom as a basketball player at Teaneck High School, moving on to Rutgers, where he earned first-team All America status. Rather than head to the NBA as a first-round draft choice after one season, which he could certainly have done, he chose instead to stay all four years. He then pulled a "Bill Bradley," and went on to Oxford as a Rhodes scholar.

When his studies had concluded, he finally moved on to the NBA, and within two years was the starting point guard for the Boston Celtics. It was during a play-off game against the Orlando Magic that on one play he cut right, while his knee cut left. He tore an ACL and MCL, which pretty much covers all the "CLs" a knee contains, and despite intensive rehab for a year and a half, he was never the same.

Confronted with physical limitations but no mental ones, Daniel Brennan went to Harvard Law, and began a rapid rise up the legal ladder.

A rise that ended in a garage, in a pool of blood and melted Fudgsicle.

"I can't make it tonight," I said.

I'm sure that my brother, Bryan, heard the news while lying in bed, because his response sounded a little groggy. "And you woke me at seven o'clock in the morning to tell me that?"

"I feel terrible about that, especially since I've been up all night. Don't you work?"

"It's Saturday, big brother."

"You don't rip off the indigent on Saturdays?" I asked, unable to help myself. It wasn't that I lacked respect for Bryan's position as an investment banker; the truth was I really didn't even understand what it involved. But it made for an easy target.

"It's way too early for occupational banter," Bryan said. "Sorry you can't join us." Bryan certainly couldn't have been surprised that I was backing out of the dinner; my cancellation rate had to be well over sixty percent. He continued. "Julie will be disappointed."

"No she won't," I said, without much conviction. As always, it was impossible for me to have any idea what

Julie might be thinking, which was unfortunate, because it was probably the thing I involuntarily pondered most.

In my mind's eye I could see Bryan turning over in bed and talking to his wife, who herself I'm sure was just waking up. She was wearing a white nightgown, low at the neckline. My mind's eye often has a very specific imagination. "Julie, Lucas can't make dinner," Bryan said. "Are you disappointed?"

"Of course."

Bryan spoke back into the phone. "You were right; she's delighted you're not coming. What's going on, Lucas? Why can't you make it?"

Bryan was one of the few people on the planet who called me Lucas; to my friends and coworkers I was "Luke"; to people I arrested I was "asshole." "Lucas" sounded formal, which I suppose made sense, since my brother is way more proper than I am. I almost expected him to call me by the name our parents stuck me with, Lucas Isaiah Somers.

"You didn't hear what happened?" I asked.

"When?"

"Last night, just before midnight."

"I went to sleep at ten thirty," he said.

"Danny Brennan was murdered."

Bryan went silent, probably mentally replaying his connections to Judge Brennan in his mind. Then, "I didn't know him that well, just met him at a few charity dinners, but I liked him. This is awful. Is anyone in custody?"

"No." I could hear him, in the background, telling Julie what had happened.

"Julie wants to know if it's your case."

It's the exact question I knew she would ask, especially since it might wind up her case as well as a prosecutor. "Technically, but not that anyone would notice. Every FBI agent in the United States is either here or on the way.

Apparently, when the President appoints a judge to the Appeals Court, the plan is that they are supposed to remain alive."

"So you local hicks should stick to traffic tickets and picking up jaywalkers?"

"Not according to the Captain, which brings me back to why I can't make dinner tonight."

"OK. Good luck," Bryan said. Then, "How did he die?"

"Stabbed to death in his garage when he got home. Thirty-seven wounds."

He paused again to relay the information to Julie, and I heard her say, "Sounds like he pissed off an amateur."

I knew exactly what she was talking about. Professional killers rarely used knives, and when they did they were precise and efficient. A blade in the heart, or a slice across the neck. Thirty-seven stab wounds meant the killer was an amateur and was venting fury. It was an emotional killing, or at least made to look like one.

I extricated myself from the call and walked over to the precinct meeting room. By that time the FBI had already assumed control of the investigation and had established a tip line. This was an irritant to my boss, Captain Charles Barone of the New Jersey State Police, though that in itself was hardly a news event. Not many days went by that something or someone didn't irritate Captain Charles Barone.

"We are going to catch this guy," is how he started the meeting he had called of the entire squad. That was no surprise; it was how he started pretty much every meeting about a specific case. But this time he doubled down. "All vacations are hereby canceled, and overtime is authorized and expected. We've got the home field advantage."

He was referring to the fact that we knew the terrain; we lived in it, while the Feds were visitors. It was bravado, and most of it was false. Everyone in the room, including

Barone, knew we were operating at a huge disadvantage. The FBI had taken over the crime scene, and was doing all the forensics. They would also be getting most of the tips, especially since a reward had already been established. It may have been our home field, but it felt like we were busing in from out of town.

Barone was right about one thing, though. Our connection to the area was a factor working in our favor. We had informants that we used with some frequency, and if those people had anything to share, they'd be leery of going to the Feds. They'd come to us, or they'd keep their mouths shut.

Assignments were given out, and I was chosen to lead the effort. I doubt if anyone was surprised by that, since even though I was one of four people at my rank, I was considered by most people to be the number two man in the department. Barone and I had worked together in one way or another for eleven of my sixteen years on the force, and he trusted me. Sometimes I wish he didn't; I'd get more sleep.

In any event, my position of leadership on this case was not something anyone would resent. Not only would my colleagues have expected it, but they'd be delighted they weren't stuck doing it.

The effort that I was going to lead would mostly include following up on those tips that were already coming in. It was a smaller amount than would usually be expected for a case that had generated this much publicity, a sure sign that most people were contacting the FBI. But some people still had it as their first instinct to call their local police, and those calls would be routed to us.

After the meeting, Barone called me into his office. "I just got off the phone with the Governor. He called me directly. He wants us to be the ones to catch this guy."

"Thanks for sharing that," I said. "Now I'm motivated."

"Don't be a wiseass, Somers. This is important."

"Right," I said. "The Governor wants to be President."

He nodded. "And the Captain wants to be chief."

I always found it refreshing that he acknowledged that, at least to me. He'd never say it to anyone else; it made me feel trusted. "So let's catch the prick," I said.

"Do we have a chance?" he asked.

"Zero."

He frowned. "That's not what I wanted to hear."

"Come on, the guy would have to fall in our lap."

"Did I mention that that was not what I wanted to hear?" he asked.

"OK, how's this? We'll get him, Captain. We're closing in on him right now."

"Good. That's what I told the Governor."

Sometimes, not often, an investigation just seems to fall into place.

This was one of those times.

The first thing I did was utilize the services of the state prosecutor's office to get a list of the cases Judge Brennan presided over in the last ten years. There are very few jobs someone can have that piss people off as effectively as judges, and sometimes the pissed-off parties have years to sit in a cell and plot revenge.

I had reached a level within the department where I didn't have a partner anymore, since most of my work was done on the inside, supervising other officers. This was a mixed blessing. On the minus side, I actually missed being on the street, closer to the action. The reason it was a mixed blessing was that sitting behind a desk significantly reduced the chance of my being shot at. Cops who are not in action are rarely killed in action.

For the Brennan case, I chose, if not a partner, then someone who I could count on to be a very willing, very competent slave. There would be quite a bit to delegate, and it was also my intention to go out on the street if a serious opportunity presented itself.

My choice was Emmit Jenkins, who at forty-eight years old had me by twelve years, and who at two hundred and sixty pounds had me by seventy-five pounds. Emmit was a walking contradiction; he was simultaneously the toughest, meanest, and most pleasant guy I've ever known.

Emmit was a twenty-two-year vet, and loved his job for every single minute of it. He had turned down four opportunities for promotions that I knew of, and probably as many more that I didn't. Emmit wanted to be where the danger and excitement was, and he excelled in those circumstances.

Emmit had the list of Brennan's cases, and therefore his potential enemies, within two hours of the request. The reason it was so quick, he informed me, was that the prosecutor's office had already prepared the same list for the FBI.

I went through the list personally, paying special attention to two groups. Those people who went to prison and got out in the past year were a priority, as were those who recently fared poorly in Brennan's court. Personally, if I were convicted of a felony, I'd be more pissed at the prosecutor, or witnesses, or jurors than at the judge, so I considered the revenge motive a long shot. But for the time being it was all we had.

As a Superior Court judge, Brennan handled a wide variety of cases, everything from high-level business fraud to low-level drug offenses. He had his share of violent crimes as well, four murders and thirty-one assaults, most of them armed, in the last five years. I instructed Emmit to find out which of the convicted defendants were out of jail.

Of course, even someone in jail could be responsible for planning the murder, since most violent felons didn't hang around with altar boys or the chess club before they went in. But we had to prioritize; if we went through the obvious candidates and got nothing, then we could widen our search. That's if the Feds hadn't already made an arrest.

There were four criminals who had been sentenced by Judge Brennan and released within the previous year. There were also five people, four males and a female, who were convicted in trials over which Brennan presided during the previous year, who were either out on bail, pending appeal, or awaiting sentencing. The most recent was a twenty-two-year-old named Steven Gallagher, a third offense for crack cocaine possession and use.

"Anything look promising to you?" I asked Emmit.

"Only one way to find out," he said. "Let's run 'em down."

That was Emmit's upbeat way of agreeing that nothing looked promising. "Go get 'em," I said.

"Who can I use?" he asked, meaning which detectives was I giving him permission to work with on this.

"Whoever the hell you want."

He thought for a few moments. "I want Garfield, Miller, Wallace, and Freeman."

"You've got Garfield, Miller, Wallace, and Freeman," I said. It may have sounded like a law firm, but they were actually four of our best officers.

Emmit went out to get started, but came back less than ten minutes later, not nearly enough time to have gotten started with Garfield and Miller, never mind Wallace and Freeman. "We may have something," he said.

"Talk to me."

"We got a tip on the hotline, anonymous, that ID'd a kid named Steven Gallagher as the killer. He's . . ."

"The user that Brennan was about to sentence," is how I finished his sentence.

"Right."

I didn't ask if the tip seemed reliable, since anonymous

tips were never reliable, except for the ones that were. They needed to be tracked down, and we were about to do just that with this one.

"Let's go," I said, standing up.

"We're on this one ourselves?" he asked.

"You got other plans?"

He grinned. "Sure don't."

We arranged for backup, and within ten minutes we were on our way to the address Gallagher had given the court. Much to my amazement, a case that had nowhere to go for us now looked to be very possibly promising.

Sometimes, not often, an investigation just seems to fall into place.

Chris Gallagher didn't need a travel agent to book his flight out of Afghanistan.

When you're Marine Force Recon on your third tour, and you're going on leave, there's no need to check expedia.com.

It was actually an emergency leave for Chris, to the extent that it hadn't been planned. But he had plenty of time accrued, and when events transpired as they did, his commanding officer expedited things and did not officially designate it as an emergency. It would have just meant more paperwork, while changing nothing.

The emergency was the arrest and subsequent conviction of Chris's brother, Steven, on a drug offense. He was a repeat offender, and this was simply another chapter in a life going downhill. Unfortunately, it was a life that Chris had spent years trying to protect.

Darlene and Walter Gallagher were killed in a car crash when Chris was fourteen and Steven was seven. The Gallaghers had never made out a will, but that was basically of no consequence, since they had no money and little of value.

The boys went to live with an aunt, an alcoholic who reacted to the added responsibility by significantly increasing her alcohol intake. Chris became the responsible adult in the house, and took it upon himself to watch out for his little brother.

For a while it went well, until real life got in the way. When Chris was twenty-three he enlisted in the Marines, and the plan was for Steven to follow suit two years later. But Chris was shipped overseas, and Steven quickly befriended the wrong people.

Chris tried repeatedly to intervene from a distance, and when he was able to get home on leave he sometimes took more forceful action. Once he arranged to be there instead of Steven when his dealer, known only to Steven as Nick, came by to drop off cocaine and collect his money.

Chris attempted to reason with Nick, proposing in a respectful manner that the man stop peddling drugs to his brother and in return Chris would continue to let Nick live. Nick was six foot four and two hundred twenty pounds, meaning he was three inches and thirty pounds larger than Chris. It was that difference in size, as well as a serious misjudgment of his potential opponent, that made Nick laugh in response to the threat.

Once he heard the dismissive laugh, there were a number of ways that Chris could have handled the matter. He could have put a bullet in Nick's brain, or slashed him across the throat with a knife, or broken his neck with his bare hands.

He chose option three.

He didn't do it in anger; Chris had lost the capacity to experience anything approaching rage in the mountains of Afghanistan. Instead he did it with dispassionate resolve, and a sense of justice that he realized was unique to himself. It was as if he watched himself do it, with a measure of approval, but felt neither triumph nor guilt afterwards.

Once Chris decided that something was right, or necessary, or both, then he did it and never, ever looked back. Nick deserved to die, so he had died, and his body was never found.

But Chris knew that there would be other dealers, each willing to take full advantage of his brother's human failings. There was a limit to how many necks Chris could break, especially since he was stationed so far away. So he tried to focus his efforts on helping Steven, rather than dispatching his suppliers and enablers.

He got him into therapy, once even a six-month program as an inpatient in a rehab facility. There were signs of hope, but months of positive progress would inevitably be undone by a single moment of weakness. And for Steven, weakness was always just around the corner.

The criminal justice system's built-in insensitivity made matters worse. It was not set up to recognize that Steven suffered from a disease, and a noncontagious one at that. It treated him as a criminal, though he was clearly the sole victim of his own "crime."

So it became a cycle of jail and rehab and progress and falling back, until the latest arrest and conviction. Judge Daniel Brennan had expressed a frustration and lack of patience with Steven, and had made it clear that he was going to sentence him to a prison term that would remove him as a problem for a very long period of time.

So now Chris was heading back home, not to pick up the pieces of Steven's life, and certainly not to put them back together. He was coming back to witness his own greatest failure.

The loss of his little brother.

Who never hurt anyone but himself.

Steven Gallagher lived in a basement apartment in Paterson, New Jersey.

It was on Vernon Avenue, in one of a dreary collection of box-like houses. They were relatively well kept; these houses likely assumed their dreary persona within an hour of the time they were built.

Emmit and I were going to be the point men; we drove through the neighborhood a few times to get the lay of the land. We'd be the ones to go in and do the actual questioning. We didn't have a search warrant with us, but one could be gotten quickly were Gallagher to prove uncooperative.

Such was the importance the department placed on this case that we had four officers with us as backup, positioned in the front and back of the house. We had no reason to believe yet that Gallagher might try to run, but if he did, he wouldn't make it fifty feet.

Emmit and I went to the front door of the house to speak to the owner, who the records showed lived on the first floor. The basement apartment had an entrance and windows only at the back, so there was no way Gallagher could have known we were there, if he was at home. But in any event, we had the back well covered.

The owner was not on the premises, and there was no reason for us to wait for him. "Let's go talk to our boy," I said, and Emmit radioed our plans to the backup officers. Emmit walked around the right side of the house to the back, and I approached from the left.

There was a door with a broken screen, beyond which there were three concrete steps down to another door. We drew our weapons and I opened the first door. I walked down the steps, while Emmit stayed at the top, which gave him a better view of the whole picture.

I knocked on the door. "Gallagher?" I called out, but got no response. "Gallagher?"

"Leave me alone!" finally came the answer from inside. "You said you wouldn't come back here!"

It was a voice filled with about as much stress as a voice could be filled with. "We're the police, Gallagher. We want to talk to you."

"NO! LEAVE ME THE HELL ALONE!"

The voice had become firmer, more decisive; this was not a guy who wanted to talk. Which, of course, made him a more interesting candidate for us to talk to.

I edged to the side of the door, in case he was planning to fire a bullet through it. "Open the door, Gallagher."

"No! I'm not going with you."

"Nobody's going anywhere. We just want to talk."

"LIAR!"

"This is not voluntary, Gallagher. We're going to talk; no reason to make this difficult. Nothing for you to worry about."

There was no reaction at all. In these cases talking is good, no matter what is said. Silence is not so good.

"Open the door, Gallagher."

Still no response. Emmit and I made eye contact, and

he spoke softly into the radio, alerting the backup officers that "we're going in. Suspect is present but uncooperative."

I edged up along the side of the door, reaching for the knob, but expecting it to be locked. It wasn't; it turned easily. This was the dangerous moment; there was no way to enter without being exposed, no matter how quickly we did so. If Gallagher had a gun, we had a problem.

I nodded to Emmit, and signaled that I would go first and he would follow. When one enters situations like this, the plan is not to saunter in saying, "Honey, I'm home." Even though there is effectively no chance for surprise, as much shock and chaos must be created as possible, to rattle the suspect.

So I slowly turned the knob, took a deep breath, threw the door open, and burst through, screaming. I felt Emmit barreling in behind me, screaming as well. When it comes to barreling and screaming, he makes me look like an amateur.

The room was sparsely furnished and dirty. A small kitchen table had partially eaten food on it, and the bed, which was more like a cot, had only a blanket, no sheets or pillow. There was a small television sitting on the floor, with a "rabbit ears" antenna, and there was a laptop computer next to it.

I didn't notice all these things until later, because my attention at that moment was on Steven Gallagher, sitting on the floor against the wall. More specifically, my attention was on his right hand, which was holding a gun, finger on the trigger.

It wasn't pointed at me, which at the moment did not provide me with that much comfort. I pointed my own gun at him and screamed, "Drop the weapon!"

He looked at me strangely, almost as if he was trying to understand what I was saying. I saw a look of pain on his face, misery like I don't think I have ever seen before, and I've seen a lot of it. Of course, everything I'm describing happened in a split second, so I could be wrong about all or part of it. But I don't think I am.

He didn't say anything, but he raised the gun. His finger was still on the trigger.

I didn't wait to see what he would do with it; I put three bullets into his chest, pinning him back to the wall. Which means I never got to find out what he was going to do with the gun.

The moment my weapon discharged, I was no longer involved in the investigation.

Instead I became a witness and had to relate in excruciating detail exactly what transpired. I also, in the minds of at least some members of the public, was about to become a suspect. I had killed a man, and the burden would be on me to show that it was a justifiable act.

Emmit called in the report, and the scene immediately became chaotic. Captain Barone arrived pretty much at the same time as the homicide detectives, which meant that he was monitoring the situation very closely. It was far more involvement than was typical for him, but then again, calls from the Governor about a case were rather rare.

After I had given the first of what would be a number of official statements, Barone came over to me. "You OK?" he asked.

I nodded. "Yeah." This was the first person I had ever killed; I had shot a previous suspect, but he was not badly wounded. I had even managed to serve in Iraq during Desert Storm without firing a weapon in anger.

I was feeling a little shaken by the experience, but I couldn't tell whether it was from having killed Gallagher or from the realization that I could have been killed myself.

"You did what you had to do," Barone said.

I nodded. "How come I don't see any FBI agents here?"

He snapped his fingers. "Damn. I knew I forgot something."

"You realize you're going to have to bring them in, right?"

He nodded. "Yeah. Once we have forensics that connect this to Brennan."

"Any indication of that so far?"

He nodded again. "Some bloody clothes in a plastic bag." Then he smiled about as wide as I've ever seen him smile. "Oh, I forgot. There was also a bloody knife in the bag."

I knew he had plenty of information to justify calling in the FBI, and so did he. He didn't even need the forensics; just the fact that we were acting on a tip that Gallagher killed Brennan was enough. "They're going to be pissed."

"Ask me if I give a shit," he said. "I don't answer to them. The President didn't call me; the Governor did."

"You da boss."

"Besides, they'll know by tomorrow morning either way."

"Why is that?" I asked.

"Because they'll see us on the *Today* show."

He wasn't kidding. The next morning a limousine was at my house at five thirty to take me into the city. Barone was already in the backseat waiting for me, wearing his Sunday best.

The publicity shit had hit the fan sometime during the night. Barone had alerted the Governor, the media, and the FBI, in that order. I was already being called a hero, which didn't thrill me and led me to believe that our hero standards are being lowered somewhat. I had shot a drug-addled kid sitting on the floor; that didn't exactly make me Davy Crockett defending the Alamo.

Lester Holt conducted the interview, which was fairly uncomfortable. He kept trying to talk to me, since I was the one who did the shooting, but Barone kept cutting in. It's not that he was imparting crucial information; he basically repeated the mantra that the investigation was ongoing, so there was very little we could say. If I were Holt, I would have asked that if there was nothing we could say, what the hell were we doing there? But he didn't.

Nor did anyone else, and there were plenty of opportunities. Barone had set up almost an entire day of news interviews, and we traveled from media location to media location, not answering the same questions, over and over again. It seems like half the people in this city are newscasters, while the other half somehow manages to have no idea what's going on in the world.

If I've ever spent a less productive or more annoying day, I can't remember when. Not only was no news being made, but the trappings were insufferable. For instance, each place insisted on applying makeup to our faces, even though it had already been applied repeatedly throughout the day. By the time we got to the fourth studio, I refused to allow it. Had I not, archaeologists would eventually have had to lead an expedition to dig down to my actual skin.

Barone handled it all with something between good cheer and outright jubilation. I wasn't quite feeling so happy, and it wasn't because of the pointless interviews. I had killed a young man, and it just didn't strike me as something to celebrate. It's not that I felt guilty about it; he had a gun and most likely would have killed me had I not shot first. My reaction was textbook police work, and would stand up to any scrutiny from anybody.

Gallagher also was likely the man who murdered Judge Brennan, so his removal from the planet was certainly not going to usher in a round of hand-wringing from me or anyone else. I expected I'd feel a little better when evidence tied him conclusively to the Brennan murder, but I was quite sure that it would. But for the moment, I was uncomfortable receiving plaudits for ending a young life.

I called my answering machine at home, and discovered it was filled. There were eighteen messages, mostly from people I worked with, calling to congratulate me, and inviting me to come down to the Crows Nest that night. It's the bar we always go to whenever there is something to celebrate, or whenever there isn't.

The only nonwork person who called was Linda Farmer, a girlfriend I had broken up with two weeks before. She hadn't seemed that devastated by the breakup at the time, perhaps because we dated less than a month. But apparently my new hero status was motivation for her to try and resurrect the relationship.

I decided that I'd go to the office and do more of the mountain of paperwork that I would have to fill out. Then I'd go home . . . no ex-girlfriends and no celebrating that night. Just me and a frozen pizza.

It was while I was at my desk that Lieutenant Billy Heyward called me. He had been assigned to take over my supervision of the case, now that I had become a key player by shooting the suspect. Billy was a good friend, and a very good cop.

"There's something I think you should know," Billy said. "They found a note."

I knew instantly what he meant, but I confirmed it anyway. "A suicide note?"

"Yeah," he said. "Looks like you may have done him a favor."

"Did the note mention Brennan?"

"No. Boilerplate 'my life isn't worth living' kind of stuff. He wrote it to his brother; said: 'Sorry I couldn't be more like you.'"

"Have you found the brother yet?" I asked.

"Working on that now. He's a Marine in Afghanistan."

I got off the phone and thought about what this meant. I couldn't get away from the realization that it was entirely possible that Steven Gallagher was raising the gun to shoot himself in the head, before I made that unnecessary. He certainly looked like he was in the kind of pain that made that possibility credible.

None of this made him less likely to have killed Judge Brennan; if anything it probably argued for his guilt. And it certainly didn't make my claim of self-defense any less justified, at least not to the legal system. Unfortunately, it did make it less justified to me, even though I believed at the time that I was about to get shot at.

I changed my mind, and as soon as I finished the paperwork I headed out to join my friends at the bar.

Not because I wanted to celebrate.

Because I wanted to drink.

The C-130 landed at McGuire AFB at one thirty in the afternoon.

Chris Gallagher got off the plane refreshed and well rested, having slept a good portion of the way. It was a trait common to Force Recon Marines, that branch's version of the Navy Seals and Army Green Berets. They had the ability to sleep whenever and wherever the opportunity presented itself. In their line of work, there was no way to know when the next chance would come.

Of course, sleeping on the plane did not require any special talent or training. There was absolutely nothing else to keep him occupied or entertained, not even conversation, since all of his fellow travelers were asleep as well.

Chris expected to hitch a ride with someone towards New York City. There were always people heading that way from McGuire; New York was the obvious first choice for soldiers coming home from Afghanistan. It was the anti-Kabul.

It turned out that Chris didn't have to look around for a ride. Waiting for him was Laura Schmitz, his brother Steven's ex-girlfriend. Chris had called and told her he was coming home, but she hadn't mentioned that she would meet his flight, and he certainly had no reason to expect that she would.

Laura and Steven had broken up two years before, but she remained his friend, and good friends were what he needed as much as anything. She was always there for him, but like Chris, she was ultimately powerless to help him turn his life around. She and Chris kept in contact because of their shared caring for Steven, and while they celebrated his successes, they more often commiserated about his inevitable setbacks.

Laura looked pained and upset, no surprise to Chris, since Steven was in such serious trouble. "Thanks, but you didn't have to come," Chris said.

"Yes, I did," Laura said, in a tone that sent a cold chill through him.

"What's wrong?"

"In the car. Please," she said, and they walked out of the building and into the parking lot.

There was absolutely no doubt in his mind that her first words when they got into the car would be, "Steven is dead." He had been dreading the words, but knowing that he would hear them, for years.

What he did not expect was her next sentence: "The police shot him."

It didn't compute. A drug overdose, that was the most likely cause. Suicide, as horrible as that was to contemplate, was always a possibility, when the pain became too much.

But shot by the police? How could that be? Steven was completely nonviolent, dangerous to no one but himself. Chris had time to speculate while Laura was crying, and the most likely scenario he could come up with was that Steven had been caught in the middle of a drug shoot-out between the cops and his dealer.

He wasn't even close.

"They shot him in his apartment," Laura said. "They said he was holding the gun when they came in."

They both knew that Steven only had a gun at Chris's insistence. In the neighborhood that he lived in, Chris felt it was necessary. But it was another example of Chris's futility in trying to protect his brother; Steven had once admitted that he usually kept it unloaded.

"Tell me everything you know," he said.

"There's a judge, Judge Brennan, who was murdered; I think just a couple of days ago. He's the one who was going to sentence Steven. For some reason they thought that Steven committed the murder, so they went to his apartment. The cop who did it said he had the gun, and that he shot Steven in self-defense. They're calling him a hero. But he's lying, Chris. The person he's describing is not Steven."

"Let's go to your apartment."

Chris said little during the ride. He had already pushed the pain and sense of loss at least temporarily to the side, as he was trained to do. That training led him to instead plan and focus on the mission, even though he was not yet sure what the mission would be. But one thing was certain; he was not going to simply accept his brother's death and head back to Afghanistan.

What he needed was information, much more than Laura could provide. And much easier to gather than most people might realize.

He had brought a computer with him; it went with him everywhere. His specialty, before he went Force Recon, was in communications, which in the modern military was totally computer driven.

Gallagher sat down with the computer in front of the TV set in Laura's apartment and got to work. It was even easier than he thought. Biographical information on Lieutenant Lucas Somers was plentiful; he had won a series of awards and commendations, and each story about them went on at length about his background.

Within a few minutes Chris knew Lucas Somers's life story, knew that his parents were deceased, that he had a brother who worked as an investment banker on Wall Street, and a sister-in-law who was a prosecuting attorney. He even had pictures of everyone, and committed them to memory. This was not a time for mistaken identity.

Amazingly, Somers's phone number wasn't even unlisted, so Chris had that as well, though there was no address shown.

The newscasts left little doubt as to how the police operation took place. Somers led a team into Steven's apartment and gunned him down. They had little interest in taking him alive; all they wanted was the kill and the subsequent glory, so that they could make their victory tour on television the next day.

Chris had all he could do not to focus on what must have been going through Steven's mind as his killers entered the apartment. He knew the intense fear he must have been feeling, with no one, especially not his brother, there to help him.

Chris had a number of ways to find out where Somers lived, but he didn't have to utilize them. That's because the TV coverage included his neighbors being interviewed. One of them referred to Somers living "right next door," as he pointed to his left from in front of his own house.

The newscast gave the man's name, and his address was listed in the phone book, which meant that Chris now had Somers's address as well.

He would be paying him a visit, and how Somers answered his questions would determine whether he lived or died.

They were easily the most devastating words Bryan Somers had ever heard.

Not even the sentences informing him of the deaths of his parents had that kind of impact. They had each been ill, and he had time to prepare for what had become the inevitable.

This came out of left field, and left him reeling.

And left him looking for his brother.

He didn't call Luke, and it was not because he had forgotten his cell phone at home when he left . . . almost staggered, out of the house. On a gut level he knew that he had to speak to his brother in person, to see his face when they spoke, even though he had no real idea what he would say.

It was a twenty-five-minute drive from his house in Englewood Cliffs to Luke's house in Paterson. He didn't even notice the time as he drove, but it wasn't because he was lost in thought. He had lost the ability to think clearly in those moments, probably the first time that had ever happened to him.

He arrived at Luke's house on East Thirty-Ninth Street and parked in front. It was a well-kept residential neighborhood, but economic light-years apart from Bryan's own home. The houses were on small plots of land, with less than twenty feet separating them on each side. Bryan's pool probably could fit on Luke's property, but only if the house were removed first.

There was a car parked in front of Luke's darkened house, unusual in that there was an ordinance prohibiting parking on the street at night. Bryan might have wondered why it was parked in that particular spot, since the street was otherwise empty and Luke did not appear to be home. Bryan might have noticed this, if he was in a mental state to notice anything.

Even though it seemed as if no one was home, Bryan got out and went to the front door anyway. He did so basically because he had nothing else to do and nowhere else to go. And no matter what happened, he was going to talk to Luke that night.

The doorbell went unanswered, so without a cell phone to call Luke and ask him to come home, Bryan stayed on the porch, sitting on the steps and occasionally getting up to pace. After a half hour, he wondered whether Luke might already know that he was there and, more important, why. Perhaps Julie had called him. Either way, there was nothing to do but wait, and he would wait as long as it took.

Bryan didn't notice Chris Gallagher sitting in the driver's seat of the car parked out front. There were no street lamps nearby, and the interior of the car was too dark to make anything out. But Chris had not taken his eyes off Bryan since his arrival.

Chris had spent that time formulating a plan. He knew from his online research that the man on the porch was Luke's brother, Bryan. He seemed agitated, but that was not Chris's concern, since it was highly unlikely that his distress had anything to do with Chris's situation, or Steven's death.

As he was trained to do, he weighed the merits of the plan in his mind, careful to keep it untainted by emotion. It seemed to Chris to be more than workable; it could provide cold justice to the cop who had killed Steven while, more important, giving Steven a posthumous exoneration.

He made one phone call, keeping the phone turned in such a way that Bryan could not see the light. The call was to a marine buddy, to ask for the favor that could make the plan workable.

It was a large favor, but it was granted, no questions asked, as Chris knew it would be.

Chris got out of his car, closing the door softly behind him, so that it was still ajar, but the light would not stay on. He approached the porch, and did it all so quietly that Bryan did not even realize he was there until he heard his voice.

"What time do you expect your brother?" Chris asked, though he knew that it was a question for which Bryan did not have an answer. Bryan would not have arrived when he did if he knew when Luke would get there. And he certainly would not have rung the doorbell, checking to see if Luke had been home.

Bryan felt a twinge of fear. He couldn't make out Chris's features in the darkness, but the voice was not familiar. Yet this man somehow knew that Luke was Bryan's brother.

"Any minute," Bryan said, annoyed with himself for using Luke for protection in that way. At that moment, with his anger at Luke so intense, he did not want to have to depend on him for anything.

"Really," Chris said. It was not a question, but rather a statement that revealed, with some amusement, his certainty that Bryan was lying.

"Do I know you?" Bryan asked.

"You're about to," Chris said, and in one incredibly quick and silent movement glided forward and rammed an elbow into the side of Bryan's head.

Bryan slumped to the ground, or would have had Chris not been there to catch him. He lifted Bryan as if he were a toy, put him over his shoulder, and carried him to his car. He looked around to see if he had been seen, though it wouldn't have mattered much either way.

Chris drove away, with Bryan unconscious in the back-seat. He took no particular satisfaction in what he had done. He and Luke were not yet even, not even close.

But they would be.

The phone woke me at five o'clock in the morning.

Cops are not like normal people when it comes to middle of the night phone calls. Most people experience a moment of panic, fearful that the hour of the call means that something bad has happened to someone they care about. And very often their fears are justified.

We cops are different in that we're positive that something bad has happened; nobody calls a cop when they have good news. For example, I've never gotten a radio transmission or call urging me to head to a place where someone has reported reading a good book, or listening to pleasing music.

The other difference is that we don't worry so much about the call when it comes, because it's almost never about someone we care about, or even know. There's no personal attachment to it; we care, and we're sworn to protect, but it's a job.

But caller ID this time told me that this was something different, and I instantly became just like every other person in this situation. It was my brother calling from home, so something had to be wrong with either him or Julie.

"Bryan?" I said when I picked up the phone.

"It's not Bryan," Julie said.

Even in just those three words I could hear the anxiety in her voice.

"Julie, what's wrong?"

"Bryan's gone, Luke. He left last night, and he hasn't come back."

"Where did he go?"

"I don't know. We talked about our marriage. I said things I've needed to say . . . I've wanted to say . . . for a long time. I told him I needed time to think about our marriage."

"Think about your marriage?" I asked. "What does that mean?"

"Thinking about whether I wanted to stay in it," she said. "God, Lucas . . . what the hell is the matter with me?"

"Take it easy, Julie." What she had said opened up all kinds of questions, none of which I was willing to ask. Instead I focused on Bryan. "So he just stormed off?" I asked. "Did you try and call him?"

"He slammed the door so hard it broke the handle. He left his cell phone here, so I have no way to reach him. He didn't go to your house?"

"No, I haven't heard from him. He's probably at a hotel, maybe in the city." In a way I was actually a little relieved. The worry of the late night phone call was at least removed; wherever Bryan was, he and Julie were physically fine.

"Luke, I also told him some things I didn't mean to say." She paused while I cringed. "Things I shouldn't have said."

"Oh, shit. Julie. . . ." Alarm bells were going off in my head.

"I'm sorry, Luke. I know I promised."

Julie and I had a brief affair, if you could call it that. I prefer to think of it as a moment of sexual weakness, even though that isn't technically an accurate description, either. It happened six years ago, a month before she and Bryan were to be married, when he was expressing doubts about going through with the wedding.

So she was angry, and we were out commiserating, since I had recently had a breakup of my own. Not that my breakups were exactly news events; you could set your clock by them.

But what happened between Julie and me wasn't revenge sex or even rebound sex. I wish it were, since that would have been the end of it. I was in love with Julie, I was before it happened, and I have been ever since. I also believed that she was in love with me.

We never talked about it again after that night, and until this phone call I thought we never would. But I learned a lesson; if you're going to fall in love with someone, your sister-in-law is not a terrific idea. Unfortunately, I was never able to put that lesson to any good use, since Julie is my only sister-in-law. And it was too late to stop loving her.

"It's OK, Julie. We'll deal with it. I'm sure I'll be hearing from him soon."

"Please tell him to come home, Luke."

"I've got a hunch that right about now advice from me isn't going to carry the day."

"Will you let me know if he calls you?" she asked.

"Of course." Then, "Julie, why did you tell him?" She had to know it would be devastating and hurtful to him, which made it uncharacteristic for her to have said it. She was also breaking a promise to me in the process, which represented another surprise.

"You know why, Luke."

The truth was that I did not have the slightest idea why. For some reason, women are always crediting me with being way more intuitive about them than I actually am.

It's the worst of both worlds; I've never had a clue what they are thinking, but because they believe I do, they're less inclined to spell it out for me.

But whatever the reason, the way she said, "You know why," made me less eager to press the issue. I was now at the place I had no desire to be, directly in the middle of their marriage. When Bryan started screaming at me, I wanted to have as little information as possible, sort of like a POW undergoing interrogation. I wanted to be on a "need to know" basis, and I didn't need to know any of this.

Julie and I once again agreed to contact each other if either of us heard from Bryan, and no longer able to sleep, I got dressed and headed for the office.

The media furor had not quite died down yet, as reporters were focused on delving into Steven Gallagher's background. His life was both short and difficult, though no one seemed to have any idea that he had violent tendencies.

Those who knew him professed shock that he could have committed a murder, but that has become standard stuff these days. For every serial killer there seems to be a dozen neighbors who swear he seemed like a quiet, nice guy, the last person you'd expect to have chopped up all those people.

Media requests for interviews were still coming in, but I declined all of them. I had "been there, done that" and I didn't want to spend the whole day refusing to answer the questions I had refused to answer the day before. Besides, it had taken me twenty minutes to remove the makeup; from now on I was going strictly "au naturel."

I had plenty else to do. I had a bunch of recent homicides to occupy my attention, and it's not like the citizens of New Jersey were going to stop killing other citizens of New Jersey any time soon.

So I tried as best I could to make the day "business as usual," but in the back of my mind was Julie's phone call, and the fact that I hadn't heard from Bryan. His silence brought home very powerfully how hurt he must have been by what he saw as our betrayal. And the truth is that he was right, "betrayal" was the correct word for it.

Bryan was not exactly the type to shy away from verbal confrontations; he believed everything should always be out in the open and discussed to death. It was one of the many ways in which we were different; I was always on the lookout for rugs to sweep things under.

So I knew we would have the conversation, he was entitled to at least that much, and that it would be a difficult one. I always felt huge guilt about the night with Julie, and while I had obsessed over it ever since, I had done so privately. Now it would be out in the open and openly talked about.

Ugh.

But I deserved whatever grief Bryan would give me.

I just wanted to get it over with.

It was a completely disorienting feeling.

Bryan Somers woke up having no idea where he was, or how he got there. It wasn't that he was groggy; he actually came to a state of alertness fairly quickly. Fear and confusion can do that.

He was lying on a couch in a dimly lit room. There were no windows, the walls were gray-painted cement, and light was provided by recessed bulbs in the ceiling. It seemed to be a small studio apartment; he was in a den-like area, which was attached to a small kitchen. There was a bar stool tucked under a counter, a dresser across from the couch, and a small television sitting on the dresser. There was also a small receiving box on top of the television.

The strangeness of the surroundings, and his lack of knowledge of how he got there, was horrifying enough. Worse yet was his discovery that a metal clasp on his leg was attached to a long chain, which in turn was attached to a radiator in the corner of the room.

He got up and walked around the room, checking it out. There was a small bathroom with a stall shower, and the kitchen was fully stocked with food and drink. He was not going to starve to death, at least not for a while.

The door was locked from the outside, and no amount of pulling, pushing, or shoving affected it. Screaming for help yielded nothing as well, and from the solid nature of the walls, he doubted that anyone outside could hear him, even if they were out there. There was no phone and no computer, and therefore no apparent way to get in touch with the outside world.

Bryan turned on the television, and was very surprised to see that it worked. It seemed to be satellite television, and Bryan quickly recognized the stations as all New York affiliates. Wherever he was, it was in the New York Metropolitan Area.

He tried to piece together how he had gotten there, but drew a blank. He remembered the conversation with Julie, and it brought back a wave of pain. He also remembered going to Luke's house, and waiting for him when he wasn't home.

But after that it was a blank. Could Luke have done this to him? Even though Julie's revelation made him question how well he knew his brother, Luke kidnapping him in this manner made absolutely no sense.

Yet the sequence of events was troubling. Just an hour or so after an earth-shaking conversation with his wife, one in which his world was turned upside down, Bryan found himself in this situation. Was it possible that the two things were not related? Could there be a coincidence that great?

Bryan was scared to a degree he had never come close to experiencing before. He found a local news program on television and started watching it, hoping that it might shed some light on what was happening. That was unlikely, he knew, since it was a morning news program, which meant he was not gone for very long. No one would have reported him missing yet, so no one would be looking for him.

So he sat down to wait. It was not a physically uncomfortable situation to be in; the chain reached to the kitchen and bathroom, and the couch was relatively comfortable. He tried to take mental consolation in the fact that someone inclined to hurt or kill him could have done so already, and would not have provided this type of environment.

But it was small comfort.

He was a prisoner.

It was three very long hours before the door opened and his captor walked in. He was a large man, at least three inches and thirty pounds bigger than Bryan. He gave off an air of physicality and toughness, even though he had a smile on his face that in other situations might seem disarming.

"You're up," the man said. "How are you feeling?"

"Who are you, and what the hell am I doing here?"

"My name is Chris Gallagher. You're here because I kidnapped you. You feeling OK? I hit you harder than I should have, and then I injected you with Sodium Pentothal. You probably don't remember any of it."

"Let me ask this again; why the hell am I here?" He tried to have his tone reflect his outrage, but the fear took the sting out of it.

"Your brother Luke killed my brother; his name was Steven Gallagher. So you have become what is commonly known as an innocent victim. Collateral damage, as it were. As was Steven."

Bryan's memory was coming back to him, and he asked, "Is this about the Brennan murder?"

Chris nodded. "That seems to be what your brother thought, but he was wrong. So he didn't ask any questions; he just went in firing. And then he went on television to brag about it. The conquering goddamn hero."

"This has nothing to do with me."

"It does now."

"What are you hoping to accomplish?"

"I'm going to be talking to Luke, and I'll instruct him to do things. If he does them, and does them well, then you've got a chance. If not, you're going to die."

He said it in a matter-of-fact, sincere way that left Bryan with no doubt that he was telling the truth. His mind was racing for something to say that might change this man's mind. "You think that killing one innocent person makes up for the killing of another?"

Chris shrugged. "It's the only system of justice I've got."

"And in the meantime?"

"You'll stay here, as you are now. You're fifteen feet underground, so there's no one to hear you, and no way out. But I guess you'll want to find that out for yourself, if you haven't already. There's a seven-day air supply. Seven and a half if you're lucky."

"What happens when it runs out?"

"You won't be able to breathe."

Bryan totally understood what was happening, but it still was somehow confusing. It was all just too surreal. "Come on, you can't do this. Please."

"We both know that I can," Chris said.

"People will be looking for me. What if they catch you?"

"They won't."

"They might. What if they do?"

Chris shook his head. "Nobody catches me if I don't want to be caught. But your brother won't even try."

"Why not?"

"Because he wants you to live." Chris laughed and said, "He does, right?"

"I don't deserve this. You seem like a smart guy, a decent guy. You've got to know that."

"Don't try to play me, OK? It won't get you anywhere, and you don't want me pissed off at you. Here's what I know; the world is one big stick, and you just got the short end of it. So your role in this is to just hang out and wait to see what happens."

Chris walked to the desk and unlocked the drawer. "There's a computer in here; e-mail service will be connected as of noon tomorrow."

He turned to leave but stopped, reached into his pocket, and put a very small plastic bag on the table; in it were two pills. "These are poison; if you start to run out of air, you'll feel light-headed. It'll be downhill fast from there. If I were you I'd take the pills; it's a much better way to die."

The panic Bryan was feeling was overwhelming, but he tried to keep himself under control in front of his captor. "Thanks a lot."

Chris laughed. "Hey, I could get in trouble for giving you those. But it's OK; I kept a couple for myself."

I wouldn't say that Bryan and I were close.

That seems an almost irrelevant way to describe our relationship. I would instead say we were brothers, which is a giant step past close. It has nothing to do with how much time we spent together, or how often we talked. Having a brother, being a brother, is in a category of its own.

Our mother, Cynthia Shuster Somers, died when I was seven and Bryan was three. Our father, Cal Somers, was not exactly the talkative type, as evidenced by the fact that I was seventeen before I learned that Mom's death was from smoking-induced lung cancer. My aunt Martha spilled the beans about that one.

I don't remember my mother much at all, so I'm certain that Bryan would have no recollection of her. But I certainly remember my father, a police captain who wanted nothing more than to have his children follow him on to the force.

I did that, of course, and I never felt coerced by his goal for me. It seemed like a natural progression, and I can't say that I remember making a conscious career decision. I also can't say that I regret where I wound up.

Bryan took a different route, and I've sometimes wondered what he would have done if our father lived past forty-one. Bryan was seventeen when Cal died of the heart attack, his third, sitting at the kitchen table.

There were no longer live footsteps to follow, and Bryan went his own way. He was always about fifty times smarter than me, and he parlayed those brains into a scholarship to Penn, followed by an MBA from the University of Virginia. From there he went into investment banking, which in my mind means he brings a basket to the office, so he can cart home money every day.

Money was always very, very important to Bryan, and that only increased when he met Julie. While he didn't follow our father's career path, he always thought he was destined to mirror his lack of longevity.

"Obsession" might be too strong a word, so I'll say that he became very focused on making sure his family was well provided for after he was gone. Bryan had to have had more life insurance than anyone, anywhere. He used to joke that his death would bring the insurance industry to its knees.

The irony was that Julie cares about money less than almost anyone I know and she would wage a constant battle to get Bryan to lighten up and try to enjoy life more.

He would say that he was working fourteen-hour days, and earning money hand over fist, so that he could retire a young man. I certainly didn't believe him, and I can't imagine that Julie did, either. His identity seemed to be his success, which is one of the ways we were very different.

There was never any doubt that Bryan would settle down and get married, just like there was never any real chance that I would. I'm not sure why things turned out that way; maybe our parents only had one commitment gene and they gave it to him. Or dumped it on him, depending on your perspective.

The revelation that Julie and I had slept together, even though it was before they were married, would be a crusher for him. I knew that, but there was nothing I could do about it, other than sincerely apologize.

It would take a while for him to get over it, but eventually he would.

That's what brothers do.

Bryan Somers slept for about two hours, only because of the leftover effects of the drug Chris had administered. It was just enough to make him forget where he was, which led to the renewed horrible realization when he woke up.

He went straight to the computer and turned it on. It sprang to life, but did not have an Internet connection. Chris had said it would be online at noon, and Bryan would have to wait until then. He searched the drawer, and then the rest of the "apartment," but he could not find a power cord. He would have only the amount of power in the battery, so he quickly turned the machine off; no sense wasting power when he couldn't use the Internet.

Bryan hoped the computer would allow him to send e-mail, and expected it would, since that's what Chris had said without prompting. It was a good news, bad news situation; Chris would allow him to be in contact with the outside world, but the reason he would was because Bryan would have no way to identify his location.

There were three pens and a pad of paper in the apartment, and Bryan decided to write out his e-mails in advance, with the computer off, so that he would not waste power while composing them.

He saw no reason to write to Julie. Though he was still in love with her, their marriage was effectively over the moment she revealed the betrayal. The truth was that it had probably been over well before that, but he had been oblivious to it.

The person he would contact would be his brother, Luke. If Chris was as efficient as Bryan believed, he would soon be telling Luke what had happened. How Luke reacted to that news would likely determine whether Bryan would live or die.

He would not be wasting time and power writing about Julie, and her affair with Luke. As horrible as that was, it took a distant backseat right now.

There would be time to hash that out later.

Or not.

It wasn't the way Edward Holland had charted his career.

The plan had been to go to a top law school, join a big New York law firm, become very powerful, and make a fortune.

And for a while everything seemed on track. Holland went to NYU, for both undergraduate and law school, and finished in the top quarter of his class. Big law firms came calling, as they are wont to do at the better schools, and Holland had no trouble getting placed at one of the biggest and best.

The beginning of his work career was less than auspicious, though predictably so. Like every other newcomer to large firms, he worked like a dog, sometimes logging sixteen-hour days. And it was grunt work, behind-the-scenes research so that the partners could look good and well prepared, and so clients could hide their wealth from US taxes in financially friendly countries. But in terms of power, Holland couldn't imagine having less.

He was an indentured servant, albeit a well-paid one. But even though the pay was very good by normal standards, New York was an expensive place to live, and Holland was certainly not getting rich.

After the fourth year, he took stock of his future, and wasn't crazy about what he saw. There was the possibility, perhaps even the likelihood, that he would make partner after eight or nine years. That would provide him with an excellent income, though he would never be mega-wealthy. And while he would be respected, he would not be powerful. That was basically reserved for the clients, at least some of them.

So he made a career move that was outside the box, way outside. The Mayor of Brayton, New York, Holland's hometown, was retiring after serving eleven three-year terms. Over drinks one night, a high school buddy, active in town politics, suggested that Holland could have the job for the asking.

So he asked. He talked to the local power players, who were impressed with his résumé, and he secured a slot on the ballot. The fact that he ran unopposed reduced the number of election promises he had to make, and within eight months of the drinks in the bar Edward Holland was the Mayor of Brayton.

He took a seventy-five percent pay cut from his previous job, not the typical path to the *Forbes* list of wealthiest Americans. But the mayoralty was not going to be the highest rung he hit on the political ladder, and you could count the number of successful, but poor, national politicians on very few fingers.

In terms of power, that would come down the road, but even now they were calling him "Your Honor," which had a nice ring to it. And he was confident that before long the power would grow greater; there was no reason they wouldn't someday be calling him "Mr. President."

The responsibilities of the Mayor of Brayton are not

exactly awesome. There's no 3 AM phone call requiring momentous decisions, and very little crisis management. Deciding whether to install a traffic light a block from the grammar school is more typical of the day-to-day crises the Mayor must confront.

And then, suddenly, a serious and very significant issue dropped into his lap.

Carlton Auto Parts was by far the largest employer in the town. Richard Carlton represented the fourth generation of leadership in the family-owned manufacturing company and wholesaler, but to that point he had presided over, if not a debacle, then a gradual decline in fortunes.

Facing daunting competition from larger US companies, and even larger foreign ones, Carlton had not weathered the recession well. Profits were down, and layoffs followed, as they inevitably do. But the town was getting by, and for the most part people were employed.

Carlton was not only the largest employer; it was also the largest landowner. Brayton was a large community geographically, and Carlton owned a lot of it. Additionally, it had recently purchased huge tracts of land from the town of Brayton. It was land that was adjacent to the town but so far mostly unoccupied, and its assessed value was reflected in the very low price that Carlton paid.

And then, suddenly, the discovery of enormous pockets of shale on the land changed everything. A process called fracking might be able to extract natural gas from the shale, depending on the type and formation of the rock. Natural gas was starting to be seen as the key to America's energy independence, and if fracking could be used on the Carlton land, the financial rewards would be mind-boggling.

But it seems as if energy development always comes with an environmental price, and fracking was the rule, rather than the exception. There were very serious concerns about its effects on nearby water supply, as well as air quality. Lawsuits were springing up around the country, with aggrieved citizens pointing to examples, some substantive and some anecdotal, of disease clusters that they felt were the result of the fracking residue.

It was a perfect opportunity for Holland. Not only could he rally the townspeople and get significant publicity throughout the state in his role as the Mayor, but he also was able to parley his legal stature into even greater prominence. Rather than forcing the impoverished town to hire outside counsel, he took on the job himself.

Win or lose, it would be a win for Holland. He could play up the heroic nature of the situation, putting it all on the line for the sake of the town. He would get great publicity, an invaluable boost to his political future.

Holland was all too aware, if no one else seemed to be, that he could not represent the town as well as a big-time firm could. The case was a long shot anyway; while fracking lawsuits around the country were finding mixed results, the majority favored the energy companies.

So Brayton lost at trial, and then subsequently appealed. Even with Holland in the counsel chair, the expenses were significant. If they lost on appeal, it would be unlikely that they would have the financial resources to go to the Supreme Court, especially if the Appeals Court made them post a bond, as they would likely do.

The arguments were made before the Second Circuit panel that included Judge Susan Dembeck. She was to be replaced by Judge Danny Brennan, but his nomination was held up in committee. If that changed before a decision was announced, then the case would have to be reargued.

Of course, Judge Brennan, murdered in his garage, wouldn't be hearing any more cases.

A media story is like a campfire.

It reaches a full blaze quickly, and then gradually starts to die down. But as you add fuel, it flares up again.

The story of the Brennan murder, and my shooting of Steven Gallagher, was running out of fuel. That was mostly because we found Gallagher so quickly, and because his death meant there was no trial to look forward to. Had the crime not been solved, or if there was a manhunt, the story could have burned for weeks.

Much was already known about Gallagher, his difficult upbringing, his subsequent descent into addiction, and his Marine hero brother, Chris. Chris had not been heard from, though it was known that he was back in the states on leave.

A funeral was being planned for Judge Brennan for two days later, to give time for the large crowd who would surely attend to make arrangements. Messages of outrage and horror had already been chronicled, and published accounts revealed how many respected legal and business leaders actually used Twitter.

Judge Susan Dembeck had not yet announced whether

she would stay in her post until a replacement for Judge Brennan was appointed and confirmed. It was expected that she would, though this represented something of a hardship for her, since her husband had a serious illness and she was retiring to help care for him.

The President would soon be appointing a new candidate to take the place of Judge Dembeck, but that person would begin at square one in the confirmation process, and the state of gridlock in the Senate would once again make it very time-consuming.

Billy Heyward kept me in touch with details of the case as it came together, and I was relieved to hear that initial DNA testing revealed that the clothes stuffed in Gallagher's closet had Judge Brennan's blood on them. That meant that the postmortem on the case would be quick and uncontroversial. It also confirmed my belief that I did the right thing.

But the day went by without my hearing from Bryan. I was surprised, but the truth was that I had little experience with a brother finding out that I had slept with his wife, so I wasn't sure what normal behavior would be.

I was disturbed by a phone call from Julie near the end of the day. She asked if I had heard from Bryan, and I told her that I had not. "He hasn't called me, either," she said. "I'm worried about him."

"I'm sure he needs the time to think this out, to digest it. Maybe to decide whether he wants to shoot me or hit me over the head with a baseball bat."

"I know it's got to be incredibly hard on him," she said. "But I want to talk to him. I feel so terrible about this."

"You could call him at work."

"I was going to, but they called me."

"What does that mean?"

"He didn't show up for work, and didn't contact anyone there. They were worried about him."

The conversation with Julie must have been even more devastating for Bryan than I imagined, and I imagined it as being hugely upsetting. Bryan doesn't miss a day of work, not ever; he's the hardest-working person I know. And to just not show up, without notification, is totally and completely out of character.

I got off the phone and tried him at home. I got the machine, and left a message that I knew what he was going through, and I was sorry and we needed to talk.

With nothing else to do, I headed down to the Crows Nest for a couple of beers and a burger. It was a comfortable place to be; there were always cops around who I knew and usually liked, though the next time we talked about work there would be the first.

I got home at a little after nine, and parked in my driveway, which is along the side of the house. I walked around towards the front and as I went up the four steps to the porch I noticed that one of the windows on the left was open.

It was only open an inch, but hey, I'm a cop, and I notice stuff. What was important was that I hadn't left it open. I'm an air-conditioning nut; I leave it on all day so the house will be cool when I get home. And this particular window was behind a table, so it's not even one that I ever open.

So if I didn't open it, someone else did. Which meant that someone might have been in my house, and might still be there.

It was safest to assume the latter, and if that was the case, then they would have heard me pull into the driveway. The smart thing for me to have done would have been to call for backup and go into the house in force.

I didn't do that for a couple of reasons. The very stupid one was that it was my house and I could defend it without help from anyone. The less stupid one was that it could be

Bryan, who found the doors locked and decided he wanted to wait for me inside. Climbing through a window would have been completely out of character for him, but with what he'd been going through, his behavior might be tending towards the unusual.

I went around to the back of the house. There was a ladder there; I hadn't put it away after a visit by the satellite TV guy. I looked in through the window, and didn't see anyone inside, so I placed the ladder against the house, as gently as I could.

I climbed up to a window in a guest bedroom, since I knew the lock on it was broken. If you're going to break into a house, it's easier if it's the one you live in, since you know the nuances.

It was difficult climbing up to the window and then through it with my gun drawn, but the potentially most dangerous part of this operation was when I physically went through the window. The truth was that if there was somebody waiting for me there with a gun, having my own gun drawn would be of little help. Of course, if it was Bryan, having my gun drawn would make me feel like an idiot.

I got into the room undetected, and made my way out to the hallway, and then to the top of the steps. There was a light on in the den, which was just to the left off the stairs, but I could have left it that way. I'd know soon enough.

Having the high ground in battle is almost always an advantage, one of the exceptions being when the battlefield is a house in Paterson, New Jersey. If there were people down there, they could have been in a number of places, pointing their weapons at the bottom of the stairs, waiting for my convenient arrival.

I edged towards the outside wall of the den, then quickly moved in, gun in firing position. There was a man sitting on the couch; he wasn't Bryan, and he wasn't anyone I had seen before. The other thing he wasn't, even though he was staring at my gun, was worried.

"You noticed the window I left open. Not bad . . . I was testing you."

I kept the gun pointed. "Who the hell are you?"

"Chris Gallagher. You killed my brother."

"The Marine," I said.

He nodded. "The Marine."

I lowered the gun, but still held it in my hand. Gallagher was far enough away from me that I'd have time to raise it and fire if he made a move. "I'm sorry about your brother."

"No, you're not."

"Think what you want."

"Steven never hurt anyone in his life, except himself."

"His clothes were hidden in his closet with Judge Brennan's blood all over them; they matched the DNA. He had a gun and raised it to shoot me when we came in. Maybe you didn't know your brother as well as you think."

"You got a brother Bryan, right?" he asked.

"Yes."

"You know him pretty well?"

"I do," I said, not liking where this was going.

"Heard from him today?"

Chris Gallagher described the situation calmly, without apparent emotion.

If that approach was to worry his audience, in this case me, it worked really well. His words reflected the fact that he was in total control, but his manner drove it home even more forcefully.

"I was here last night, looking for you. Your brother was on the porch; wrong time, wrong place. Not that it matters, but there's a certain justice to it, don't you think?"

"I don't. Bryan has nothing to do with this."

"And my brother had nothing to do with Brennan. But you made sure he'll never have his day in court, so the world can always think he's a murderer."

"I didn't to shoot your brother. I wanted to talk to him, to question him and, if the facts warranted it, to arrest him. He made that impossible, and I'm sorry about that. I was sorry about it before you came here."

If I was getting through to him, he was hiding it well. "You're full of shit."

"Where's Bryan?" I asked.

"In major trouble."

"What does that mean?"

"He's in an underground room, with no way out. Plenty of food and water, and a seven-day air supply, a little less now. If anything happens to me, that's how long he'll live."

He was telling me that I couldn't arrest him if I wanted to, because it would be a death sentence for Bryan. For the time being at least, I couldn't see any flaws in that logic.

"Why did you come here yesterday?"

"Probably to kill you. So in a way he saved your life."

"So why don't you ditch 'Plan B' and start over? Let my brother go, and then come after me."

He smiled. "You think you can handle me?"

"Only one way to find out."

"Luke, you have no idea what you're dealing with. You're sitting there holding a gun, and I'm unarmed, and if I wanted to kill you right now, you'd be dead in thirty seconds."

"Let my brother go and you can prove it."

"All right, that's enough of this bullshit. Your brother has a hell of a lot more chance than my brother had. It's up to you."

"How is it up to me?"

"You know the investigation you didn't do before you went in shooting? Do it now. Prove Steven didn't do it; find the real killer and announce to the world that you were wrong. That you killed an innocent man."

"And what if I find out he did do it?"

"He didn't."

"What if my investigation shows that he did?"

"Then we're both short one brother."

In a way this was a positive development, but a small one at best. While there was no chance that I was going to actually find information to exonerate Steven Gallagher, this at least gave me some time to try to figure out another way.

"OK, what are the ground rules?" I asked.

"There aren't any. Do your job."

"What if I have to reach you? Give me your cell number."

"I'll reach you," he said.

He was no doubt aware that every cell phone has a built-in GPS signal that can be traced and located. My hope had been that I could find out through the signal where my brother was, when and if Gallagher went there.

"Can I use other detectives to help in the investigation?" I asked.

"I don't care how you do it; just make sure you do it."

"This won't bring your brother back."

"Really?" he sneered. "I wasn't aware of that." Then, "It's my fault what happened to my brother. I wasn't there for him when he needed me. That's something I have to live with. Make sure you don't know what it feels like to be responsible for your brother's death."

He started towards the door, and then stopped and turned. "Your brother's got seven days, so don't waste any time."

I called and made an appointment to see Julie at 10 AM.

I wanted to break the news to her in her office, where things would seem less personal. I was aware that either way things were going to be intensely personal, but I needed Julie's professional help if we were going to succeed.

Julie is an assistant prosecutor for the state of New Jersey. We worked together on a couple of cases a long time ago, but not since we had our sexual indiscretion. I assume she has structured things deliberately to not work on my cases; I'm just not sure why she's done that, and I haven't been about to ask.

I had met Julie while working on a case, and I was the one to introduce her to Bryan. I was in that phase of my life whereby a long relationship lasted three weeks, and in fact I'm still in that phase. Julie wasn't the three-week type, that was immediately clear, and Bryan was looking for someone to settle down with. So I introduced them, and if there has been a twenty-four-hour period since in which I haven't regretted doing it, I can't recall one.

There was and is something special about Julie. She has the ability to see through me, but in a way that I never seem to mind. I've always thought she felt something for me as well, though I can't pinpoint why I thought that. Our way of dealing with all of this was never, ever to deal with it.

When I called I spoke to Julie's assistant, who had no reason to think it was strange that I was setting the meeting. Julie meets with cops all the time. But I knew that when Julie heard that I was coming in, she'd realize it was about Bryan.

I couldn't sleep after Chris Gallagher left my house, so I tried to be productive, filling the time by analyzing the options that I had. I was positive that everything he said was true, and that he was fully capable of killing Bryan.

Goal number one had to be keeping Bryan alive until I could achieve goal number two, which was to free him. I had no idea yet how to get him out, but keeping him alive seemed achievable, as long as I followed Gallagher's instructions.

So I would conduct the investigation into Brennan's death that Gallagher was demanding. There was no doubt about that. The only questions to be resolved would be how I would go about it, specifically who I would recruit and confide in.

I couldn't do it alone, and I certainly couldn't do it in secret. I needed the access to information that my job provided, but people would inevitably become aware of my actions. I just had to make sure that they were people I could trust to exercise discretion. If the particulars of this situation got out, then I would have lost control, and Bryan would have lost a lot more.

I was going to conduct a serious investigation, though I had no expectation of proving Steven Gallagher innocent. My hope was to find information that proved his guilt so conclusively that even his brother would accept it as the truth. Chris Gallagher seemed capable of anything, and that included rational thought.

My first stop was to my office to speak to Emmit Jenkins. I needed him to be my right hand, if he was willing, and I was sure he would be.

I told him the story, and watched him get furious as I told it. I'm not sure what it says about me, but Emmit was far angrier at the situation than I was. Gallagher thought I killed his brother with no justification. If I were in his situation, and I recognized the irony that soon I might be, there would be no place the killer could hide.

"Give me ten minutes with him," Emmit said. "He'll be begging to tell me where your brother is."

I have great respect for Emmit's physical prowess, but I didn't think there was anyone, anywhere, who could get Chris Gallagher to do much begging.

Then Emmit asked the key question, or at least the key question of the moment. "Who else are you going to tell?"

I had my thoughts on the matter, but wanted his view. "What do you think?"

"We gotta be careful," he said, already using the pronoun that made us a team. "This gets out, somebody is going to want to arrest this guy for kidnapping."

I nodded. "I know. But I need to tell Barone."

He frowned his disagreement. "I'm not so sure that's a good idea; the Captain will want to cover his ass."

"No doubt. But I need the resources of the department."

Emmit left and I went in to see Barone. There were two officers in with him, so I said, "I need to see the Captain alone."

They agreeably got up and left, and once they did, Barone said, " 'I need to see the Captain alone' is not a phrase I like. The next thing I hear after that is usually a problem."

"This one's a beauty," I said, and proceeded to lay it out for him.

"Damn," he said when I was finished. "What are you

going to do?" he asked, demonstrating that he and Emmit had little in common when it comes to pronoun usage.

"I'm going to do what he says, while at the same time trying to find my brother. I don't see any other way."

He nodded, but didn't say anything.

"I can't do it alone, or just with Emmit," I said. "I need the resources of the department."

"I'm listening," he said. "I'm cringing, but I'm listening."

"No one except Emmit, you, and I will know about my brother. Everyone else involved will just think we're covering our bases on the Brennan murder."

He still wasn't answering, so I said, "It's just seven days, Captain."

Finally he said, "You know the part you said about the three of us knowing the situation with your brother?"

"Yes."

"Make it the two of you," he said.

"Did I say three? I meant two."

Barone nodded his approval. "So listen carefully. I am authorizing that you investigate the Brennan murder; I feel it's important that we dot every 'i.' I am unaware of any secondary motives that you and Emmit might have."

"You're a profile in courage," I said.

He nodded. "It comes naturally."

He was still doing me a big favor, and he and I both knew it. "Thanks, Captain."

"Keep me posted," he said. "Unofficially."

Were Richard Carlton to describe the citizens of Brayton in one word, it would be "ungrateful."

The Carlton family, through their auto parts manufacturing plant, had been employing almost a third of the town for close to sixty years. Without it, it was fair to say that Brayton would have ceased to exist, at least in its present form, a long time ago.

Yes, there had been some layoffs in recent years; that's what struggling businesses do. But for the most part Carlton took care of its employees, and did as much as it could for them.

Richard Carlton, in his five years since inheriting the leadership role from his father, had continued the tradition. His was an open door, though one had to get through quite a few other doors to reach it. But he was going to do what was best for his company, and that in turn would benefit Brayton.

A win-win all around.

But now there was the opportunity for a huge win, a game changer. Carlton had purchased enormous tracts of land from the town of Brayton, for the purpose of someday building housing units. Since the town had not been thriving in recent years, there would have been no one to live in new housing, so it hadn't yet been built.

Not long after, it was discovered that the land contained enormous shale deposits. Carlton had contacted Hanson Oil and Gas, a company that had become a leader in natural gas in the US by taking a preeminent position in the fracking industry. It was the wave of the energy future, seen by many as our key to independence from the Middle East.

Hanson's chief engineer, Michael Oliver, conducted a study that confirmed the shale was porous enough, plentiful enough, and configured in such a way as to be a prime candidate for fracking. It was one of the largest and most promising finds ever, and Hanson immediately made a preemptive offer of three hundred and fifty million dollars for the land, contingent on legal approvals.

But outside environmental groups came in and spread fear within the Brayton community of water contamination and air pollution. The Mayor, Edward Holland, took up the fight, and as a lawyer actually handled the lawsuit himself. He chose to file in Federal rather than state court, on the assumption that it would be a more favorable venue for Brayton.

Not many legal analysts agreed with that decision, and Brayton lost in District Court. They then filed their appeal, and the results would be known soon. Holland had already privately indicated that a loss there would unfortunately be the end, that the town simply did not have the resources to pursue it further.

So for Carlton it was a waiting game, but he looked at the big picture. And the big picture contained a lot of money.

I was not looking forward to my conversation with Julie.

She was in the reception area waiting for me when I got off the elevator. I could see the tension on her face, but I couldn't hear it in her voice, because she didn't say a word. She just turned and started walking back to her office, a silent invitation for me to follow. It was as if she didn't want to delay hearing whatever news I was about to deliver by engaging in idle chitchat, like saying "hello."

We went into her office, and she closed the door behind us. "How did it go?" she asked.

"How did what go?"

"Didn't you speak to Bryan?"

"No."

She seemed confused. "You never heard from him? Then why are you here?"

"Julie, I've got something important to tell you; this goes way beyond the level of marital spat."

"It was more than a spat, Luke."

"Then this goes way beyond the level of marital earthquake."

"What is it?" She took a deep breath, as if bracing herself for the news.

"Bryan has been kidnapped by the brother of the kid I shot."

I watched as her mind tried to compute what I was saying. It was so unlike what she expected that it took her a few moments to process it, and even then it didn't make sense. "What the hell are you talking about?"

I went on to tell her the story, exactly as I related it to Emmit. I watched her intently as I spoke; Julie watching is something I've spent a lot of time doing over the years. She seemed to go back and forth between horror-stricken wife and law enforcement professional. It was the latter I needed to help me.

Her first words when I finished were not the ones I wanted to hear. "We need to go to the FBI with this."

"I've thought about that, Julie, but I don't see the upside, at least now."

"The upside is that maybe they'll catch him; maybe they'll save Bryan. How can you not see that?"

"Catching him doesn't save Bryan; it probably does exactly the opposite."

"You don't know that."

"Maybe you're right, and we need to get as much information as we can about Chris Gallagher so we can make that judgment. But for now Bryan is alive, and our doing what Gallagher asks keeps him alive."

"Maybe he'll kill him . . . ," she said, as her voice cracked and I thought she was going to break down. But she pulled it together. ". . . No matter what we do."

"If that's the case, then Bryan is probably dead already." When she reacted, I added, "I'm sorry, Julie, but that's the truth."

She nodded her understanding, but said, "We have knowledge of a crime, Luke. It needs to be reported."

"I'm a cop; consider it reported."

We talked about it some more, and she reluctantly agreed to go along with my approach. I was relieved, but not as much as I expected. I was not confident that I was right; I just couldn't think of a better way to go. With my brother's life on the line, I would have liked to have greater conviction.

"So what can I do?" she asked, the professional in her kicking into gear.

"Can you start gathering information on Chris Gallagher?"

"Of course," she said. "And I know a judge advocate at Quantico. We worked on a case together last year; a Marine got into a fight at a rest stop off the Jersey Turnpike and killed a guy. I let the military handle it, so he owes me a favor."

"Great; call it in," I said. "We need to know who we're dealing with."

"What are you going to do?"

"I'm going to investigate a murder and pretend it's not already solved."

The door opened and I was looking straight ahead at a man's chest.

I was at the late Judge Daniel Brennan's house in Alpine, and I expected to be greeted by his wife, not a man who looked to be seven feet tall. But he obviously expected me, because the voice from up there asked, "Lieutenant Somers?"

I looked up. Way up. "Yes," I said, to a face I recognized but in the moment couldn't place.

He held out his hand. "Nate Davenport. Friends call me Ice."

I shook his hand. We were just meeting for the first time, but I knew all about Nate "Ice Water" Davenport. He was the center for the Detroit Pistons in the late seventies and early eighties. He was one of the early big men who was also a great athlete; he could grab a defensive rebound and lead a fast break up court.

The "Ice Water" nickname came from the coolness that was said to run through his veins when it came time to take the key shot at the end of a game. He was a great clutch player, and though I wasn't sure if he was in the Hall of Fame, he was certainly a candidate for it.

I'm not a huge pro basketball fan; I prefer football and baseball. But I read enough of the sports pages to have in the back of my mind that Davenport became an agent for players after he retired, though I wasn't aware of a relationship with Judge Brennan when he played for the Celtics.

"Come on in," he said. "Denise will be down in a minute."

Denise was the recently widowed Mrs. Brennan, and my starting point in the investigation. "Good. Thanks."

"I'm a longtime friend of the family; would you object to my sitting in on your talk? She would prefer that."

I saw no problem with that, and said so. I wasn't trying to trap her; I just wanted information, and the more at ease she was the more likely she was to provide it. "Whatever makes her comfortable."

It was almost fifteen minutes before Denise Brennan came down the stairs, and if she spent that time trying to make herself appear not to be devastated, it was a wasted effort. She was a small, thin woman, and my guess was she looked a lot smaller and thinner than she had before her husband's murder.

She apologized for keeping me waiting, and offered me coffee, which I accepted. Then, "Thank you for your efforts, Lieutenant. I share my husband's disdain for capital punishment, but I must admit I wasn't sorry to hear about the resolution of this situation."

By "resolution," she meant my putting three bullets into Steven Gallagher. "I understand," I said, because I did. "I'd just like to ask you a few questions about your husband."

"You don't have any doubts about who committed the crime, do you?" asked Davenport.

I shook my head. "None. But in a situation like this, we have to tie up all loose ends," I said, neglecting to mention that among the loose ends here was the fact that my brother had been kidnapped and in six days wouldn't be able to breathe.

"What do you want to know?" she asked.

"Had your husband ever mentioned Steven Gallagher, in any context?"

She shook her head. "No, he didn't bring home his work. Once he took off the robe, that was it. His life on the job and his life at home were separate."

"So he never felt threatened by anything that happened in court?"

She thought for a moment. "Yes, a few times. He never spoke about it, but I could tell."

"How?"

"Sometimes he didn't want me to go out somewhere, or he would go with me, even if it was shopping, or something else he didn't like doing. And a few times I noticed some people that I think were security."

"But he never told you why he was concerned, or who he was concerned about?"

She shook her head. "No, I'm sorry. He never addressed it in any way."

"Was there anything unusual about the way he was acting recently? Any changes in mood? Anything that you noticed?"

She considered that for a few moments, and said, "I think he was feeling some stress, good kind of stress, over the Appeals Court appointment. When he testified before Congress, he was a little nervous. Dan rarely got nervous, so it surprised me. But it was more excitement than anything else."

I basically asked the same questions a few more times, but this woman obviously had no information that would help me. I told her I appreciated her talking to me, and let Davenport walk me to the door.

"Thanks for your time," I said.

"Strange way to spend yours."

"What does that mean?"

"It means that you're not sure the Gallagher kid did it. Otherwise what would be the difference if Danny had enemies?"

"Gallagher did it."

"I hope so. But if the real son of a bitch is out there, let me know how I can help."

"Will do."

When we got to the door, he opened it and I stepped outside.

"Danny was a complicated man, but a good one," he said. "A very, very good one."

It was a strange thing to say. "Complicated how?"

He just shook his head very, very slightly. "He was my friend."

I took one of my cards out of my pocket and handed it to him. "Call me if you want to talk about your friend some more."

Tommy Rhodes considered that night's job beneath him.

It wasn't a big deal, and he certainly wasn't going to complain about it. He was only thirty-four years old, but he thought of himself as an old-school guy, which meant that you did your job and moved on to the next one.

Of course, the fact that he was being paid enough money to last him until he was a hundred and thirty-four years old made him even more sanguine about the situation. He was a mercenary, pure and simple, and that was fine with him. As such, it wasn't his job to strategize; it was his job to accomplish the mission.

This was an easy assignment. He didn't really need Frankie Kagan there. Kagan had no experience in these kinds of operations; his talents were more in the areas of guns and knives. In this case he was there to provide protection for Tommy while he worked, though it was extremely unlikely that any problems would arise.

Tommy was resentful of Frankie's role as leader of their end of the operation, but he realized that it was Frankie who had the connection, and who brought Tommy in. There might be a time when Tommy would try to move up in the hierarchy, but he would have to be careful; Frankie was very, very dangerous.

So for now Tommy just focused on the work. The jobs he would be doing would grow progressively harder, and considerably more dangerous, but nothing that Tommy couldn't handle.

The toughest part was learning the terrain. His employers were smart enough to go outside the area to recruit, and had done their homework. Tommy was from Vegas, as was Frankie, or at least that's the place they had been working. So finding their way around upstate New York was not that easy.

They didn't want to use a GPS; if it was ever confiscated, the fact that it contained addresses of all of these criminal acts would be rather incriminating. So they did it the old-fashioned way, with a map, which was a bit of a pain in the ass.

Tommy didn't really know what was going on, and he didn't care. He had vaguely assumed that it had something to do with this mining thing, something about natural gas, and the fight that was going on over it. His target tonight confirmed that suspicion, but it really didn't matter to him either way.

The house was on a secluded street, which was understating the case. It wasn't really a street in the normally accepted sense; it was an estate with no other houses within a quarter of a mile. Tommy parked outside the property, and they walked towards where they were told the house would be, though it couldn't be seen from there.

It was a long walk, and only when they got close did the lights from the house pierce the total darkness. It was certainly not a hardship for Tommy, who was in extraordinary physical shape, even though he was carrying a bag that weighed the equivalent of two bowling balls.

The house looked massive, triggering a vague child-

hood recollection of his parents taking him to Virginia to
see where Thomas Jefferson lived. Tommy remembered
seeing the slave quarters on the property, and thinking
that Jefferson must have been an asshole.

Lights were on in the house, so Tommy assumed that
people were home. He had no idea if Richard Carlton was
there or not, and it didn't matter to Tommy at all.

The guesthouse was off to the left, and that was where
Tommy headed. It was dark and hard to see; the sky was
cloudy and moonlight was almost nonexistent. Tommy was
sorry that he didn't bring his night vision glasses, but it
wasn't a big deal either way. He could see well enough to
know that he had never lived in a house as nice as this
guesthouse.

But those days were in the past. In six months he'd be
living in a palace or, better yet, in a suite at the Bellagio.

The windows on the main floor were unlocked, as
Tommy expected they would be. He opened one and
climbed inside, signaling Frankie to stay outside and watch
for intruders. Tommy did not wear gloves, and was not
concerned about fingerprints.

Once inside, he entered an interior room and took out
his small flashlight, shining it into the bag he was carrying.
He emptied the contents, and spent the next twenty minutes positioning the explosives strategically around the
house.

The army training had served him well; Tommy oper-
ated with an expertise that was instinctive, and a complete confidence that he was doing things correctly. The
fact that there was no basement in the house made it easier, though only marginally.

Once he was finished, he did a check of his work, to
make sure everything was in good condition. There was
no hurry; he was not going to be detected. The only reason for moving quickly was that there was a basketball

game on television later that night that he was anxious to see. He had a bet on the game, for an amount of money that in the future he wouldn't be wasting his time on.

Tommy left through the front door, closing it and all the windows behind him. He didn't want there to be anywhere for the air to escape, though that was just him being more cautious than necessary. He took pride in his work, and even though there was no chance of failure, he still wanted to do it exactly right.

"All good?" Frankie asked softly once Tommy was outside.

"All good."

Thirty feet in front of the guesthouse, they stopped and Tommy took out the remaining items in the bag that he was carrying. They were a can of red paint and a brush, and he slowly and methodically painted letters on the driveway. It was difficult because of the darkness and the small light given off by the flashlight.

Once he was finished, he took his time to make sure the message was legible.

You will not hurt our children.

Satisfied with his work, Tommy took the now empty bag with him. He jogged back to the street, not because he was fearful of being caught but simply so he could get to his television and basketball game sooner. Frankie, not being a basketball fan, was not pleased, but since Tommy had the keys to the car, he was obliged to jog as well.

Once in the car, they drove about a half a mile, and then stopped. It would be close enough to confirm that the operation was a success, but far enough to ensure an easy getaway.

Tommy opened the window and dialed a number on his cell phone. Within two seconds of his pressing the last digit, he saw the flash of light in the distance, and then heard the explosion.

"All good?" Frankie asked.

"All good."

If Richard Carlton was going to have guests any time soon, they'd be staying in a hotel.

Michael Oliver had a very important job.

It didn't make him famous; it didn't make him stand out at all. He could walk down the streets of Tulsa, Oklahoma, as he did every day on the way to and from work, and never be recognized.

Oliver was chief engineer of Hanson Oil and Gas. They didn't have traditional titles there, but if they did, he probably would have been a Senior Vice President, or maybe an Executive Vice President. Which made him pretty high up the ladder.

But his significance was even greater than it appeared. As the head of a very small department, Oliver's job was to analyze land for its potential to provide energy, be it oil or natural gas. Once this was completed, a cost-benefit analysis was done to determine how expensive it would be to extract that energy, versus how much it could be sold for.

Hanson was a middle level player in the industry, but it still had a market capitalization of over six billion dollars. It didn't get that big by making mistakes, and Michael Oliver was the mistake preventer in chief.

When Oliver gave the go-ahead on a find, Hanson literally would take it to the bank. And if Oliver said the potential was not there, they did not go near it.

It was Oliver who personally did the analysis of the land near Brayton. It was he who determined that the shale was porous enough to yield natural gas and that it was set in a formation that could be harvested efficiently and very profitably. And it was he who estimated the immense amount of energy that could be derived.

For doing this, he was very well paid. But now, by simply putting another set of diagrams in an envelope and sending them off, he would have taken the final step towards ensuring he would get far more money than that.

So he put them in the envelope, and then drove an hour and fifteen minutes to a UPS store in Stillwater. He sent the package under an assumed name; it was the first illegal act he had ever committed, and he was not about to take any chances. It was why he did not simply e-mail the diagrams; e-mails lasted forever, and could not be shredded.

Oliver was not recognized in Stillwater, just as he was not recognized in Tulsa. But that didn't make him any less important. And what he had just done, simply sending that package, had been the most significant act of a very significant life.

"Nothing has changed," Barone said. "Overtime expected, vacations postponed, until we wrap this up."

I had requested that he call the meeting, and he didn't hesitate. There had been a letdown in effort on the case; cops have a tendency to stop focusing on a case when they believe it's been solved and the bad guy killed.

Detective Johnny Pagan asked the obvious question. "Wrap what up?"

"The Brennan murder," Barone said. "We want to nail Gallagher on the facts, not just because he pulled a gun on Luke. Shit, you know how many times I've wanted to shoot Luke?"

"What about the bloody clothes, and the DNA?" Pagan asked.

Barone hesitated for a second, so I jumped in. "It's evidence, significant evidence, but it's not everything. There's a huge amount of attention focused on this case; we need to be right, and we need to demonstrate it beyond any doubt. So the Captain wants to handle it as if it's going to trial, and that's what we're going to do."

Nobody in the room except Emmit had any idea what

the hell was going on, but nor did they want to question it any further. They would work on the case, that's their job, and the opportunity to get some overtime was just an added plus.

Emmit took over the meeting and gave out the assignments we had discussed. He would ride herd on them; Emmit was good at that. I saw no reason to tell anyone the seven-day deadline, but Emmit would see to it that they would be very busy days.

It was on the way back to my office when I felt a buzzing sensation in my pocket. All Sergeants and up are given BlackBerries, the purpose being to eliminate any semblance of a private life. The buzzing meant that I had an e-mail.

We are prohibited from using the devices for personal matters, so very few people outside of the department had this e-mail address. The only ones I could think of were Julie and Bryan, three or four prosecutors, an aunt in Florida, and a woman named Jeannie who I dated for four months. I gave it to her because she set what remains the record for my longest relationship, crushing the previous record holder by six weeks. The way things were going, you could say Jeannie was the Joe DiMaggio of my girlfriends.

I took the device out of my pocket and looked at it. I got what felt like a physical shock when I saw that it was Bryan's e-mail address. My first thought was that it was Julie using it, though it would have been the first time that I was aware of.

I clicked on it.

Lucas . . . I've been kidnapped and imprisoned by the brother of the kid you shot. He said he was going to find you and demand that you do something before he will release me. He is dangerous. Don't

*know where I am . . . he said it was underground. I
only have seven days of air. Limited power on computer . . . don't want to waste it . . . will check every
three hours.*

Tell me whatever you can . . . please.

Bryan.

I read the message twice. It didn't really tell me anything I didn't already know, but the fact that Bryan sent it
was enormously significant. It opened up the possibility
that he could aid in his own rescue; there might be something he saw or heard that could help us find him.

There might also be a way for us to locate him through
the e-mail itself, though that was way out of my area of
expertise. To that end, I wasted no time in heading for
Deb Guthrie's office, which was located one flight up, at
the far end of the building. I took the stairs two at a time.

Deb was a state police Lieutenant, as was I, but she
occupied an entirely different world. She was in charge of
the cybercrime unit, which is to say that I did not understand a single thing that she did. My computer proficiency
was such that it was lucky I was able to open the e-mail.

I could see through the glass into her office; she was
meeting with some guy in a suit, a meeting that was about
to end. I barged in and said, "Deb, I need to talk to you."

Deb and I have a really good relationship, and she could
tell from my entrance and the tone of my voice that this
was serious. "Kevin, let's pick this up later," she said, and
the guy obligingly got up and left.

"What's up, Luke?" she said when the door closed behind him.

"If someone sends you an e-mail, can you trace it to
where they are located?"

"We can get their IP address, if that's what you mean," she said.

"I don't even know what an IP address is. Is it like a real-world address?"

She shook her head. "No, but it's close. We can certainly narrow it down to a specific area. What have you got?"

"Deb, I'm about to show you something that I need your help on. But in the process I'm going to be putting you in a difficult position, because you cannot tell anyone about it."

"It's business?" she asked.

"Yes."

"Does the Captain know about it?"

"He officially knows nothing."

She smiled. "His favorite official posture. Let's have a look, Luke."

I showed her the e-mail, and she took her time reading it. "I assume you don't want to answer any questions," she said when she was finished.

"Correct."

"Luke, the person that e-mailed you can find out the IP address himself, as long as he has Internet access."

I hadn't known that, but in any event it didn't solve the problem. "No good," I said. "His e-mails might be being read."

She nodded. "OK. Give me your e-mail password."

I did so, and she said, "I'll call you as soon as I have the address."

I left Deb's office and went back to my own. By that point logic had overtaken optimism, for a number of reasons. For one, there seemed no possible way that Chris Gallagher had made a mistake in allowing Bryan to have the ability to e-mail. He had to have been completely confident that Bryan would not be able to aid in his rescue.

There was also a very significant possibility that it wasn't

Bryan e-mailing at all, but rather Gallagher using his account. He could be hoping to gain access to information in that manner. I would have to come up with a way to test that theory, and learn if it was really Bryan I was communicating with.

Even if it was Bryan, I had to assume that Gallagher had a way to monitor the account, and read our correspondence.

We still had a lot to learn about Chris Gallagher, but I suspected that we were going to learn he was smart, not the type to have made such a significant mistake. At the very least, he had to believe that he could not be hurt by Bryan being in contact with us, and more likely he saw it as a positive for himself.

As with our investigation, I would play it out the way Gallagher set it up, at least for the moment. I had no other choice. But first I had to answer Bryan.

Bryan . . . I spoke to Gallagher, and I'm working to get you released. Who was your favorite baseball player growing up?

Jonathon Stengel was a combination idealist/realist.

Certainly the prospect of a financially successful career influenced his decision to go to law school, but that wasn't all it was about for him. He also respected the justice system, and thought he could do good and worthwhile work within it.

That was a significant factor in his decision, after graduating from NYU Law, not to head for the financial security of a large firm. Instead he was awarded a position as a clerk on the United States Court of Appeals, working for Judge Susan Dembeck.

And the time he spent there was all he had hoped it would be, and more. He got to work with brilliant people, on important matters, all the while getting a look at the intimate workings of the system. He decided he would stay for only a year, leaving when Judge Dembeck left, but felt and hoped that he would someday be back, with clerks of his own.

But Stengel also had a need to earn money, and a clerk's pay was not going to get it done. Which was why he was susceptible to an approach from a fellow NYU alum, Edward Holland, the Mayor of Brayton, New York.

No money would change hands, but Stengel would supply information to Holland, who was arguing the fracking case before the court. Stengel rationalized it with the knowledge that it was not information that would give Holland an unfair advantage; all it would do was provide a "heads-up" for Holland. Advance information would then allow him to position things politically, since his audience was the electorate.

In return, Holland would use some of his significant connections in both the legal and political communities to aid Stengel in his career path.

A simple transaction with no losers, only winners.

To this point, there had been little for Stengel to provide, but now he finally had something. He did not want to make the call from home, and he certainly couldn't do it from the court, so he found a rare pay phone on the street.

Holland answered on his home number, and immediately recognized Stengel's voice. "What have you got?" he asked.

"Nothing good, but I thought you should know," Stengel said.

"She's staying on?"

"Yes, and she's the deciding vote."

Both men knew what that meant. The only chance Holland had to win the case on behalf of Brayton was for Dembeck to leave the court and be replaced by Brennan. Once Brennan was murdered, Dembeck's deciding to leave anyway would have left the court deadlocked.

But the die was cast; Dembeck was staying, and Holland was backing a losing horse.

"I'm sorry," Stengel said.

"Yeah. Me too."

I never got to ask Steven Gallagher if he had an alibi.

My shooting him three times in the chest effectively derailed prospects for an in-depth interrogation.

What would otherwise have taken place was my asking him where he was at the time of the Brennan murder. He could have said that he was home, or at a bar, or performing *La Traviata* at the Met. Whatever he said, I'd then be able to check it out, with the remote potential to exonerate him, or the far more likely potential to implicate him by proving he had lied.

But all of that never happened, and with him in a drawer at the coroner's office it wasn't about to. So part of our investigation had to include trying to discover where Steven was at the time of the murder. The fact that we already knew he was in Judge Brennan's garage swinging a knife was a complicating factor, but one that we had to overlook.

Emmit's role was to sift through the investigative information coming in, alerting me to things I should personally follow up on. Unfortunately, we were learning that Steven was a young man who had pretty much cut himself off from the world, once he descended into his drug use.

A notable exception to that seemed to be Laura Schmitz. She was said to have been Steven's girlfriend, though that relationship had apparently ended quite a while before his death. Steven's phone records showed calls from Ms. Schmitz with some frequency, calls that continued pretty much until the time I shot him. So she was someone we needed to talk to.

Laura worked as a waitress at the Plaza Diner in Fort Lee. Emmit and I stopped at the cash register in the front, where the manager was handling the register. When I flashed my badge and told him we needed to talk to Laura, he pointed to a woman behind the counter.

"Laura, these guys are here to see you."

She looked up, saw us, and quickly left the counter area, through an open door to the back. Emmit and I took off in pursuit.

It wasn't a long pursuit. Laura was standing in a corridor, adjacent to the kitchen, staring at the floor and looking angry.

"You son of a bitch," she said to me when we reached her. "You son of a bitch."

"I'm sorry, Laura. I know Steven was your friend."

"He was a beautiful person. And you shot him like an animal."

"It was not something I wanted to happen," I said.

She shook her head sadly. "You and me both."

"We just have to ask you a few questions."

"I've got nothing to say to you."

"Laura, don't make this harder than it has to be. If you won't answer the questions here, then you'll have to go down to the station with us. You could be there a very long time."

She seemed to consider this, but didn't say anything. I took it as an invitation to continue. There was an open office off the corridor, and I suggested we go in there. She didn't answer, but went into the office, and Emmit and I followed.

"Laura, do you know where Steven was on Friday night, just before midnight?"

"He was home."

"You saw him there?" I asked.

"No, but I spoke to him on the phone at about seven o'clock."

"What did he say?"

"I don't know," she said.

"You don't remember?"

"He wasn't making much sense," she said, then added grudgingly, "He was using."

"Did he say what he was planning to do later that night?" Emmit asked.

She frowned at the question, as if she considered it stupid. "He wasn't planning anything. When he got like that, he didn't go out. He stayed in his apartment and wasted his life." Then she looked at me. "Until you ended it."

"But you can't say for sure that he stayed home that night?"

She wouldn't give in. "I'm sure."

"Did he sound angry?"

"The only person Steven Gallagher was ever angry at was himself," she said.

"Can you give us the names of some of his other friends? Maybe people who saw him or spoke to him that night?"

"I was his only friend, besides his brother. And I wasn't there for him."

"Do you know where his brother is?" I asked.

"No."

"Have you seen him in the last couple of days?"

She nodded. "The night before last, but I haven't seen him since."

I asked if she had an address for him, but she said that

she didn't, and I believed her. Then I asked her if she had anything else to say.

She did.

"The idea that Steven Gallagher found out where that judge lived, that he even remembered the judge's name, is ridiculous. The idea that he went to his house that night is even dumber. The idea that he killed him is beyond stupid. And the fact that you murdered Steven Gallagher means you are going to rot in hell."

As interrogations go, that one was not great.

Bryan Somers couldn't wait three hours to check e-mail.

He made it to two hours and fifteen minutes, and turned on the computer, simultaneously vowing to himself to wait the full three hours next time. This was extra important, he said, because it would reveal whether Luke was getting the messages.

When the machine powered on, the first thing he looked at was the percentage of power remaining, displayed in an icon near the top. It said "96%," which pleased Bryan. He had been afraid that the simple acts of turning the machine on and putting it to sleep might have caused a more precipitous drop. If he was disciplined about using it, the computer would last longer than he would.

The e-mail from Luke was incredibly relieving for Bryan. While the situation with Julie had caused him to question how well he knew his brother at all, Bryan had no doubt that he was a terrific cop. If anyone could find him, it was Luke. Whether anyone could find him was an open question.

He rushed to respond; not knowing whether Luke would

answer, or what he would say, had made it impossible for Bryan to write out his message in advance.

He understood the question about his favorite ballplayer growing up. Luke had to make certain he wasn't communicating with Chris Gallagher, though Bryan knew Luke would be aware that Gallagher could easily be monitoring the e-mails.

> *Gary Carter. Keith Hernandez. Ron Darling. Take your pick. Lucas, even though Gallagher might be reading these e-mails, keep me as updated as you can. I'm scared and running out of time.*

> *I don't think Gallagher was making empty threats.*

Bryan was a Mets fanatic growing up, and he knew that Luke would view the list of ballplayers as evidence that it was really Bryan conducting the correspondence.

Very familiar with computers, Bryan next typed in a website that would let him find out his own IP address. He was sure that Luke was already trying to do the same, but he could do it more easily.

Except that he couldn't. Much to his disappointment, he discovered that he did not have access to the web at all, simply to the e-mail account. For whatever reason, Chris had wanted him to be able to communicate with Luke and the outside world but not be able to browse sites. The disconnect from Internet access would substantially limit his ability to help Luke find him, but there was no way for him to override it.

He still had television as a way to learn what was happening outside, but his situation had not hit the news.

So there was nothing to do but wait for another e-mail from Luke. He assumed that Luke had not brought in the FBI, or other authorities, or it would have made it into the media. So Luke was his contact with civilization, and his only hope to rejoin it.

Bryan decided that he would write out questions for Luke for his next e-mail, though Luke would have to be discreet in answering them, since Gallagher was probably reading them.

He might also eventually write out an e-mail to send to Julie, but first he would have to sort through his feelings about her. With no parents, and no children, Luke and Julie were all he had in the world, and they had betrayed him.

It made Bryan feel very alone, and the worst part was that he knew it was not just a feeling.

He really was alone.

One hundred and sixty-eight hours.

That's how I thought about the seven days that Bryan had been given. Somehow thinking about it in those terms made me press that much harder. But in the back of my mind, in the front of my mind, was the knowledge that I was wasting my time. I was not going to be able to prove that a guilty man was innocent.

Unless I lied.

Perhaps I could describe progress to Chris Gallagher that wasn't real but would seem to exonerate his brother. I certainly had no moral qualms about doing so, but it would really have to be convincing.

I would need to fake some evidence, and come up with someone I could hold up as the real killer. It would take some creative thinking, but if I wasn't making progress in the investigation, it would be a fallback position I would turn to.

So for the moment, I had to focus on the real-life investigation, and I was heading back to the office to get updated by Emmit. I turned on the radio, and they were still talking about the Brennan murder. One of his former basketball teammates was reflecting on his life, and the fact that he was a winner in everything he did.

"The fact that this happened just as he was reaching a goal, the Court of Appeals, makes it a particularly unspeakable tragedy," the friend said.

I had never focused on that fact before. If Steven Gallagher committed the murder, it had nothing to do with Brennan's appointment to the Appeals Court. Clearly Steven could not have cared less about that, if he knew it at all.

Instead, Steven's stabbing Brennan to death would simply have had to do with the fact that Steven was bitter and vengeful about his drug conviction.

So it was an apparent coincidence. Brennan was ascending to his new position, and receiving substantial publicity for it, just before his murder. Except I don't believe in coincidences, and had I not focused on Steven, I would have been cognizant of the fact that this one was a whopper.

So stepping back and looking at it, there were only two choices. One, that Brennan's judicial appointment and murder coincidentally happened at the same time. Or two, that the appointment and murder were related. For my purposes it did me no good to assume the former; I had to go with the latter.

That realization opened up a new line of inquiry. Rather than analyze only Judge Brennan's previous cases to find someone with motive, I could look at his future cases, or at least those in what was supposed to be his future.

It was well outside of my area of expertise, but I was sure there must be many cases awaiting Brennan when he arrived at the Appeals Court. Maybe someone didn't want him helping to decide them, and killed him for it.

I was about to call Julie when she called me. I could hear the strain in her voice.

"Talk to me, Luke. I need to know what's going on."

"I heard from Bryan. For some reason Gallagher is allowing him to e-mail."

"Is he OK?"

"So far. Julie, can we meet later, maybe have a quick dinner? I'll download you on all that's happening, though I wish it were more."

"Of course. And I have some information on Gallagher I can give you then. I wish there were more also."

"In the meantime, I need to talk to someone who would be familiar with the cases that Brennan would have heard on the Appeals Court."

"Why?" she asked.

"Because I'm flailing around, trying everything."

"OK. Call Lee Bollinger. No, don't call him; go see him. He's at his office in Teaneck; I spoke to him an hour ago. I'll call ahead and tell him to get started on what you need."

"I'm particularly interested in situations where someone knowledgeable would think that Brennan would have voted differently than Susan Dembeck."

"OK, I'll tell him that."

"How do you know he'll see me if I just show up?"

"Trust me, he'll see you," she said. When Julie sounds that certain about something, you can take it to the bank. In this case I would take it to Teaneck to see Lee Bollinger.

Bollinger is about as big an attorney as you can find on this side of the George Washington Bridge. Most of his clients are corporations, but he also handles some celebrities, especially sports figures. Somehow his cases often make it into the headlines; if a legal case becomes a hot publicity ticket, Bollinger is usually at the center of it.

But except for when his celebrity clients get hit with DUIs, or a domestic abuse offense or two, Bollinger rarely gets involved in criminal cases, which was why I was surprised that Julie knew him as well as she seemed to.

Bollinger's firm has its own three-story building off Route 4 in Teaneck, and if he's able to fill it with lawyers, then business must be pretty good.

When I walked into the reception area, I didn't have to say a word. The receptionist preempted that with, "Lieutenant Somers? Mr. Bollinger is waiting for you."

Within forty-five seconds I was sitting in the great man's office, having just been provided with a cup of the most delicious coffee I'd ever tasted. Bollinger was not yet there, but he came in a few seconds later, carrying a folder and offering a big handshake.

After our hellos, I said, "Boy, Julie must have pictures of you in a closet with a goat or something."

He laughed. "Better than that. She had discretion on a case involving one of my more famous clients, who shall remain nameless. She could have turned it into a huge PR fiasco, or quietly accepted a no contest plea."

"So she took the plea?"

He nodded. "After telling me this morning that she wouldn't." He holds up the folder. "So this must be pretty important."

"Not as much as you'd think."

He smiled, obviously not believing me. "Yeah, right. So Brennan's killer was a kid strung out on drugs, who was worried about how Brennan might decide future Appeals Court cases?"

"You remember what you said about Julie using discretion when it came to your client?"

"Of course."

"You might want to use some of your own, or she'll change her mind and discretion your client's ass onto every tabloid front page in the country. "

He looked surprised, so I continued. "Just tell me what

you have, and then don't talk to anyone else about it, counselor."

He smiled. "I am a model of discretion."

"Good. What have you got?"

He shrugged. "I have no idea. It's only been forty-five minutes since I spoke to Julie, and I put four lawyers on it. This is what they came up with, but I haven't gotten a chance to look through it. There will be more."

"How soon?"

"End of the day. I'll messenger it to your office."

I thanked him and took the folder.

"I hope you got the right guy," he said.

"Me too."

Bryan . . . he wants me to clear his brother and find out who really killed the Judge. I'm working on it now . . . the whole department is on it. We've got some good early leads. You feeling OK? Anything you can tell me about where you are? Gallagher says he's not reading these e-mails but he probably is. In any event, tell me whatever you can.

You can punch me in the mouth when I get you out.

Keith Hernandez couldn't carry Don Mattingly's glove. Mattingly belongs in the Hall of Fame. Hernandez belongs on Seinfeld.

In all the time I was a cop, I never framed anyone.

I'm not just talking about out-and-out frames, where evidence is created and planted to implicate an innocent party. I'm talking about shadings, about things like not aggressively pursuing evidence that might help the accused, when I thought the accused was guilty.

I always prided myself on going after the truth whether or not it might butt up against my preconceived notions; I'd much rather adjust my point of view than adjust the evidence in any way.

I'm not looking for praise in saying this; it's my job, and I could say the same of every cop I've ever worked with, with the possible exception of one or two. Or three at the most.

But I'd never been faced with a situation like this before, and my strategy was evolving. And it was becoming increasingly clear to me that in order to succeed, I was going to have to frame someone for the murder of Judge Danny Brennan.

My victim wouldn't be going to jail; he or she wouldn't even be going to trial. The sole judge and jury who would decide the case was Chris Gallagher. I had to credibly make a case to him that someone, other than his brother, committed the murder.

But I couldn't come up with a perpetrator out of whole cloth. I also needed a motive, and an ability for someone to have committed the crime. And that was basically why I had gotten the information about the Appeals Court cases. I did not believe that anyone involved in those cases had slaughtered Danny Brennan in his garage. But I needed to make Chris Gallagher believe that they did.

I spent a few hours going over the information in the folder, plus additional material that Bollinger, as promised, messengered over. Much of it was legalese, which I only partially understood, but I identified at least three possible cases to pursue. I would bring it to dinner with Julie, since she was far more knowledgeable about this stuff than I was.

We met at Spumoni's, a casual Italian place in Englewood. I'd eaten there a number of times with Julie and Bryan; sometimes I brought a date, and sometimes I didn't. I even remember some of their names.

I got there first and took a quiet table near the back. Julie came in a few minutes later, the strain evident on her face. She still looked fantastic; that was a given. But this time she looked fantastic and very, very stressed.

We didn't kiss hello; we never did. I don't think I know another woman in the world, outside of work, who doesn't kiss me hello, but Julie never did. At least not since the night we did a lot more than kiss.

She just about grabbed the waiter and ordered a drink, a favorite of hers called a "Dark and Stormy." She asked for it the way she might ask for a life preserver on a ship about to go down, but didn't wait for it to come before handing me the envelope she had brought.

"Everything you ever wanted to know about Christopher Gallagher," she said.

"Summarize it," I said.

"No, it's bedtime reading for you, but you won't sleep much after you read it. You do the talking."

I took her through everything that had transpired since we last talked, including showing her printed copies of the e-mails that Bryan and I had exchanged. It was depressing in the telling, as it drove home the reality that we were getting nowhere.

I was getting nowhere.

"Do you think I should bring in the Feds?" I asked.

"I've been thinking about that," she said. "And I don't think you should."

"Why not?"

"Because they're a machine, and they will do what they're programmed to do. They'll try and catch Gallagher, though I don't think they'll be able to. But if they did catch him, it wouldn't go the way that we want."

"I'm chasing something that doesn't exist," I said.

She nodded. "I know."

"I'm going to have to fake it," I said.

She nodded again, and pointed to the folder that I had brought. "Which is why you wanted the case information from Bollinger."

"Right. I need you to go through it. I saw a few possibilities that we can go after, maybe find a credible villain . . ."

"So I've got my own bedtime reading," she said.

"Yeah. Julie, is there anything you want me to say to Bryan for you? Or you could e-mail him yourself."

"I don't think I should. This is a nightmare for him, and I want it to be as bearable as possible. If he wanted to hear from me, he would e-mail me. You think I'm wrong?"

I nodded. "I think you're wrong."

She thought about it for a while. "Tell him I love him. And tell him I'm sorry."

Chris Gallagher was waiting on my porch when I got home.

He was sitting there, not a care in the world, like he belonged and was thinking of organizing a neighborhood block party. I wasn't particularly surprised.

"How come you didn't break in?" I asked.

"No need for the drama anymore," he said. "You want to talk inside, or out here?"

"Inside."

We went into the kitchen, and I stopped at the refrigerator. I took out two bottles of beer, and tossed one to Gallagher.

"The gracious host," he said.

"Hopefully you're doing the same for my brother."

"I assume you're asking him in your e-mails," he said.

"And I assume you're reading them."

He shook his head. "No. I could, but I'm not."

"You're full of shit," I said.

He smiled. "I am many things, but I am not full of shit. I don't say words unless I mean them."

"So why are you letting him e-mail?"

"Steven e-mailed me in Afghanistan; it's the way we

kept in touch. I heard from him just six hours before you killed him. Unfortunately, all I did with his e-mails was read them."

"So Bryan being able to e-mail me satisfies some sense of justice you have?"

He shrugged. "I guess so. I don't try to figure myself out much."

"So what are you doing here?" I asked.

"Checking on your progress, assuming you're making some."

"It's been one day," I said.

"You've only got seven."

"That's not enough."

"On behalf of your brother, I'm sorry to hear that. Now tell me where you are."

I was having a tough time deciding how much to tell him, since at that point I didn't even know enough to come up with a credible fake scenario. I decided to be as nonspecific as I could get away with.

"There's an entire task force working on this, though they are not aware of the situation with you and Bryan. We're taking a two-pronged approach. We're attempting to establish an alibi for Steven, trying to find out where he was at the time of the murder, and whether anyone can place him away from the scene."

"How is that going?"

"We're not there yet. But I have a proposition for you. I am willing to go on national television and say that Steven was innocent, that I shot the wrong man. And when Bryan is released, I won't go back on that. I promise."

"No good," he said.

"Why not? It will clear Steven's name in the eyes of the world. Isn't that what this is about? You already believe in him; he doesn't need to be cleared in your eyes, does he?"

He ignored this. "You said two-pronged approach; what's the other one?"

"We're trying to identify other suspects. These could come from defendants in Brennan's courtroom who might have carried a grudge against him, or people with a reason to fear how Brennan might help decide cases before the Appeals Court."

Gallagher nodded, apparently agreeing with the approach. "And where are you on all that?" he asked.

"We're one day in, Gallagher. One day."

"It took less time than that for you to go after Steven," he said.

"We were there to question him, that's all. He had a gun, and he raised it."

"That's bullshit."

It hit me that Gallagher knew less than I had imagined. "He left a suicide note."

Gallagher reacted angrily. "Be careful, Luke. I am not someone you want to bullshit."

"I'm telling you the truth. It said that he couldn't take it anymore. And he said, 'Tell Chris I'm sorry.' "

"Shut your mouth."

"So you're better at telling the truth than hearing it? I can get the note and show it to you, if you'd like."

He was quiet for a few moments, sort of bowing his head. I couldn't tell whether his eyes were open or not. The really unsettling thing was that I had no idea how he would react; he was a complete mystery to me. Bryan's life would ultimately depend on whether I figured him out.

When he finally spoke, it was softly, and the words did not seem to come easily. "He was scared. He was alone, and he was scared, and everything ahead of him seemed awful. But you made sure there was nothing ahead of him."

"That's what Bryan is going through right now."

"It's different for him," Gallagher said. "He's got someone to help him. Don't blow it."

"Let him go, and I promise I'll work just as hard to
clear Steven."

He stood up. "Six days," he said, and then left.

*Lucas . . . I'm feeling OK . . . I'm comfortable. He's
got me chained, but I can get around, and there's
plenty to eat and drink. Can't access the Internet,
but obviously can e-mail. I have television, local NY
stations, and it seems to be satellite, if that helps.*

*I watched a clip of you doing a TV interview . . .
you might want to spend some time on the tread-
mill.*

*The idea of punching you in the face is what keeps
me going.*

*Remember the time Dad took us to a Mets game for
the first time and we were amazed at how green the
grass looked? I'd sort of like to see grass again
sometime.*

Please get me out of here.

Julie was right that reading about Chris Gallagher would not be fun.

She had somehow gotten his service record, plus letters written about him by his commanding officers and others he encountered during his military career.

The service record itself was scary, as much because of what it didn't say as what it did. There were large gaps that did not detail where he was or what he was doing for months at a time. Instead the only listings during these periods categorized him as being TAD, which I knew to mean Temporarily Assigned Duty.

Having served in the military myself, I had no doubt what this really meant, and the dates confirmed it. He was Black Ops, meaning he was put into both Iraq and Afghanistan before we entered those countries. They would have been mostly reconnaissance missions, to prepare for our full-scale military entrance.

While Black Ops are there to scout the enemy, terrain, etc., they are quite prepared to engage any hostile forces they might meet. If they are captured, the US Government will not acknowledge their existence, which in and of itself is not that significant, since they would certainly be killed anyway.

Suffice it to say that our government uses very few wimps for these missions. They send the toughest of the tough, the most well-trained, disciplined soldiers we have. That was who Chris Gallagher was, and that was who Bryan and I were up against. And if Iraq and Afghanistan did not prove daunting for him, it was unlikely that New Jersey would fill him with fear.

Gallagher joined the Marines at the age of twenty-three, and was trained as a communications and electronics expert. Eighteen months later he applied for Force Recon status, which involves training in everything from parachute jumping to underwater demolition to enhanced combat techniques in extraordinarily difficult conditions.

His psychological evaluations seemed unremarkable, though they were filled with words like "resolute," "determined," and "purposeful." The only relative he listed or apparently ever mentioned was his brother, Steven. Their parents were long deceased.

Nothing about Gallagher, or anyone else for that matter, frightened me physically. I think I was born without the "personal danger" gene; I just never get fearful about my own physical safety. It's not necessarily a good quality for a cop.

Physical fear is as important as physical pain. People who can't feel pain aren't able to be protective; for instance, their skin could be being burned and they might not know it. In a similar fashion, fear acts to help one avoid dangerous situations, and my lack of fear is a negative for that reason. I don't instinctively avoid danger; instead I must force my mind to be logical about it.

But I can feel fear for others, and I was feeling it big-time for Bryan. He always had the fear gene; we were very different in that way. He once confessed to me that it was a major reason why he didn't follow me and my father into police work. And at the moment he had to be really, really scared of what was going to happen, so I was scared on his behalf.

One of the most disappointing things about the information Julie had given me on Gallagher was his lack of connections to anyone but his brother. I had hoped for friends, or other relatives, who he might be in contact with. They might have led me to Bryan; they might even have been helping to keep him captive. But at least for the moment, that avenue was closed.

I decided to focus on something more upbeat, though pretty much anything would have qualified. I again dove into the Appeals Court cases, since I needed to pick one to focus on. I wasn't necessarily looking for the one most likely to tie in to the Brennan murder, but rather the one I could make Gallagher believe. They might have been one and the same, but maybe not.

I narrowed it down to two possibilities, and then chose the one that made the most sense. It was a case in which the town of Brayton was suing to prevent a company from doing something called fracking on land adjacent to the town. Fracking, which was the extrication of natural gas from shale, was claimed by the town to be environmentally devastating.

I chose the case for four reasons. One, it was relatively nearby. Two, there was close to four hundred million dollars at stake, just representing the purchase price of the land, and maybe billons more once the drilling took place. Three, the case was nearing a completion and Brennan's addition to the court could have upset the applecart. And four, emotions in the town were running very high; there had even been violence that was being attributed to the situation. The guesthouse of the man who owned the land had been blown up.

All of this seemed to add up to a believable set of circumstances to lead to a murder.

Bryan, I will get you out . . . you have my word. Knowing about the NY stations is helpful; think hard about anything else you can tell me. Maybe something you saw or heard on the way there. No matter how insignificant it might seem, it can help.

Also look for serial numbers on any of the appliances.

That wasn't me doing the interviews . . . it was a fat actor they hired to play me. Someday I'll work myself into shape, like you investment bankers.

You'll see grass again soon, but it will be in Yankee Stadium. Only the best for my brother.

"I am with you one hundred percent," Edward Holland shouted.

He had just said pretty much the same thing, albeit more softly, at the council meeting inside the Brayton Town Hall. There he had been talking to the elected town officials, as well as the small number of citizens who could fit inside the cramped quarters.

But this was a much bigger gathering, and in many ways a more significant one. It numbered more than fifteen hundred people, holding signs and chanting their determination to protect their families and their lifestyle. For Brayton, it qualified as something akin to a Million Man March.

They were also voters, and they had put Holland in office. They had supported him throughout the fight against Richard Carlton and his company, trying to prevent the fracking that they all believed, that Holland had in fact told them, could threaten their health and well-being.

But they had to be handled, and Holland was the guy to do it. He was their hero, fighting valiantly against the corporate villains. It was an image that he had carefully cultivated throughout the battle, so much so that his "soldiers" were apparently getting carried away.

"I know how you feel, and I share your passion and your anger," Holland said. "And I know you agree with me that violence is not the answer. It is not what we are about; it is not what Brayton is about."

There had been no arrests made for the destruction of Richard Carlton's guesthouse, but it was commonly believed that the perpetrators did what they did in retaliation for Carlton's attempt to sell the land for fracking.

Holland's call against violence was greeted by a mixture of cheers and angry yells; it was clear that not everyone in the audience was inclined to take the high road.

"The moneyed interests and many in the media are trying to paint you as vigilantes, as outlaws who are dangerous and disrespectful of the process. We cannot let them do that."

This seemed to get a more enthusiastic response, so Holland continued. "We don't need bombs, or guns, or violence of any kind. We have a greater power on our side; we have the truth."

This was greeted with a roar of approval; Holland now had them under control. He turned to look at Alex Hutchinson, who had emerged in recent weeks as an unelected leader of the townspeople. Alex was nodding approval.

"We are law-abiding citizens," Holland continued. "All we are seeking is justice and the ability to protect our children and our families. We will get that justice; I will accept nothing less.

"So have faith in the process. Have faith in the American system. Have faith in God. Your faith, our faith, will carry us through to victory."

By then the crowd was completely with Edward

Holland; they hung on his every word. They trusted him; if he said they would win in the courts, then they would win in the courts.

The only thing he failed to mention was what he knew to be the truth.

They were going to lose.

The drive to Brayton took an hour and ten minutes.

It would ordinarily have taken me an hour and a half, and with it raining like it was, maybe even longer than that. Which was why I brought Emmit along, and let him drive.

Emmit drives like an absolute maniac, and he rode the siren most of the way. He did this even though we had no jurisdiction in New York, figuring we could handle any local cops who had a problem. None did.

My first stop was going to be at the town hall to see the Mayor, Edward Holland. We had a brief conversation over the phone, but if I was going to pin Judge Brennan's murder on the situation in Brayton, I needed as much firsthand exposure to it as possible. I was hoping Holland could draw me a road map.

Holland originally thought I was investigating the explosion at the house of Richard Carlton, his adversary in the legal proceedings concerning the proposed fracking. He quickly realized that it made no sense for the New Jersey State Police to have an interest in a New York crime, and asked why I wanted to meet.

"We believe that a case we are working on here may intersect with the controversy you're involved in."

"Can you be more specific?" he asked.

"I can, and I will when we meet."

He made it clear to me how busy he was, as a way of telling me that the meeting would not be a long one, but he ultimately agreed. I made a similar call to Richard Carlton, who it turned out was in Manhattan for business meetings. I arranged to see him there the next day.

I liked Brayton a lot. It was a sort of sleepy place, with a town center consisting of basically three streets of shops. It was the kind of place where the superstores have not made their appearance, probably because the economics don't warrant it.

All in all, a nice place to grow up, provided the water was safe to drink and the air breathable. I could see why people would be upset that big industry might damage the cocoon they had constructed around their families. It wasn't Mayberry; it was considerably more sophisticated than that. But it felt right.

Emmit dropped me off at the town hall, while he went on ahead to the Brayton Police Station to get as much background as he could on the violence. Edward Holland had left instructions for me to be ushered into his office immediately upon my arrival, and that's what happened.

"Is this about the Brennan murder?" he asked right away, surprising me.

I nodded. "Yes, but very loosely at this point. We're covering our bases, and as part of that we're looking into the cases he would have been involved in on the Court of Appeals."

"That could take a while. He would have had a full caseload," Holland said.

I nodded. "And we're checking as many as manpower allows. The fact that there has already been some violence in connection with your case puts it near the top of the list."

"Somebody blew up Richard Carlton's guesthouse in frustration and anger. It is extraordinarily unlikely that whoever did it had the sophistication to try and control which judges would rule on the Court of Appeals."

"I'm sure you're right," I said, and in fact I was sure he was right. But that didn't mean I wasn't going to implicate the "Brayton bomber" in the court run by Chris Gallagher. "But I've still got to ask the questions."

He shrugged. "Ask away."

"Do you have any idea who set the explosion?"

"Not the slightest. You'd be better off asking the police."

I nodded. "My partner is doing that right now. I'm asking if you have any instincts about it."

He shook his head. "I don't; this has been a peaceful community for as long as I remember. But people are very, very upset, and rightfully so. Having said that, there is no one I know in this town that I would consider capable of such an act."

"Are you going to win your case?"

"I have every confidence," he said, without much conviction.

"Is that your official position?"

He smiled. "It is."

"What impact would Brennan replacing Judge Dembeck have had on the case?"

He shrugged. "Hard to say, which is one of the reasons you're wasting your time."

"So you as the lead lawyer, and Mayor, had no preference for either Judge Dembeck or Judge Brennan?"

He thought for a moment, as if deciding how honest to be. "I doubt that Judge Dembeck is favorable to our position, based on her previous rulings, and her questions during oral arguments. Brennan would have been a wild card, hard to categorize."

"Why?"

"A couple of reasons," he said. "First, it was in his nature to be unpredictable; I think he relished it. Second, I'm not aware of any similar cases he had ever heard, and he had never written on the matter."

"So you researched it?"

"Of course. Not to do so would have been unprofessional and borderline negligent."

"So net-net, Brennan would have been better for your side than Dembeck? That's your view?"

"Probably, but it's all very, very speculative. Other lawyers might feel completely differently about it. Anticipating judicial decisions is no way to make a living."

I was pretty much running out of questions, mostly because of his answers so far. If he was right that Brennan's joining the court would be a possible problem for Carlton's side, then they would have been the ones most inclined to prevent him from doing so. Which made them my most likely suspects.

I thanked him and walked over to the police station, which was in the same complex. Emmit was just coming out, having spoken to the lead detective assigned to the bombing of the Carlton guesthouse.

"They've got zip; the perp left nothing behind at the scene," he said. "Which surprises them. They think it's an amateur who behaved like a pro."

"Why are they thinking amateur?"

"Because everybody in the town is pissed at Carlton and they aren't the types to go out and hire professional muscle. So somebody got frustrated and angry, and did the job. They were just lucky."

Holland had described the perpetrator in similar terms;

no doubt he was in touch with his officers. "Is there a leader in the town on this issue, other than Holland?"

Emmit nodded. "According to the detective, the unofficial leader is Alex Hutchinson."

I thought about it for a few moments, then shook my head. "Doesn't work for us."

"What do you mean?"

"According to Holland, the town's side would have had reason to be in favor of Brennan joining the court. They might have bombed Carlton's guesthouse, but killing Brennan is a tough sell. It would run counter to their interests. If there's a killer we can point to, he's on the other side."

Emmit nodded his understanding. "Makes sense."

"So let's go talk to Alex Hutchinson."

"You just said that doesn't work for us."

"We're here anyway; maybe Hutchinson will say something to change my mind. Can't hurt to talk to him; where is he?"

"She's at the diner," Emmit said.

"What?"

"Alex Hutchinson is a woman."

Lucas . . . something happened this morning. I was watching television at about ten forty-five, and the satellite went out for about five minutes. Then, maybe twenty minutes later, it went out for three minutes. Could it be the weather? Would that have happened everywhere, or just certain areas?

Sorry to say serial numbers have been scraped off. He's smart. Please be smarter (just this once).

Let me hear from you.

"What was the weather like there this morning?"

"The weather?" Julie asked, obviously puzzled as to why I had called to ask that question.

"Yes. Bryan's satellite television went out for a few minutes twice this morning. It was out for five minutes at ten forty-five, then for three minutes at eleven ten."

"I don't know . . . I was in my office. I know it was raining; Danielle went out for coffee and took my umbrella."

"OK, we—"

Julie interrupted me, knowing exactly where I was heading. "I'll get a subpoena and get the satellite companies to give me any information on disruptions this morning. Maybe it's isolated to a specific area."

"That's why Bryan told me about it."

"I'll get right on it," she said. "It will give me something to do."

I could hear the stress in her voice, and I felt for her. I also felt for me. But I especially felt for Bryan. "Julie, you OK?" I asked.

"Yes, other than the fact that my head feels like it's going to explode."

"I know the feeling. Did you get a chance to look through those Appeals Court cases?"

I could hear the sudden anger in her voice. I had always been struck by her ability to change moods on a dime; some people found it intimidating, but I was not one of them. "Did I get a chance?" she asked. "No, I went miniature golfing instead. Of course I got a chance."

"Sorry. Unless you have a better idea, I'm focusing in on Carlton versus the town of Brayton, NY. Emmit and I are there now."

"The fracking case. That's the one I would go with as well."

"Good. I need to know what impact Brennan not joining the court would have been expected to have on that case."

"You think that could have something to do with Brennan's murder?"

"In real life? No. But it could serve our purpose."

She promised to dig more into the case immediately, and then asked, "How's Bryan holding up?"

"Seems OK," I said. "He's tougher than I would have thought."

"Doesn't surprise me at all," she said.

We got to Alex's Country Diner at around one thirty, at what should have been near the end of the lunch hour rush. There were three cars in the parking lot; my guess was that Alex's Country Diner hadn't seen an actual rush in a very long time.

There were only ten tables in the place, and two were occupied, plus another three people were eating at the counter. In terms of employees, there was a woman behind the counter, and another at the cash register. Each was in her thirties; they could have been sisters.

It turned out that Alex Hutchinson was the cashier, and when we identified ourselves she nodded as if she was expecting us. She called out to her colleague to cover the register, and we went to a booth near the back.

"I've got nothing to tell you now that I didn't tell you last time," she said.

"This is the first time we've spoken to you," I said.

"Don't you guys talk to each other? Two other officers questioned me the other day."

"They were local; we're New Jersey State," Emmit said.

She laughed a very likable laugh, one that said she couldn't have been less intimidated by us. "New Jersey? What is it you think I did in New Jersey?"

"Actually, this works better if we ask the questions, so let's start over," I said. "Did you supply the other officers with your whereabouts when the explosion took place?"

"I told them I was at home, reading a story to my kids. The kids that Carlton is trying to poison."

"You seem angry at him."

"Duhhhh," was her way of telling me I made a stupid statement. I almost laughed myself, because she was right, and called me on it.

"But not angry enough to blow up his guesthouse?" I asked.

"If I thought blowing up his guesthouse would protect my family, I'd blow up his guesthouse. But it won't, so I didn't."

"Maybe you thought it would scare him into keeping the land pure."

She laughed, quickly and derisively. "The only thing that scares the Richard Carltons of the world is not having a lot of money. What scares me is not being able to keep my family healthy."

"Just so I understand, you're not opposed to violence, as long as the cause is just?"

"What they're trying to do is violence, and the worst kind. It's murder for money."

I liked her a lot, and in the moment identified with her. I was having some family protection issues myself.

I changed the subject. "What do you know about Judge Danny Brennan?"

"The basketball player who got murdered?"

"That's the one."

"My husband played against him in college, and he got stabbed to death, I think it was in his garage. And he became a judge. That exhausts my knowledge of him."

"Do you have any thoughts about how he might have ruled in the case your town is involved in?"

"Not a clue, and I had no idea he'd be involved in our case. But if he would have been on our side, then Carlton's the killer. Go get him."

I turned to Emmit. "Might as well."

Before we left I gave Alex my card, and said, "Please make me your first call if there's anything you think I should know. Anything at all. I'm here to help, and to put the people that are doing this away."

She nodded and said, "I will." I believed her, and I thought she believed me. It seemed like Alex Hutchinson only said things if she meant them.

On the way out, Emmit smiled and said, "I don't think it would be a good idea to get on her bad side."

"You got that right."

While we were at the diner, I had gotten a message from Deb Guthrie, asking me to call her back. I did so as soon as we got into the car.

"You're up against somebody that's good," she said.

"How so?"

"We traced your brother's e-mail back to the IP address. It's in Afghanistan."

"That's crazy, Deb. There's no way he's in Afghanistan."

"I didn't say he was. It's a trick that's used. Not to make it too complicated, they route the traffic through servers set up for the purpose of concealment. He's probably using multiple servers in different countries; the next e-mail your brother sends could come up with an IP address in some other country."

"So no way to crack it?"

"Not likely," she said. "But your brother could find it out himself; there are websites he could go to. He'd get the address before it's routed."

"He doesn't have web access, only e-mails."

"Like I said, you're up against somebody that's good."

There really wasn't much for Chris Gallagher to do.

He had accomplished his initial goal, which was to send Lucas Somers out in search of Steven's exoneration. He had no idea what Somers would come up with, but he had no intention of extending the deadline.

After seven days, if the goal had not been achieved, Lucas Somers's brother would die. Gallagher didn't see that as revenge; he saw it as justice, as a form of equality. He wouldn't be happy about it; he'd much prefer to have Somers succeed. But nor would he feel any particular remorse. He had seen plenty of innocent people sacrificed for a mission; it was simply a fact of life.

If Somers failed, an outcome probably more likely than not, Gallagher would have to come up with another way to defend Steven in death. But he had confidence that he'd figure out something, and wouldn't worry about it until events dictated it.

Which left him with some time on his hands, a situation that Gallagher was neither used to nor comfortable with. He wasn't in hiding; there was no need for that. Somers was obviously smart enough to realize that he had nothing to gain and everything to lose by putting out an arrest warrant, so the police were neither after him nor looking for him. If Bryan Somers wound up dying, then of course that would change. No matter; Gallagher could handle it either way.

But hanging out and watching television while Somers was doing the work wasn't quite Gallagher's style, so instead he decided to more closely monitor the situation. He would follow Somers from a distance, to see firsthand what he was up to.

The act of doing so would not be difficult. Gallagher had trailed the enemy through mountain terrain in Afghanistan; by comparison the New York State Thruway was a piece of cake. And Somers would not be alert to the possibility; he would have no reason to think he was being followed.

The purpose was not just to kill time, nor to make sure that Somers wasn't able to locate his brother. The house and shelter was owned by a marine buddy of Gallagher's, but there would be no record of them having been together in the service. They were both Black Ops, which in army terms was to say that they barely even existed.

Gallagher's buddy had done what buddies do; he didn't ask questions when Gallagher asked for the use of the place for ten days. It even gave the guy an excuse to visit his sister in Syracuse.

Gallagher was going to follow Somers to gather information and help him judge the veracity of what Somers was telling him. He fully expected Somers to dramatically exaggerate his investigative progress, thinking that it would make Gallagher inclined to spare his brother.

So Gallagher followed Somers and his partner out to Brayton, and waited as he went into the town hall, and then on to the diner. Gallagher had no idea who he met with in the town hall, but saw that the cashier in the diner accompanied them to the booth in the back as soon as they walked in. Clearly they were not there for lunch, they were there to talk to her.

When they left, he decided not to follow them, but rather to enter the diner. The place was almost empty, and he found it easy to strike up a conversation with the woman who said her name was Alex Hutchinson.

She was more than willing to talk about her crusade to protect her town and family from the environmental disaster she was sure they were facing. And when she mentioned the fact that it was before the Court of Appeals, Gallagher knew why Somers had gone there in the first place.

He left to head back to his motel room, where he would research the case on the Internet.

It would give him something to do.

I asked Emmit to gather any information detectives had uncovered regarding an alibi for Steven Gallagher.

I had not been paying much attention to that part of the investigation for a couple of reasons. First of all, I strongly believed he was the killer, so by definition there could be no credible alibi. But secondly, I feared that just an alibi and a proclamation of Steven's innocence would never be enough for his brother. We were going to need to come up with an actual guilty party, and just developing an alibi for Steven didn't get us there.

"Nothing good to report," Emmit said when he entered my office carrying a large folder with the accumulated information. "Nobody has come forward claiming to having seen Steven Gallagher that night. He made a couple of phone calls, but they were three and four hours before the murder. The last e-mail he sent was earlier that day, to his brother."

For some reason, when I heard that information, it struck me differently than it had Emmit. But before I voiced my point of view, I asked Emmit to give me a half hour with the detectives' reports to go over them.

When he came back I said, "Somebody saw Gallagher that night."

"Where did you see that?" he asked.

"The nine-one-one call. Whoever made that call must have seen him."

"Unless Gallagher told him about it the next day."

I shook my head. "He was a loner, had almost no friends, but he happened to see someone the next day and mention that he murdered a judge? Doesn't make sense."

"So someone saw him come home with blood on his clothes, made the anonymous call, but hasn't come forward," he said.

"It was nighttime, Steven was wearing dark clothing, but somebody saw the blood and knew that's what it was? And then connected Steven to a judge's murder twenty miles away?"

"Maybe they knew Steven, and knew Brennan had sentenced him."

"It's a stretch, but maybe," I said. "How did Steven get to and from Brennan's house? He didn't own a car."

"That's bothered me as well," Emmit said. "Brennan lived miles from a bus stop, and there's certainly no bus that goes anywhere near a route from Steven's house in Paterson to Brennan's neighborhood."

I nodded. "Have them check the buses anyway, and every cab company that services the area."

"Will do. Maybe Steven has a friend that gave him a ride, then realized what had happened and called nine-one-one anonymously."

"So how come we haven't found the friend?"

Emmit shrugged. "Doesn't mean he doesn't exist. Somebody called nine-one-one, and we found the bloody clothes. With Brennan's DNA. You can't wish that away, Luke."

Right then all I was wishing was that I hadn't been so intent on developing a lie, because it had stopped me from searching for the truth. "Emmit, this kid was strung out on drugs. He lived in a dump with no locks on the windows. Almost never went out of the house. He had no friends. No support structure. Danny Brennan was about to sentence him to prison."

"And?"

"And I'm not saying it happened, but can you think of an easier person to frame?"

Emmit didn't seem convinced, which was OK, because I wasn't, either. "This murder was done in the dark, with no one around. As far as we know, there wasn't a single piece of evidence at the scene which would have led us to the killer."

It was my turn to cut the speech short. "So?"

"So why bother to frame him at all? The killer got away clean. Why go to all this trouble? It would only add to the risk."

"Why do you ever frame someone? So the dumb cops would stop looking for the real killer. And in this case maybe there was another motive. Maybe it wasn't just the killer they were protecting. Maybe they were protecting the reason for the killing."

"You mean one of Brennan's cases?"

I nodded. "Maybe we've been looking in the right place all along."

Emmit was clearly skeptical. "You believe all this?"

"Probably not, but there's one other thing that bugs me," I said.

"What's that?"

"That the informant called us. The Feds had a hotline being advertised constantly on television; they even had a reward offered. But someone anonymously calls us. If it were one of our regular informants, I could understand it. But it obviously wasn't. So why did he call us?"

"You have a theory on that?" he asked.

"I do. They thought we could be more easily manipulated than the Feds. That we'd take the bait, and maybe even go in shooting. They thought we'd be dumb enough to take it all at face value.

"And you know what?" I asked. "They were right."

Bryan . . . we're checking into weather patterns. Did you hear any thunder? Can you hear anything outside at all? Making progress, Brother . . . hang in there.

Julie said to tell you that she loves you. It wasn't her fault . . . it was mine. You need to know that.

Finally Tommy Rhodes believed he was earning his money.

Well, maybe not all that money, but a lot of it. Because this was one of the most difficult things he had ever had to do.

Once again Frankie Kagan was along to provide protection against any unexpected intruders. Tommy would have preferred that Frankie help in the actual operation, since it involved some heavy work, but it also required a technical sophistication and expertise that Frankie didn't possess. Frankie's expertise was better suited to stabbing judges to death in their garages.

Explosives, by definition, are designed to destroy, to obliterate. As such, they often don't have to be placed with great precision; if the bomb is big enough, the job will get done.

Sometimes, of course, the placement of explosives becomes an art. For instance, in the implosion of an aging building or sports stadium, they must be placed strategically, so that not only will the target come down, but it will come down in a specified and predictable manner.

Tommy had a great deal of military experience with

all kinds of munitions, but this assignment was particularly challenging. It had to be done in darkness, in a period of a few days, but that was not what made it difficult.

Man-made structures are finite; like baseball managers who are hired to be fired, structures are built to eventually come down. Explosives can eventually hasten the process, but the end result is inevitable.

This was different. Nature was the target, at least the primary one. And the goal was to inflict damage that would take years, if not decades, to overcome.

He finished the job and set the timers for Saturday at 8 PM. For Tommy Rhodes that moment would be his crowning achievement, albeit a secret one.

But he would certainly have earned his money.

My dislike for Richard Carlton was pretty much instantaneous.

He deigned to see me in his suite in the Pierre Hotel on 61th Street, between 5th Avenue and Madison. I was greeted at the door by a guy who identified himself only as William, and who seemed to be an assistant of some sort. Or, more likely, based on the way William fit into his jacket, a bodyguard.

He led me into a private dining room, said, "He'll be right out," and left the room. Carlton came in a few minutes later.

In a bathrobe.

"You didn't have to get dressed up," I said.

He chuckled an annoying chuckle, which made me sorry I hadn't been the one to blow up his guesthouse. Then, "What can I do for you, Lieutenant?"

I had decided to be aggressive about this interview. Since there was a very good chance that I was going to claim to Gallagher that the real killer was somewhere on the Carlton side of the court battle, I needed to act as if that's what I believed.

I had to keep asking myself how I would proceed if
this were a normal investigation, and in this case, if I suspected Carlton, I would try to shake him. He was obviously complacent and feeling in control, so I would scare
him as best I could.

"I am conducting an investigation into the murder of
Judge Daniel Brennan."

He looked surprised. "I thought that crime was solved
rather violently. Wasn't a young man shot to death?"

"If the crime were solved I wouldn't be here," I said.

"Then why are you here?"

"We have strong reason to believe that the murder of
Judge Brennan is directly connected to the fracking case
before the Court of Appeals."

"What the hell does that mean?"

"It means that the Judge was considered a solid vote on
behalf of the town of Brayton." I was vastly overstating it;
Julie had solicited opinions that confirmed Holland's view
that Brennan was more likely to side with the town than
Judge Dembeck. But it was far from a slam dunk.

"So?"

I decided not to answer that directly, at least not right
then. "You share ownership of the land in question with
an offshore company, Tarrant Industries."

Carlton was clearly annoyed with my impertinence. "My
company shares ownership, not me personally."

"You own eighty percent of your company."

"Is that a question?" He made a motion to look at his
watch, as if he was late. It would have been more effective
had he been wearing a watch.

"Tarrant Industries has set up a structure which is difficult to penetrate. Can you tell me the names of the prin-
cipals of that company?"

"No," he said.

"You can't, or you won't?"

"I can't, but I wouldn't if I could."

"Are you denying that you own Tarrant as well?"

"I do not own Tarrant; that much I can tell you," he said.

"Mr. Carlton, are you familiar with the concept of motive?"

He was now openly hostile. "What are you saying?"

"Your chances of making hundreds of million of dollars have increased dramatically now that Judge Brennan will not be on that court."

He stood up. "You clearly have no idea who you are talking to. This interview is over. Direct any further communication to my attorney."

With that he strode out of the room, and William entered moments later. "If you'll follow me, Lieutenant . . ."

"Just a heads-up, William. Carlton seems a little pissy today."

I can't hear anything . . . total silence. It's as if I'm at the bottom of the earth.

It was her fault, Lucas, and it was yours. But I can't deal with that now. All I seem to be able to do is watch television, and the clock. I don't think five minutes has gone by without me looking at the clock.

Please tell me about your investigation. I need something to think about that doesn't involve me worried about being able to breathe.

"Three areas in New Jersey and one in Long Island experienced outages," Julie said.

"But the Long Island one lasted for twenty minutes, so it doesn't seem to fit what Bryan said. All the documents from the satellite company are in the folder, and I included a map showing where they are. The supervisor for that area was very helpful."

Julie and I were having a quick dinner at a coffee shop near her office. Everything seemed to be quick these days, including the days themselves. Bryan was running out of time, so every second seemed precious.

"Terrific," I said.

"What does it do for us?" she asked, picking at her French fries. Julie is the healthiest eater I know; she throws down broccoli and brussel sprouts like I do M&M's. But this time she ordered a burger and fries, which probably said something about her mental state.

"At this point not enough. But if we get more information, we can cross-check it against this."

She asked that I bring her up to date on the status of the investigations, which I did, starting with my concerns about Steven Gallagher's ability to get to and from the crime scene.

"You really think he could have been framed?" she asked, her tone clearly displaying her skepticism.

"I think there's a lot that a defense attorney could have used, if I had let it get to that."

"He could have hitched a ride with a friend. He could have stolen a car and then dumped it."

"There is no evidence that this kid ever harmed a fly in his entire life. He had probably been before a half-dozen judges on drug offenses in the past. All of a sudden he tracks down this one and becomes Jack the Goddamn Ripper?"

She seemed exasperated. "Come on, Luke, you've never arrested a first-time murderer? People snap, and drugs make them even more unstable."

"You seem anxious for me to be wrong about this," I said.

She shook her head. "I actually don't care either way right now if Steven Gallagher was a killer or an altar boy. But I want you to focus on the prize, and not waste your time on re-solving the case."

For some reason while she was talking I was looking at the wedding band she wore on her finger. I'm not sure why; I don't think I'd ever noticed a ring on a woman in my life.

"You know, when I got there that day, the first thing Steven yelled was something like, 'You said you wouldn't come back here.'"

"So?"

"So maybe he thought he was talking to people that had framed him. Maybe they left the bloody clothes there, and he thought they had come back."

She sighed. "You need to separate the facts there are from the facts that you wish there were," she said.

"What does that mean?"

"It means he had motive. It means he probably couldn't think clearly because of the drugs. It means he had the Judge's blood on his clothes. And it means there's not a jury in America that wouldn't have convicted him."

"That's all true." She was right in that I was having some difficulty in separating what I wanted to be facts from what I knew to be facts.

"But you're not buying it?"

"Not entirely, no. I think there is a chance that Steven Gallagher was innocent."

Julie seemed to decide there were much better things to do than continue pursuing that topic. "Let's talk about the court case," she said. "I've done some work on that."

That sounded promising. "What did you come up with?"

"Carlton's got some financial troubles."

"His company? Or Carlton personally?" Remembering him in his robe in that hotel suite did not conjure up a picture of a guy worried about where his next meal was coming from.

"Both. The company has been bleeding money for quite a while now; it seems that each new generation of Carltons is less competent than the one before it. And Richard is in the middle of a tough divorce, which is sure to cost him a bunch of cash."

"Interesting," I say. "If he wins the court case, he gets four hundred million dollars. If he loses, he keeps a tract of undeveloped land near a depressed town. Pretty powerful motive. Not beyond a reasonable doubt, but definitely strong stuff."

"Are you trying to convince a jury, or Gallagher?"

"Gallagher. Which might be harder."

We got quiet for a while, neither of us eating our food. We were frustrated with each other, because neither of us could make the situation better.

Finally, she said, "Luke, I know it's a long way from happening, but if you are able to do this, to prove his brother innocent, will he let Bryan go?"

"I might be crazy, but I believe that he will. He's got a sense of justice that he follows, like an internal road map that tells him right and wrong."

"But that would mean you would have killed an innocent man, his own brother. Wouldn't he have to do the same to Bryan to satisfy that sense of justice?"

What she said made sense yet didn't ring true. "I don't think so; these are the rules he's set up, and I think he'll follow them."

"And what if you can't convince him that you have the proof? Will he . . . ," she said, unable to finish the sentence.

"I think he will."

We were both quiet for a few moments, and then she said, "And then what will you do?"

"I'll hunt him down and kill him, if it takes me twenty years," I said. "So maybe he and I are not that different."

She looked me in the eyes, so intensely that I thought she could see through the back of my head. "You're very, very different. Did you tell Bryan I was sorry?"

"I did. Should I tell him you want him back? Back with you?"

She hesitated. "This is ground I've never covered before, Luke. Do I say what will make him feel good? Or do I tell the truth?"

"It depends what the truth is," I said.

"The truth is that right now, at this moment, if you told me the only way to save his life would be for me to go on with our marriage, I would do it in a heartbeat. I care very deeply for him, and I would do anything to protect him. But if he comes back, and we resume as if nothing has happened, it ultimately will not work. He'll know that as surely as I would."

She smiled, and continued. "That's how I feel right now, at this moment. Tomorrow, who knows?"

"Maybe you can make it work. Maybe you owe him that."

"The problem is I don't love him, Luke. I love you."

That was something I had both waited a long time to hear and never wanted to hear. And under these circumstances, it was actually hard to process. I'm a disaster at being in touch with my feelings, and in this case my feelings and I weren't on the same planet.

A hundred things raced through my mind as to how to respond to what she said, and I just as quickly rejected each of them. Finally, I settled on the only one I felt comfortable with.

"Oh," I said.

But I said it with feeling.

We're getting closer, Bryan. And there's a definite chance that Steven Gallagher did not kill Brennan. I was played for a sucker . . . they sent me in there and I did their killing for them.

This is going to end well, Brother. I'm not saying we'll laugh about it someday, but we'll get through it.

Richard Carlton was worried and annoyed.

He wasn't about to panic; that really wasn't in his DNA. Things had always worked out for Carlton, and this situation would be no exception.

But it was very irritating, mainly because he thought this issue had been put to bed. With Brennan out of the way, there was nothing standing in the way of the Court of Appeals decision. That would end the legal battle, which would trigger the sale of the land, which would make Carlton unbelievably wealthy. The last roadblock had been removed, but the cop, Somers, was single-handedly dragging it back into the middle of the highway.

The implications were ominous. Cops were loathe to reopen solved cases, especially ones in which they had gunned down the alleged killer. For them to admit an error in a situation like that would be to expose themselves to outrage and ridicule, not something they were inclined to do under any circumstances.

So Somers must have something significant, Carlton figured, or he wouldn't be going down that path. And he came on so strong, almost accusing Carlton of involvement in the murder, that it left no doubt he was ready and willing to cause problems. And anything that interfered with the sale, for any reason, was an unacceptable problem.

Hanson Oil and Gas was a committed buyer, but deals are not closed until they are closed. The kind of publicity that Somers might bring to bear, talk of murdering Federal judges, could spook them. They had a Board of Directors to answer to, and were listed on the New York Stock Exchange. Companies like that have to be careful of ugly controversy, and Daniel Brennan's murder was as ugly as it gets.

The only saving grace, it seemed to Carlton, was that Somers appeared to be on something of a solo crusade. The fact that he showed up at the hotel alone was somewhat revealing, but the key fact was that Somers was the one who killed Steven Gallagher. Maybe he was haunted by that, and feeling a need to find out whether Gallagher deserved his fate.

Carlton and his partners were close, way too close for things to get derailed now. So Carlton made the phone call, and explained the situation.

"It's not a problem," said the voice on the other end of the phone.

"Easy for you to say; he didn't come to see you. He knows something, and he's not the type to let it go."

"I'll take care of it. Don't call me on this line again."

"What are you going to do?"

"I'm going to take care of it."

"Don't overreact," Carlton said, but by then he was talking to a dead phone.

He hung up, already regretting that he had made the call.

It was "unofficial update" time.

I had promised Captain Barone that I would keep him informed about what was going on, and I entered his office to do that.

"How's your brother?" was his first question.

"Hanging in. He's got four and a half days to live; if I was in his position I'd be doing a lot worse."

"So you're not making progress?" he asked.

"Actually, more than I thought I would. I think there's a reasonable chance that Steven Gallagher did not kill Daniel Brennan." I hadn't planned to share that with Barone at this point, because I didn't think he'd react well and I had more important things to do than manage his moods. But he was a partner in this, he had a stake in the outcome, and he had a right to know.

"Can you rephrase that?"

"What do you mean?"

"Well, maybe it's just semantics, but it would be better if you could say it this way: 'I've confirmed beyond a shadow of a doubt that Steven Gallagher killed Daniel Brennan.'"

I smiled for the first time in a while. "So these unofficial updates are not supposed to be accurate?"

"It's not a requirement, no. But since we've started down this path, tell me why you feel this way."

I went over basically the same items I had discussed with Julie. Barone kept shaking his head; I couldn't tell whether he was disagreeing or just upset by the possibility that we, that I, had tracked down and killed the wrong man.

When I finished, he said, "Maybe the *Today* show was a mistake."

"You understand I've got more important things to worry about than how this is going to look."

He nodded. "I do understand that. How can I help?"

"I think we need to put more pressure on Carlton, maybe plant some items in the press. We need to force him into making a mistake."

"Luke, you're guessing on this thing, and it's not even a particularly educated guess."

"I know that, Captain. But the jury here is Gallagher; I don't have to go by the strict rules of evidence."

"Carlton is not without resources; we start libeling him in the press, we could be bringing problems on the department, on me, without any benefit coming from it. I can handle the hassle, and I'm willing to, but I need to see more potential upside."

I was annoyed by his attitude, even though I expected it, and even though I knew he was basically right. "OK, so we don't mention him by name; we just let the word get out that we're still checking some key leads in the Brennan murder. And we say the focus of the investigation has switched to Brayton."

"Even though we already shot the guilty party." It wasn't a question; it wasn't even said to me. Barone was sort of rolling it around in his mind, trying to see how it would play.

"I shot him," I pointed out. "Captain, even if my brother was sitting on a beach on the Riviera sucking down piña coladas with umbrellas in them, I wouldn't let this go." I was basically telling him that he had no choice, that I was going to keep pulling on this string until I got to the end.

"You're a pain in the ass," Barone said.

"I'm aware of that."

"Do it."

"Thanks. I will."

"You probably already have," he said.

"Yes, I have."

"Did I mention that you're a pain in the ass?"

"I'll check my notes, but I believe you did."

"So now what?"

"A tour of New Jersey."

The decision was announced on the court website and made available in the clerk's office.

The three-judge panel of the Second Circuit Court of Appeals had issued their ruling in the matter of Brayton vs. Carlton Industries.

In boxing parlance, it was a split decision, the court coming down 2-1 on the side of Carlton. But this wasn't boxing, and there was no provision for a rematch. Simply put, while a close call, the net result for Brayton was devastating.

Judge Susan Dembeck wrote the majority opinion. While acknowledging the legal right, in fact the duty, of a town to protect its citizens, she argued that Brayton had failed to establish that the fracking would cause real damage. She felt that the purchasing company, Hanson Oil and Gas, had in their brief established a regimen that would adequately monitor the environmental effects. The data would be shared with the town, and the court would be receptive to reconsideration, if circumstances warranted. But, she felt, the town had simply not met its burden.

Judge Richard O'Brien, in a blistering dissent, said

that Carlton and Hanson had not come close to meeting their own burden of guaranteeing that the health of the innocent citizens of Brayton would not be irrevocably damaged. He even trotted out the "can't unring a bell" cliché, meaning that once the damage was done, it could not be effectively removed.

But by far the most devastating aspect of the ruling was the requirement that Brayton, if they were going to appeal to the Supreme Court, would have to post a bond in the amount of five hundred million dollars. There was no way that they could afford to do so; they did not even have the resources to make the appeal, no less post the bond.

Left unsaid in the opinion, of course, were the actions that the decision would trigger. Within thirty-six hours, the sale of the land to Hanson Oil and Gas would close; the documents were already signed and sealed. The money would automatically transfer to Carlton and the company that shared ownership of the land, Tarrant Industries.

Richard Carlton had known that the decision was coming, down to the time of day it would be released. He also knew that it would be a favorable one, yet he still felt substantial relief that it had come to pass.

Edward Holland issued a terse press release, saying that he needed time to study the decision and analyze the options. He spoke of the need to protect the families of Brayton, and promised further announcements soon.

Alex Hutchinson was already rallying the very disappointed citizens, planning demonstrations and vowing to continue the fight. Her outrage was palpable, so the media naturally gravitated to her.

Richard Carlton expected all of those reactions, and none of it bothered him. What did bother him was a report in the *Daily News*. Citing unattributed sources, it said that the investigation in Judge Daniel Brennan's murder was still ongoing, and that the focus of that investigation had moved to Brayton.

No details were given, and neither Richard Carlton, Luke Somers, nor anyone else was mentioned by name. But Carlton recognized it for what it was, the first salvo in a pressure campaign that Somers was planning to mount.

Dealing with that pressure was now effectively out of Carlton's hands, which worried him. With victory at hand, any overreaction had the potential to be terribly counter-productive.

But all Richard Carlton could do was watch.

Who are "they"? Who is behind it? And more importantly, will Gallagher believe it? He gave me suicide pills, Lucas. They're sitting on the table. I don't want to suffocate. Remember that time at the lake? I know what it feels like to be without air to breathe.

You saved me then, Brother.

This is Act Two.

It's only about a half hour from Paterson to Morristown.

That's mainly because the drive is on Route 80, the only highway in America that never, ever seems to have any traffic on it. I don't know why that is, but whoever planned and designed Route 80 should be anointed as the official National Emperor of Highways.

Within that half hour you can see the state take on a completely different character. People generally don't think of New Jersey as particularly beautiful, but those people might change their minds if they drove to the northwest portions of the state.

Of course, Emmit and I weren't on a sightseeing trip. It was in the northwest, Morris, Warren, and Sussex counties, that the satellite company reported weather interruptions of service that matched what Bryan had reported.

We had called ahead and set up a meeting with Captain Willis Granderson of the Morristown police. We picked Captain Granderson because he had served on the force the longest, thirty-seven years. It was important that we talk to someone who had a history in the area.

Granderson was an immediately likable guy, and one

who seemed genuinely glad to have company. I got the feeling that he was sort of out of the law enforcement loop, and was just putting in the time until retirement. But based on the interactions he had with fellow officers on the way back to his office, it seemed he was treated with deference and respect.

After making sure we had cold sodas, Granderson asked us what he could do for us.

"We want to talk about bomb shelters," I said.

"Just goes to show if you hang around long enough . . . in thirty-seven years, nobody's ever asked me about bomb shelters."

I smiled. "Well, you can check it off your list. Are you aware of any in this area?"

"Course I am. Why do you want to know?"

"We have reason to believe that someone is being held against their will in this part of the state. We further believe that they are underground, and cannot hear outside noise, nor themselves be heard outside the room. It's not necessarily a bomb shelter, but it's a good guess."

He nodded. "Sounds right. The good news is that we do have bomb shelters in this area; the bad news is that there's a whole shitload of them."

"Why so many?" Emmit asked.

"Because in the sixties, there were a bunch of missiles here, sitting in silos, pointed at the dirty Commies. So people figured that if the other side shot first, they'd try and hit the missiles before they got in the air. So here is one of the places the Russians were aiming first."

"So people built the shelters to protect themselves from a direct hit," I said.

He laughed. "Yeah. Like if I shot a bazooka at you, and you protected yourself by wearing a heavy sweater."

"They weren't safe?" I asked.

"They were safe if there was a tornado, or a hurricane.

But a nuclear missile landing nearby? No way. And you know what? If you were sitting under a nuclear attack, you'd never want to come up for air, because you'd be sucking poison. If you ask me, instant incineration is the way to go."

"Have you ever been in one of the shelters?"

"Are you kidding? We had one under our house; my father built it himself. I took girls down there until I was twenty-two. I wish I lived there now." He smiled at the recollection.

"Is it possible that there is one with satellite television hooked up?" I asked.

He shrugged. "Sure. Why not? Have the satellite on the house, or a nearby tree, and run the line down to the shelter. No problem. It could even be in a silo."

"What do you mean?"

"Some people bought old silos, for beans, once the missiles were taken out. I've never seen one, but I've heard they turned them into like underground apartments." He laughed. "I even heard some people built homes next to them, and use the silos as guesthouses." He laughed again. "I got some family I'd like to put underground when they visit."

"Is there a map of where the shelters are?"

"No, not that I know of. I'm sure some of them would be registered in town halls, or something. You know, if people had to get permits to build them. But I'm sure most of them just went ahead and did it."

"What about the silos? Is there a map of where they would be?"

Another shrug. "Must be. The Defense Department keeps records of everything."

I turned to Emmit. "Let's make sure we get that."

Emmit wrote it down, which meant I could forget it. Once Emmit wrote something down, it happened.

"I can tell you where a couple of them are, if you want to see them," Granderson said.

"How far from here?" Emmit asked.

"Twenty minutes."

Granderson told us where they were, and how to get there. We thanked him and left.

True to his word, we were there in twenty minutes, an old sign directing us off the road to a US Military Installation, apparently unnamed. We drove on a dirt road towards it, and in less than five minutes we were there. It was a group of small buildings, maybe barracks, and six small towers.

We parked near one of the buildings, and walked towards the towers. Everything was old and dusty, metal was rusted . . . it sure didn't feel like a place that once contained enough power to wipe out a good part of the world.

Emmit and I walked towards one of the towers, and saw what used to be the hole in the ground. It was very, very large, maybe thirty feet across, and it was covered by what could best be called an enormous concrete manhole cover.

There were still warning signs, some alerting to the dangers of radiation. It didn't seem like a current worry, since the area hadn't been roped off, but I did feel a flash of concern.

"You think this stuff could still be radioactive?" Emmit asked.

"Let's put it this way," I said. "You've been impotent since you got out of the car."

He laughed, but the laugh was cut short by the bullet smashing into him. He fell backwards, and I dove on top of him, rolling us over to some level of protection, behind the tower.

"Emmit, you OK?"

He didn't answer me, but his eyes were open, and the

bleeding was coming from just below his shoulder. I balled up his shirt and pressed down on the wound with one hand, as I tried to peer out to where the attack had come from. I had my gun out in the other hand, but I had no target to shoot at.

Another round of weapons fire shattered the quiet, and dirt and concrete kicked out from all around us. We were in a completely untenable position; any effort to find the person shooting at us would leave me totally vulnerable.

But I had to do something, because Emmit could well have been dying. And the way things were setting up, I was going to join him.

I started to work my way around the tower, but more shots cut me off. Then I heard a sound; it was a human sound, maybe a small shout of surprise. Or pain. Or both.

I waited sixty seconds, which in that situation was an eternity. Then I started to make my way around again, bracing myself for more gunfire.

But there was only silence.

So I kept going, gun at the ready, prepared to shoot at anything I saw. And what I saw was a man, standing off in the distance near a building, looking down.

I raised my gun, but I didn't shoot, because the man was Chris Gallagher. And he was looking down at a body.

Gallagher looked up at me, clearly not afraid of the gun in my hand.

He bent over and seemed to be searching the pockets of the person lying at his feet. I wanted to ask him what the hell was going on, but I had Emmit to worry about.

I took off in a run towards my car, and as I passed by Gallagher I yelled, "My partner's been hit!"

Gallagher nodded and started running back towards where we had been. I continued on to my car, and drove it to where Emmit was lying, now with Gallagher beside him and pressing down on the wound. As I approached, Gallagher picked Emmit up. It seemed effortless, amazing since Emmit weighed more than two hundred and fifty pounds.

I helped Gallagher put Emmit into the backseat, closed the door, and ran back around to the driver's side. As I passed by Gallagher, he slipped something into my hand. I didn't look at it; I was too busy programming the GPS to find the nearest hospital.

It was seven miles away, and while en route I called in to Barone's office to report what had happened, and to tell them to have the hospital waiting for our arrival.

I called to Emmit a few times, but he didn't answer. I was hoping that he was just unconscious.

When we got there, I pulled up and was immediately surrounded by emergency personnel. The hospital appeared unimpressive, a one-level place that looked more like a veterinary hospital, but the people there had their act together.

Emmit was out of the car, on a gurney, and in the hospital within a minute. By the time I got inside, he was gone, and I had to ask the person behind the desk where they had taken him.

She asked me to fill out some papers, but I refused, at least for the time being. I wanted to be with Emmit, and she understood and directed me to the area where he was being treated.

I was in the waiting room for over an hour when Captain Barone and three other cops from our station showed up. "How is Emmit?" Barone asked.

"He's in surgery. They're not telling me anything, but he lost a lot of blood. Did you reach his wife?"

He shook his head. "She's on a plane to Seattle to visit her parents. There's a message for her to call in when she lands. Who did this?"

It was then that I realized that I hadn't looked at whatever Gallagher had given me. I took it out of my pocket. It was a Nevada Driver's License, in the name of Frank Kagan.

I showed it to Barone. "He did."

"How do you know that? Where is he?"

"He's dead. Chris Gallagher killed him."

"Excuse me?"

"This guy had us pinned down. Emmit was hit and I was next. Gallagher was there, I don't know why, but he killed him."

I told Barone where it happened as best as I could, and

he made a phone call to dispatch officers to the scene. Then we waited on Emmit.

It was another hour and forty minutes before the doctor came out to talk to us. "He's going to make it. He may not go dancing any time soon, but he's going to make it."

He went on to say that no major organs were hit, but that Emmit had lost a lot of blood, and if he had gotten to the hospital ten minutes later, it might have been too late.

The bottom line was that Gallagher had saved Emmit's life.

And mine as well.

Gallagher instantly regretted what he had done.

Intervening had not been a mistake, even though he was operating mostly on instinct. Kagan was going to kill those two cops, and Gallagher was not about to let that happen.

What he regretted was killing Kagan. He could have knocked him unconscious as easily as he broke his neck, and if he had, Kagan would have remained alive to answer Gallagher's questions. And Gallagher had no doubt that Kagan would have found it in his best interest to answer them; Gallagher could be very persuasive that way.

But now it was too late for that; Kagan's question-answering days were behind him. So now Gallagher would have to do the answering for him. He'd find out why Kagan was there to kill Somers and his partner, and he had no doubt it was related to the Brennan murder investigation.

Gallagher had a strong feeling that Kagan was military, just based on the way he handled his weapon, and how he chose the optimum spot and position to take out the cops. If he was right, it would make it easier for Gallagher to find out what he needed to know.

But Somers certainly had more resources at his disposal, which was why Gallagher gave him the driver's license. They'd be able to track down Kagan's history, and find out a great deal of information about him.

But Gallagher kept a prize for himself. It was a hotel key, a card that would provide entry to Kagan's room at Cod Cove Inn. At that moment Gallagher had no idea where that was, as there was no address on the key. But he'd find it, and he'd get into the room. And once he did, if he learned anything that made sense to share with Somers, he could do so.

Gallagher placed a phone call to Lieutenant Linda Worley, a military police officer assigned to the Intelligence Unit at Quantico. Worley and Gallagher had briefly been stationed together in Germany about eight years prior. They almost had an affair, and would have, had not Worley remembered that she had a husband back in the states. They'd run into each other a few times in the intervening years, but not for long enough for anything to have happened.

"This is Gallagher," he said, when she got on the phone.

"And this is a happy coincidence," she replied. "I've been divorced six months."

He laughed. "Well, if you give me some information, I just might work my way down there to see you."

They bantered some more, until he got around to telling her what he needed. "There's a guy named Frank Kagan, last known address Las Vegas; I need to know all there is to know about him."

"What else have you got?"

"I think he was military."

"Well, that narrows it right down," she said.

"He's maybe forty-two, and probably has a criminal record."

Gallagher had a pang of conscience in asking her to help. She had no way of knowing that he had gone renegade;

if she checked, his records would simply say that he was on leave. But before long the police, military and civilian, would be after him. It would come out that she'd helped him, and at the very least wouldn't look good in her file.

She said that she'd get back to him, so he turned to his computer to find out where the Cod Cove Inn was. There were three of them in the Northeast, the closest being near Brayton. Having followed Lucas to Brayton and met Alex Hutchinson, he knew there wasn't any need to check out the other Cod Cove Inns. That was the one.

Knowing that time was of the essence, Gallagher set out to drive to Brayton. He certainly wanted to examine the room, and there was always the chance that the police would find out where Kagan had been staying and seal the place off.

On the way, Gallagher thought about the possibility of extending the seven-day deadline, of bringing a replacement tank to supply air for Bryan Somers. Luke was making headway, and since the goal was to clear Steven, ending the process prematurely was counterproductive. Complicating the situation was Gallagher's concern that when Somers was at the missile shaft he was also just six miles from the place his brother was imprisoned.

Gallagher wasn't sure how they got so close, but he was confident they were still operating mostly in the dark. And close was not going to get it done for them.

Gallagher rejected, at least for the moment, any extension of the seven-day deadline. Either Luke would get it done in time or he wouldn't. And if the latter was the case, then Gallagher would finish the job.

Bryan wouldn't get an extension, because Steven did not get one.

The Cod Cove Inn could not have been set up better for Gallagher's purposes. It was a relatively small, two-story place, with maybe fifty total rooms. The main office was in a small separate building, so there was really no way to monitor movement.

He decided to try the upper floor first. If Kagan was military, and had any concern about his safety, he would instinctively want the higher ground. The jump down was a small one, easily navigated, so escape would have been just as easy as from the ground floor.

He started in the back, near the exit, since that was where he would want to be. The parking lot had not seemed crowded, and the vacancy sign confirmed that the place was not filled. Kagan, within reason, should have been able to choose his location, and most people would have wanted to be towards the front, closer to the elevator.

He found the room on the second try; the little green light went on and the door opened. He entered and found it to be very neat, every piece of clothing carefully folded and placed in drawers. Definitely military.

But it was also a suite, or at least connected to an adjoining room, with the door between the two open. It didn't take much examination of the belongings to know that two men were staying here, Kagan plus one other.

Gallagher started searching carefully but quickly. On the desk in one of the rooms was a briefcase, locked, which was no problem for Gallagher, since among his talents was one for picking locks. In this case he didn't bother; he was able to rip the briefcase lid off with sheer strength.

Inside was a thick envelope containing copies of media reports of the court case in Brayton, biographical notes on the various players, what seemed to be land maps, and some kind of geological reports. This was outside of Gallagher's area of expertise, but he would look at them later, when he had more time.

A short while later, in the adjoining room, he reached one of the closets and saw a large suitcase standing on its side. He felt that it was quite heavy, which surprised him, since both Kagan and his partner had obviously unpacked.

The suitcase was locked, and it took Gallagher only a couple of minutes to pick it. Inside was a large, metal box, which was also locked. After another three minutes, Gallagher had that opened as well, and he recognized what he was looking at immediately.

The box was divided into twelve compartments, all the same size. Two were filled with a substance that Gallagher recognized very well, C-245, one of the most powerful plastic explosives ever developed.

The other ten were empty.

Gallagher heard a noise out in the hall, and waited a moment to see if someone was going to enter the room. He hoped it was Kagan's partner, because he would keep him alive until he answered every question Gallagher could think to ask. But it was a chambermaid, who recoiled in surprise when she saw Gallagher.

"Can I clean the room?" she asked.

"Yes, I was just leaving," Gallagher said. He grabbed the envelope, the suitcase with the remaining explosives, and left.

I got your back, Bryan. Big news on this end. Someone shot at us today. My partner got hit, but he'll be OK. Gallagher was there, and killed the shooter. I'll get him to understand that we've scared some people and they want to shut us down.

The truth is in Brayton, New York. There's a case that Brennan would have ruled on if he got to the court; they made sure he didn't. Don't know exactly who "they" are yet, but I will.

Before you know it you'll be back at work, enriching yourself and stealing from the little people.

And all I remember about that day at the lake was giving you mouth-to-mouth . . . I still have nightmares about it.

Don't touch those pills, Brother. We'll flush them down the toilet together.

I waited to talk to Emmit.

The doctor said he should be awake and coherent in about an hour, and I figured I could use the time to plan out my next moves.

My assumption was that Frank Kagan had been following us. Gallagher might have been following Kagan, but more likely he was following us as well. It was an embarrassment to me that we were obliviously leading a goddamn caravan around, but I'd get over it.

I had to assume that Kagan shot Emmit and had us pinned down. Gallagher must have come up behind him and killed him. I didn't see any blood on Kagan, so it must have been done with bare hands. Gallagher's reputation appeared justified.

I didn't delude myself into thinking this changed the dynamic or balance of power between us. He didn't save us because we were best buddies; he did it so I could continue my efforts to exonerate Steven. That's why he gave me Kagan's driver's license; he was helping us along in the investigation.

My hope was that he would realize that we were getting

somewhere, that Kagan came after us because he or, more likely, people who sent him were getting worried. My other hope was that Gallagher would move the seven-day deadline back, but I knew I couldn't count on that.

But it wasn't just a question of whether Gallagher thought we were getting somewhere; the fact was that we were. There could be no other explanation for it. Kagan would have been worth more to us alive, but just his identity might be enough to unlock the puzzle.

I didn't want to jump to conclusions, but there was only one person we could be scaring, and that was Richard Carlton. If I could establish a tangible connection between him and Kagan, I'd nail him to the wall with it. He could go fracking in his bathrobe on Rikers Island.

The nurse came out to tell me that Emmit was alert, and I went in. He looked pale, but better than I expected, and he greeted me with a small smile.

"That really went well, huh?" he asked.

"Smooth as silk."

"What exactly happened?"

"You got shot; I had a couple of beers, and then drove you back here. Ruined my whole day."

The banter out of the way, I filled in all the details about Kagan and Gallagher. He seemed to be straining to listen, as if just doing so required an enormous effort.

When I finished, he said, "So you kill his brother, he threatens to kill yours, and then he saves your life. Complicated guy."

"Yeah."

"So what are you going to do now?"

"I called in to find out what I can about Kagan, see if it leads us back to Carlton."

Emmit nodded. "It might just do that," he said. "I can't think of anyone else we've pissed off, at least not in the last few days."

"That's how I figure it."

"You think you can get me something to drink?" he asked. "I'm thirsty as hell."

I went out to tell the nurse the request, but when I came back Emmit was sound asleep. There was no sense waking him, and no reason for me to hang around. I didn't know what I was going to do next, but I knew I was going to do it quickly.

Complicating matters, of course, was the need to now be careful. There were people who wanted to kill me, and if Frank Kagan was any indication, they were people with experience at it. I'd never had a particularly well developed self-preservation instinct, but in this case I knew that my death would ensure Bryan's.

I called in to the office to get updated on what they had so far uncovered about Frank Kagan. He was a hit man out of Vegas, which was not quite as interesting as something else they learned. He was known to partner with an old army buddy named Tommy Rhodes. It turned out that Rhodes was an expert in bomb making and, more important, bomb using. It was those kinds of devices that were responsible for Richard Carlton no longer having a guesthouse.

As soon as I hung up, the cell phone rang. "Lieutenant Somers. This is Ice Davenport."

Because of the strange name, it took me a moment to make the connection. It was Nate "Ice Water" Davenport, longtime friend of Daniel Brennan and unofficial counselor and confidant to his wife.

"Yes. What can I do for you?"

"You said I should call you if I wanted to talk some more about my friend."

"I remember."

"Well, I'm ready to do that."

"Ice Water" Davenport lived on 88th Street and Riverside Drive in Manhattan.

To my amazement, I found a parking spot. The sign said that parking was OK except on Monday and Thursday mornings, which is when street cleaning allegedly takes place. I have my doubts about that, since I've been there on Monday and Thursday afternoons and suffice it to say that the streets do not look spotless.

He greeted me with a fairly tense, "Thank you for coming," and offered me something to drink. I took coffee; it had not been a great week for sleep.

We sat in the living room. The apartment was huge; I hadn't seen other doors when I got off the elevator, so it was possible that it occupied the entire floor of the building. The furniture was extremely modern, mostly glass and stainless steel, and the place was spotless. The doorways were higher than usual, in deference to the inhabitant.

"I'd like to establish some ground rules," he said, which is one of my least favorite ways to begin a conversation. "I will provide you with some information, which may or may not prove relevant to your investigation. You in turn will keep Denise Brennan out of this, and will do nothing to damage Daniel Brennan's impeccable reputation."

"I'll do my best," I lied. The stakes being what they were, the last things I'd be concerned about were reputations or public personas. If I had to publicly brand Daniel Brennan as a Taliban-loving pedophile to save Bryan, I would not hesitate.

It seemed to satisfy him. "I'm speaking to you on behalf of Denise Brennan," he said, continuing one of the longest preambles to an interview in recent memory. He spoke carefully and precisely, as if each word had been vetted and cleared before takeoff.

"Why isn't she speaking for herself?"

"Believe me, I tried. Her allowing me to speak represents a major concession. But almost all of what I will tell you represents her feelings and relates events as she experienced them."

I didn't understand why "Ice" needed someone to "allow" him to speak, but I figured I'd find out soon enough, so I waited.

"In the weeks prior to his death, Judge Brennan had seemed under stress. I noticed it, but I didn't spend much time with him. Denise saw it much more clearly, and was quite worried about it."

"What was the cause?"

"She initially believed it to be financial. Despite an amazing career, Judge Brennan was not a wealthy man. He was injured before he could attain a large salary in basketball, and judges certainly earn far less than what would be commensurate with their importance to society. And I include Appeals Court judges in that."

"With his name and reputation, I assume he could have earned far more practicing law?"

He nodded. "Without question. But he wanted to contribute to the greater good. So he was happy in his work, but concerned that he would not leave Denise financially stable upon his passing. His father died a very young man."

I needed to move this along. "What does this have to do with his murder?"

"Perhaps nothing. And perhaps his increased stress was simply a result of the Appeals Court nomination process, testifying before Congress, and the like. But now there is this."

He got up and walked over to his desk, opening the drawer and taking out a small folder. He opened the folder and took out a piece of paper, handing it to me.

I looked at it, but he told me what it was as I did. "It is a bank account in Judge Brennan's name, opened six weeks ago in the Central Bank of Belize. There is one deposit, made two weeks later, in the amount of two hundred thousand dollars."

"And Denise has no idea where the money came from?"

"She does not. And she tells me that there were no secrets between them, that they discussed finances and everything else as equal partners."

I held up the paper. "How does she reconcile that with this?"

He shook his head. "She cannot. Which is why we are having this conversation. If it is somehow related to his death, then the likelihood is that the real killer has not been apprehended."

"Where do you think he got the money?"

"I simply cannot imagine. My hope is that you will come up with a benign explanation."

"You'd be amazed how few benign explanations I run into in the course of a day."

I left there thinking that Judge Daniel Brennan may not have been the total paragon of virtue that his wife and friend believed him to be. I was also thinking that there was a damn good chance that the two hundred grand, however he got it, played a role in his death.

Given his job and position, my initial instinct would have been to think of the money as a bribe. But his taking the money would likely have signified his agreement in the matter, so why would he have been killed? Had he reneged, and was going to rule the other way?

I certainly did not know the answer to that, but there was one thing I did know.

Steven Gallagher did not give Daniel Brennan two hundred thousand dollars.

I never thought I'd say this, but I was happy to see Chris Gallagher.

He was sitting in his car in front of my house, probably in deference to the fact that it was raining outside. Apparently the great man was not impervious to water.

In any event, I needed to talk to him, to find out what, if anything, he knew. And, just as important, to impress him with how much I had learned.

I got out of my car and we made eye contact, which was enough to get him to follow me into the house. He was carrying a suitcase; I hoped he wasn't planning to move in. The first thing he did was walk into the kitchen and take a beer out of the refrigerator.

"Have I said or done something to make you think we're buddies?" I asked.

"Not that I recall. I also don't recall you thanking me for saving your life."

"What were you doing there?"

"Following you, as was Kagan. You're not that hard to keep track of; does your car have a rearview mirror?"

"That explains why you were there. Why are you here?"

"It's time for an exchange of information. We seem to be getting somewhere, and the deadline is approaching."

"It can be extended," I say.

"No, it cannot. Everything we discover makes your killing Steven even more unforgivable. Now tell me what you've learned."

I brought him up to date on everything I knew and suspected about Richard Carlton and the situation in Brayton, as well as my belief that it was my nosing around there that got Kagan after us.

He nodded. "The answer is definitely in Brayton."

"You're taking my word for it?" I asked, surprised at his certainty.

"No chance," he said. "I paid a visit to Kagan's hotel room, which was just outside Brayton. I found some explosives, but more important were the explosives I didn't find. The box was mostly empty."

"What kind of explosives?"

He opened the suitcase and showed them to me. "C-245," he said. "You can keep it."

I knew what that meant; I had quite a bit of experience with munitions in the army. "Shit."

"And Kagan was not working alone. I believe the guy he is working with—"

I interrupted. "Tommy Rhodes."

Gallagher smiled. "Very impressive. What have you found out about him?"

"They were army buddies. Rhodes would know how to use the C-245; he was a munitions expert in the service. Our information is that he was considered as good as it gets, that if you gave him some hairspray and a bottle of Drano he could demolish Argentina."

He nodded. "That fits. You should also have someone

take a look at this." He handed me some drawings, which seemed to be some kind of geological maps. "I think it's the land area that Carlton is selling, but I don't know what it all means."

"Beats me, but I'll find someone who understands it. What I can't figure out is what Rhodes could have been looking to blow up. If he's working for Carlton, they've already won in court. Who could they be after?"

Gallagher frowned. "I should have stayed there and asked Rhodes when he came back to the hotel."

"I'll send some people to pick him up."

"They may not find anyone," said Gallagher.

"What does that mean?"

"There were empty timer cases in his room. He might have already planted devices on timers. If not, he could detonate them remotely. He may have been staying around to make sure that there were no hitches. But with Kagan gone, he might bail out of the area. Probably depends on when the next device is set to go off."

"It's probably soon," I said. "Rhodes was booked on a plane back to Vegas Saturday night. I'll have cops at the airport, but he'll be aware that we know his name, so I imagine he won't show up."

Gallagher smiled. "Then Saturday is a really big day all around. Keep your priorities straight, Luke."

He was telling me that I shouldn't spend too much time worrying about what Rhodes might or might not have been targeting, because Saturday was already a big day.

It was the day Bryan was scheduled to die.

One thing you need to do, Lucas . . . you need to tell me the truth. It's hard enough for me to prepare for this; I just can't be taken by surprise. I've been thinking about my will . . . my life insurance . . . right now everything goes to Julie. Not sure if I should leave it like that. Of course, when you change a will, you need two witnesses to sign it. That might be a little tough in this case.

The moment the court decision was announced, Alex Hutchinson was on the move.

More accurately, she was on the phone, planning a strategy of action to prevent Hanson Oil and Gas from starting to drill on the land they had just purchased. Richard Carlton, as much as she loathed him, was no longer the enemy. He had sold the land to Hanson, which made them the threat.

The loss in court was far from unexpected. Alex was smart, and informed, and she was a realist. Similar cases were being decided with some regularity in favor of energy companies, in New York and around the country. And they had already lost in District Court; the appeal had been something of a long shot.

Her first call was to Mayor Edward Holland. He had been a stand-up guy throughout, even taking on the legal work himself, in deference to the town's shaky finances. It had served him well; the publicity he received was national, and he was portrayed as a heroic figure fighting big business on behalf of the little people. While she recognized his ambition, in her mind he still deserved most of the accolades, even in a losing effort.

It became obvious early in the conversation that he had no more bullets left in his legal gun. "We don't have the money to take this any further," he said. "It's not the legal fees; hell, I'm working for nothing. It's the bond."

As he had privately predicted to her, the court had imposed a bond requirement of five hundred million dollars that the town would have to put up, should they try to delay matters with a further appeal. It was the court's way of saying that their case would not win on appeal, and that Hanson would suffer financial damages if the process caused a delay in drilling the land.

"We need to take action outside the system," she said.

"What does that mean?"

"It means that we have to prevent the fracking from beginning. Once it does, we've lost."

"Alex, we've already lost. Now we need to work with the EPA and other regulatory authorities to minimize the damage."

"Great, we'll just partially pollute the air and water supply. That way only half the town will get cancer."

"You know that's not what I meant."

"Mayor, I personally appreciate all that you've done. But it's moved to the next level."

"Which level is that?"

"We are going to organize, we are going to take action, and we are going to stop this."

"Those are just words," Holland said. "And with all due respect, they're not the brightest words I've heard."

"There will be more than words. We have a rally planned for tonight. We'll have made decisions by then."

"No violence, Alex. It will be self-defeating."

"Letting our children die is self-defeating," she said. "The rally is at the high school at six o'clock in the evening.

You are the Mayor, and our leader, so you should be there. People will want to hear you."

"I'll be there, but you may not like what I have to say, Alex. I'll be preaching restraint, and lawful behavior. I share your anger, believe me, but there is no other way."

"See you tonight," she said, and hung up.

Holland took some time to think about the phone call, and to decide what to do. He then picked up the phone and dialed his police chief, Tony Brus. "Tony, I think we've got a problem."

"What's that?"

"People are upset, and I think more violence is a possibility. You'd better be ready."

"Have you got any specific information?" Brus asked. He was not a big fan of politicians in general, and Holland in particular.

In addition, Chief Brus was harboring hopes of running for Mayor himself in the next election, and had no interest in doing anything that would make Holland look good. He saw no irony in the fact that he frequently expressed his disdain for politicians while angling to become one himself.

"No, but if they blew up Carlton's guesthouse before we lost, there's no telling what they'll do now," Holland said.

"OK, I'll keep an eye on it."

Holland got off the phone and started thinking about public relations. So far the entire situation had been a political plus for him, even with the court defeat. He had been the hero fighting the good fight; it was the other side, and the judges, that bore the blame.

But he was sure there was more violence to come, and he needed to come out against it before it happened.

So he called his high school sweetheart.

Adrienne Horton and Edward Holland had repeatedly expressed their undying love for each other throughout high school, but their commitment actually lasted only a few days past the Senior Prom.

She had only spoken to or seen him a few times in the past couple of decades, mostly at reunions. But they had spoken five times in the last couple of months. She had made the first call, in her role as a producer of prime-time CNN programming. The fight between Big Energy and the people of Brayton made for a compelling human interest story, and she wanted to get Holland on to talk about it.

He had been receptive, but preferred to wait until the legal proceedings had run their course, so as not to appear to prejudice them. She was so sure that he would eventually come around, regardless of the outcome of the case, that she had done background work. Camera crews had been sent to the town, and interviews were conducted. The piece was done and ready to go, and probably would have aired with or without Holland.

But he was a politician, and Adrienne knew that no politician would be able to resist such a platform. So when the call came to tell her that he was ready, she set it up for that evening, and Holland was there at 6 PM.

The interviewer was Anderson Cooper, and he first ran the taped piece providing background for the viewers who had not been familiar with the story. It included the interviews with local people in Brayton, expressing heartfelt concern for their children and their way of life.

The piece tersely said that Richard Carlton and representatives of Hanson Oil and Gas had both declined to comment on camera but had released packaged statements vowing that they would protect the environment while supplying much-needed energy resources.

It was obvious that the compilers of the segment were on the side of the people of Brayton, which provided an easy segue into Holland's interview.

But he was not there to mouth platitudes; he was there to make news, and he did so right away. "Anderson, I have asked privately, and now I am asking publicly, for state and federal authorities to come in and provide protection for the people of Brayton. There is a significant danger of violence."

"Why do you say that?" asked Cooper.

"Well, as you noted in the piece you just ran, there has already been violence, a house was blown up. And now the anger, the totally justified anger, has been ramped up to a much higher level. I've put our police force on high alert, but we are a small town, and can do just so much. I want to do everything I can to protect the people of Brayton; they are not just my constituents, they are my friends."

Cooper pointed out the obvious. "But it's those same people that are angry. So the constituents and friends who you are trying to protect are the ones that might commit the acts you're worried about?"

"Anderson, I don't know who committed the previous act, and I certainly have no knowledge of who might do something illegal or dangerous in the future. But people are very, very angry and upset. When parents feel that their children's lives are in danger, they will do anything they can to protect them. In a situation like this, the frustrations can boil over, and the actions of one or two can hurt many."

"So you've not been able to provide specifics to the authorities?"

Holland shook his head. "I have not. What I have done is caution everyone to remain calm and not take any rash actions. At the same time, I repeat that I have asked for state and Federal intervention to help defend our community. These are dangerous times, and I don't want to be in the position of wishing we had all done more."

Holland was more than satisfied with the interview. He

felt that he came across exactly as he hoped, as an intelligent, rational public servant who cared only about the people he represented.

He did not delude himself into actually believing that anything he said made anyone safer.

Holland went directly from the studio to the rally in Brayton. It was at the local high school, but was far too large to be contained by that building, and was being held on the football field.

A podium was set up with a loudspeaker, and various citizens were taking turns speaking and voicing their outrage at what the courts had decided. Among the listeners there was some anger, but the place had a sort of festive atmosphere, and the watching police had absolutely no need to intervene.

When Holland arrived, Alex Hutchinson was talking to the crowd. "So we will have people on the site twenty-four hours a day, seven days a week. Carl Hamilton will set up the schedule; so contact him and tell him your availability. We need everyone to contribute their time. Saturday evening will be our big rally; please call everyone you know, not just citizens of Brayton, and ask for their support. It will start at four o'clock, but come as early as you like.

"We want fifty thousand people on their land, telling them to go away. We can still win this thing, but we have to stick together."

When she saw that Holland had arrived and was listening to her, she called him up to the podium. Neither she nor anyone else had been able to watch his CNN interview, so of course they did not know that he had expressed concern that they would commit violent acts.

He spoke briefly, cautioning everyone to be calm and to write their Congressman and Senators. He spoke of understanding their anger, but said that it had to be channeled in a law-abiding fashion. There were no TV cameras, so no need to speak with any particular passion.

He also was not inclined to tell them that he had decided to get a court order to remove them from the land, if they did not go peacefully. He did not want any of the people in his town getting hurt or worse.

roled on a low shelf nearby. There were no TV cameras so no need to sneak with any furtive glances.

Rhodes was not deterred as . . . felt them that he had d . . . ted to get . . . enter well in . . . . . . then from the mind . . . day did not recognize . . . He did not want any of the people in town getting hurt, or worse.

Tommy Rhodes had only himself to blame.

He should have gone with Frankie Kagan after that cop, even though Frankie had said he could handle it alone. Frankie was the boss, so Tommy let it go, but he should have insisted. But he hadn't, and the results were disastrous.

Just how disastrous remained to be seen, but he already knew enough to be very worried. Someone had gotten into his hotel room, and had gone through his and Kagan's things. They had also taken the documents relating to Rhodes's ongoing operation, though the likelihood was strong that they would not understand them, at least not in time to cause a problem.

Kagan hadn't returned, and hadn't checked in with Rhodes for six hours. That was such a violation of procedure that it could only mean one of two things; either Frankie Kagan was captured, or he was dead.

Rhodes was very much rooting for dead.

In any event, Rhodes needed to get away, so that he would have time to assess the damage, report in to his boss, and figure out his next moves. He had wanted to usurp Frankie's position and deal directly with their employers, but now that it seemed to have happened, he wasn't pleased.

It was very likely the police would search for him at the hotel; in retrospect he was surprised that they weren't waiting there for him when he returned. It might mean that it wasn't the cops at all who had broken in, though Rhodes could not imagine who else might have done it.

So Rhodes packed his things quickly and left. It wasn't safe to go to another nearby hotel; there were so few that the cops could easily check each one. So Rhodes drove south, towards New York City, and checked into a Hilton in northern Westchester. He further assured his anonymity by using a fake ID, which he carried for emergencies. He would not cancel his plane flight on Saturday, but since the police would find out about it, he just wouldn't show up.

A radio news report as he was leaving Brayton provided some level of reassurance. A cop had been shot, out near the abandoned missile silos, and the shooter had been killed. Rhodes thought with relief that at least Frankie hadn't talked, which meant there was no way the cops could react quickly enough to stop the operation.

Of course, Tommy's future was altered forever. His identity would certainly become known, and he was going to be a target of the police. He was confident that he'd have the money and resources to never be found, but it was not the way he wanted this to go down.

He was already a wanted man, and in forty-eight hours he'd likely be the most wanted man in America.

Julie Somers was not used to feeling helpless.

It wasn't her style to just sit back and watch events unfold. It's why she went into the public defender's office after graduating from law school; she always wanted to be where the action was.

After a couple of years, she decided she wanted to be on the right side of the action, so she moved over to the prosecutor side. It's not that she didn't believe all defendants were entitled to excellent representation. She just got worn down from the belief that the majority of her clients were in fact guilty of the crimes with which they were charged.

She wanted to win; she was as competitive as anyone. But she wanted to feel good when she won, and that was not often the case as a defense attorney. So she switched sides, and hasn't looked back. In her new role, she controlled the action. She called the shots, and was on offense rather than defense. Just the way she liked it.

Bryan's kidnapping left her in the exact opposite position. Except for finding out some information for Luke when he requested it, she was sitting on the sidelines and waiting for him to update her.

She loved Bryan and always would; whether or not she could still live with him as his wife was an entirely separate issue. She also felt guilt over having somehow caused the current situation. She was the reason that Bryan was at Luke's that night, when Gallagher showed up.

She still agreed with Luke's decision to not call in Federal authorities to go after Gallagher. She and Luke had access to the same information that they would have, but they had different goals. The Feds would have shared their desire to get Bryan back unharmed, but would have gone after Gallagher as well. Julie and Luke simply did not feel that was the best approach towards keeping Bryan alive.

But she knew one thing; if anything happened to Bryan, Gallagher was going down. She wouldn't rest until that happened, though she knew it wouldn't be easy. From what she had read about him, Gallagher was as good as they come at the art of survival. He was trained in living off the land, and could probably melt into some undeveloped area and never be found.

So she called Lou Rodriguez, an investigator she had frequently employed while on the defense side of the system. Rodriguez was smart, tough and reliable, and better than anyone she had used since moving to the prosecutor's office. Now, whenever she opposed him, she found herself cringing at what he might find.

She asked Rodriguez to meet her away from the office, and they had coffee at a diner near the courthouse. "I need to hire you," she said.

He was surprised; prosecutors had no need to go outside to get investigative help. "What about that army you've got working for you, Jules?"

He always called her "Jules," and was the only one to do so. She had no idea why, but sort of liked it. "I meant personally."

"Personal issues? Jules, you know how I feel about you, but—"

She cut him off. "It's not that." Rodriguez took pride in never working on cases involving marital problems. Getting pictures of husbands with other women was simply not his thing. "It's not on the same planet as that, but it does involve Bryan."

"Sorry," he said. "Tell me about it."

So she did, after first soliciting his promise that whatever she said would remain confidential. After describing the situation in as much detail as she knew, including the progress Luke had been making, she said, "I want you to follow Gallagher. If things don't go well . . ." She stopped to compose herself. "If things don't go well, I want to know where he is, and how to pick him up."

He didn't hesitate. "I'm in."

She exhaled in relief. "Great. Thanks, Lou. Just bill me at your normal rate."

He shook his head. "This one's on the house; you've done enough for me. Any idea how I find him?"

"It shouldn't be hard. He spends some time following Luke, and even shows up at Luke's house sometimes, mostly at night. He's not worried, because he knows Bryan is his trump card."

"I'll start tonight."

She gave him a folder with copies of all the information she had. "I'm having dinner with Luke at Morelli's tonight at seven. Maybe he'll follow him there."

"I'm on it," he said. "Just one question, Jules."

"What's that?"

"It doesn't matter, but I'm curious . . . did Gallagher's brother do Brennan?"

She thought for a moment. "I'll know more tonight, but gut instinct? I don't think so."

No surprises, Bryan . . . I promise. I'm meeting Julie tonight, to tell her what's going on. It's driving her crazy to just sit and wait. I guess you know the feeling. Anything you want me to tell her?

I'm proud of the way you're holding up, little brother.

Michael Oliver would have preferred being anywhere but Brayton.

He had last been there when he studied the land that his employer, Hanson Oil and Gas, was considering buying. He had recorded all the data, taken all the pictures and measurements, and gone back to Tulsa to analyze the information and write his report.

It was that report that convinced Hanson to make the purchase, and which in effect started the entire controversy. Hanson had great confidence in their chief engineer. Once Oliver said there were huge amounts of natural gas to be gotten efficiently from the shale under the ground, they relied on it without question.

Now that the purchase had just been finally approved by the courts, Oliver was brought into town for meetings with the engineers who would conduct the actual fracking process. Some of the equipment was still in place from when the tests were conducted, and the drilling that had been done put them ahead of the game.

But for all the violence that critics said the fracking did to the environment, it needed to be done with some care, almost delicacy. Mistakes could be costly, in both time and money. And despite what the citizens of Brayton claimed, the engineers also were concerned about the environmental impact. Everyone in that room, except Oliver, had children of their own, so they understood.

Oliver laid it all out for them, providing a road map for what they were going to find underground. They met for six hours, and he assured them he would be available by phone and computer back in Tulsa to answer any further questions they might have.

Oliver couldn't wait to get back home, but felt compelled to accept the invitation of the executive in charge of the project to have dinner that evening. It would be an early one, and Oliver would get a late flight to Chicago afterwards. He'd stay overnight there, and get a short flight to Tulsa in the morning. It was not ideal, but anything was better than staying in Brayton.

When he arrived the previous evening, he had made the mistake of turning on CNN in the hotel and watching the interview with Edward Holland. The situation was dangerous, or at least Holland made it sound like it was. The only saving grace for Oliver was that he was anonymous; there was no way that anyone in Brayton knew who he was, or what his crucial role in the situation had been.

After the meetings he went back to the hotel and packed, putting his one bag into his rental car and heading for the restaurant. It was a Japanese steak house in Central Valley, one of those places where they cook for you right at the table. There were six of them there, the executive, four senior engineers, and Oliver.

His dinner companions were in a great mood, but all Oliver was focused on was getting out and on that plane. The only good thing about the dinner was that it was not in Brayton; Oliver was out of there and would never be back.

So at seven thirty, he said his good-byes, pretending that he wished he could stay longer. He knew it would be the last time he would ever see these people, but he certainly didn't tell them so. They would likely be lifers at Hanson, while his time there was coming to an end.

Once out the door, he went to find his rental car in the parking lot. For a few moments he forgot which car was his, but rather than figuring it out, he just pressed the button on the key that unlocked the door. It also caused the rear lights to flash on and off, providing an easy way to identify the car.

Oliver trotted to the car; he hadn't left that much time to get to the airport, and was not about to miss that flight.

He got in, turned the key, and ended his life. The explosion took out three cars on either side of him, and brought everyone in the restaurant running outside to see what had happened.

His colleagues were afraid that his was the car that blew up, but there was no way to know, because it would take an army of forensics people to find any sign of what used to be Michael Oliver.

I heard about the latest violence on the way to meet Julie.

The explosion was followed by a second explosion, this one in the media. It firmly put Brayton onto the national map, in a way that hadn't happened before. Edward Holland had been on some TV shows making his case, but it hadn't really registered on anything but a local level.

That was then.

The main difference was that this act, unlike the guesthouse destruction, took a life. In fact, the purpose of it was to take a life. Michael Oliver was not collateral damage; he was the target. It was an execution, pure and simple, an act of domestic terrorism.

Moreover, it was a sophisticated act. The perpetrator knew who Oliver was, even though he was an obscure part of the process. That is not to say he was an unimportant player; the reports were crediting him with making the determination that the land contained natural gas in amounts worth literally billions of dollars.

But he was barely known; he was not the head of Hanson Oil and Gas, nor a public spokesman for them. He was actually based in Tulsa, and was simply in town for meetings. For the killers to have known that, and to have isolated him as a target, represented a level of planning and calculation that was as impressive as it was ominous.

There were signs that this was going to trigger a national debate about fracking itself. It was an incredibly important factor in the energy landscape, and had already prompted countless lawsuits. Yet it had stayed somewhat below the radar, a place where it would never reside again.

The various players in the drama were already reacting in an expected manner. Carlton issued a vehement condemnation of the "terrorists," and Hanson's spokesman did the same. They said that they would not back down in the face of the unlawful acts and would take additional steps to beef up security, in order to ensure the safety of their employees. Nothing would stop Hanson from pursuing their goal of providing affordable energy to the American people.

Alex Hutchinson, the de facto leader of the protesting townspeople, also condemned the action, and claimed that neither she nor anyone in her group had anything to do with it.

Edward Holland, trying to remain above the fray, added his strong disapproval of any violence, and pleaded for calmer heads to prevail. He talked of his own anger at what was happening to his town, and the need to protect the children, but added that this was not the way to go about it.

Holland went on to remind everyone that he had asked for preemptive state and Federal intervention to cool things off, but that his requests went unfulfilled. He once again renewed those requests publicly, and media reports were very favorable to him.

"How does all this help Bryan?" were Julie's first words when she saw me.

I had been thinking about it, and wasn't pleased with my

own point of view. "I don't think it does," I said. "At least not much."

She seemed surprised. "Why?"

"Well, first of all, keep in mind that the entire jury here is composed of Chris Gallagher. And the fact that there has been some violence is not a surprise to him; he already knew that Emmit and I were targeted to be killed."

"So, if he's a jury, treat him like one, Luke. Make a persuasive argument; make him understand. Put the facts out there in a clear, concise manner; that's what is done for juries. Let me do it; I'll convince him."

"I've been trying, Julie. And I'd be happy for you to try. But there's a logical flaw in our argument."

"What's that?" she asked.

"Our focus, Gallagher's focus, is on the Brennan murder. Brennan was considered pro-Brayton, or at least more pro-Brayton than Judge Dembeck. So the side that might have had any interest in killing him would have been the company side, not the town."

She had to know where I was going with this, but I spelled it out. "This new violence is being committed against the company, most logically by people who would have wanted Brennan to take the seat. The people that killed Michael Oliver would have placed Brennan in a protective cocoon if they could have."

"And Gallagher is smart enough to see that?" she asked.

"Without a doubt."

She seemed lost in thought for a few minutes. I had no idea what she was thinking. I had known Julie for almost seven years, and this made the seventh consecutive year that I had no idea what she was thinking.

"I did something you're not going to like." She said it in a challenging way, as if she was comfortable with what she did, and not worried about my reaction.

"I already don't like that sentence."

"I hired Lou Rodriguez to find Gallagher."

"Shit, Julie . . . what do you mean 'find'?"

"He's not going to do anything, just keep track of where he is."

"Keep track of where he is? He's been following me. He's probably at the bar in the next room right now."

"Then Lou's on the stool next to him," she said, obviously annoyed by my attitude.

"Great. So the bad guys are following me, Gallagher's following them, and Rodriguez is following Gallagher. I'm leading a procession. I'm like the goddamn Grand Marshal of the Rose Bowl Parade."

"Maybe he'll lead Rodriguez to Bryan. Probably not. But he's not going to walk away from this, Luke. No matter how it turns out. I wouldn't be doing my job if he did. Nor would you. He's a kidnapper, at a minimum."

She didn't say what the maximum was, but she didn't have to. She was right, of course, but on some level it didn't sit well with me, and she could see it.

"What's your problem with this, Luke? That he'll make Rodriguez, and take it out on Bryan?"

"No, he couldn't care less who's following him, or why."

"Then what?" she asked.

I wasn't sure how to answer that, but my mouth seemed to make the decision for my brain, and started talking without permission. "I killed his brother, Julie. I guess on some deep level I understand what he's feeling. I don't know what I'd do in his shoes, but it wouldn't be pretty."

She spoke in a much softer voice, trying to keep herself from crying. "You might find yourself in his shoes."

I nodded. "And then I'd feel completely different. Then I'd find him and kill him. And on some level he'd understand that completely, and he'd be fine with it."

"What do you mean?"

"I think he's decided that his life is over, one way or the other."

"If he hurts Bryan," she said, "it will be."

Got your e-mail too late . . . you've already had your dinner. Not much for me to say to Julie, anyway. Just tell her not to feel guilty about this; she had nothing to do with it.

Remember the time you were going to have a fight with Randy Singer after school? Nobody could believe I wasn't going to watch, but I didn't because I didn't want to see you lose, and I thought you might.

I never remembered you losing at anything, and I wanted to keep it that way.

I still do.

This was not going the way Chris Gallagher expected.

It was actually going far better, which was causing him to reassess. Nothing wrong with that, not in his mind. A battle plan only lasts until you first meet the enemy. Then you make the necessary adjustments in the field.

Luke Somers was better than he thought, far better. He had dug deeply into the investigation, and was on his way to creating reasonable doubt as to Steven's guilt. Which might have been enough, had Steven been allowed to go before a jury.

Somers had recognized the inherent difficulty in proving Steven innocent without finding the real guilty party. Because whoever killed Brennan had also set Steven up to take the fall; they had planted the bloody clothes, and called in the anonymous tip.

The violence interested him in that it was counterintuitive. It was targeted at those intent on mining the land, yet if Somers was right, Brennan was likely to be opposed to the miners' position. Why would the same killers be going after players on both sides?

He discounted the possibility that there were two separate sets of killers; the world didn't work that way. And the fact that Brennan was killed in a knife attack, rather than the type of explosions that did the subsequent damage, did not surprise him. On the Brennan hit, they wanted someone to blame, and Steven was in the wrong place at the wrong time. Had Brennan's garage been blown up, Steven could not have been set up as easily.

The fate of Bryan Somers, in Chris's mind, still very much hung in the balance. Someone was going to die for Steven. If it had to be Bryan, that was fine with Chris. Justice would be served, since no matter who killed Brennan, it didn't change the fact that Luke Somers had gunned down Steven.

But if the real killer was found in time, then he would have been the one to set Steven up. And then Chris would see to it that he would die, and Bryan would be spared.

One way or another, Steven would get his justice.

So the goal was still to find out who killed Daniel Brennan, and to do so fast. Somers would do what he would do, but Chris could operate in a way that Somers could not. And he was about to do exactly that.

Chris believed that the one person most likely to have all the answers was Richard Carlton. The money was always the key, and Carlton was the one who had walked away with a fortune.

So Richard Carlton was the person who was about to receive a visit from Chris Gallagher.

Why was Michael Oliver chosen to die?

That was the question I was interested in, partly because I had run out of other things to be interested in. But on any level it was strange, which made it something I needed to understand.

I had Julie run a search on Oliver on something called LexisNexis. She had once assured me that if anyone was mentioned anywhere at any time for any reason, it would show up there. Ten minutes later she called to tell me that Oliver had never been mentioned in connection with the situation in Brayton anywhere in the media, at any time.

But he was very specifically targeted. He was at a dinner with five other employees of Hanson Oil and Gas, all of whom would be involved in the actual drilling operation. It would have seemed that from that group Oliver would have been the least likely candidate to be attacked.

He had merely performed his analytical function, and had done so in anonymity, at least as far as the people of Brayton were concerned. Between the Hanson and Carlton companies, there was a target-rich environment of

people who were about to do damage to Brayton, yet
Oliver was plucked from obscurity to die.

Frank Lassenger spent thirty years in the Army Corps
of Engineers, retiring as a Lieutenant Colonel six years ago.
He had done it all, building and repairing dams, creating
structural solutions for buildings that were in earthquake-
threatened areas, advising mining companies on safety and
structure, and even providing expert guidance for underground rescues. After leaving the service, he had done
some private consulting, but nothing that kept him away
from his kids and grandchildren for any length of time.

I know all this because we both like bagels.

There's a bagel store I stop off at almost every morning
on the way to work, and Frank is usually there. We got to
talking about each other's jobs; he was more interested in
mine, and I was more interested in his.

I instructed officers to contact Frank and tell him that
I needed to speak to him about a matter of great urgency.
I knew Frank would respond, and he was waiting for me
at the precinct when I got there. Frank is the type that if
you need him, he is there. I really like that type.

"You know anything about fracking?" I asked.

"Some. I've never done it myself, but I'm familiar
with it."

"Ever heard of a guy named Michael Oliver?"

"The guy that got killed? Sure."

"Did you know him before that?" I asked.

"By reputation."

I was glad to hear that Frank was familiar with him.
"What kind of reputation did he have?"

"Let's put it this way," he said. "These companies are
spending hundreds of millions, billions, of dollars to take
energy from under the ground, sometimes under the ocean.
They know it's there, but until they go after it, they don't

really know how much or, more importantly, how easy it will be to get to."

"So it's a crap shoot?"

"Ever hear the term 'dry well'? Anyway, people have to make the judgment about what's there and what isn't, and there are maybe fifteen people in the industry who are considered the best at doing that. Michael Oliver was one of those people."

"Could he be wrong?'

"Sure, anything's possible. But if Michael Oliver said 'drill here,' I'd invest my money in it, no questions asked." He laughed, "Well, of course I'd have questions, but you know what I mean. And I don't really have any money."

I showed him copies of the information that Gallagher had gotten from Kagan and Rhodes's room, except for the information about Carlton and the Hanson executives. He seemed most interested in the schematic layouts of the land, as I knew he would.

"Oliver prepared these?" he asked.

I shrugged. "Not sure. Why?"

"They're well done, very thorough, so it was probably him."

"Does it show where the natural gas is?"

"It shows where Oliver thought it was, and based on what I see, I would say he was right."

"So there's nothing unusual about it?" I asked. "I was struggling to come up with a reason that Oliver was a specific target, but that reason probably did not exist."

"Well, there's one thing that surprises me, but there's probably a good explanation for it."

"What's that?"

He pointed to the map. "You see these arrows? That's where Oliver was telling them to drill."

"So?"

"So I don't know why they'd drill in that many places,

and it's too spread out. You drill in the best spots, and then expand if you have to. He was telling them to start out wider. He must have had his reasons, but I don't know what they were."

"Would Oliver be important to the process from now on?" I asked. "Would they have needed him to do the drilling?"

Frank shook his head. "I doubt it. I'm sure he'd told them all he knew, and they had his notes and reports. Now it's just a question of going down there and sucking the stuff out. Guys in his role become expendable once they've finished their analysis."

I nodded. "Expendable people seem to have a short life expectancy."

Bryan . . . I'm not going to lose this time, either.

There's been a lot of violence surrounding this Brayton situation. You may be seeing it on television. Gallagher is going to understand that it's all tied in to Brennan's death. I will make him understand, and at the very least he'll give you more time.

Do not give up hope. We've been through a lot, Brother, and we'll make it through a lot more.

It took Bryan almost six hours to break into the box.

That was not a lot, when you consider that it took almost five days to even notice that it was there. It was a fairly large metal box, technically a strongbox, and it was in the kitchen pantry, partially hidden by shelves and dishes.

The reason it took so long to break open was not just that it was locked with a fairly good-sized padlock. It was also just at the end of the range that Bryan's chain allowed him to reach, so prying it open became that much more awkward. But with the help of a heavy screwdriver that was in a kitchen drawer, he was finally able to get it done.

The result was something of a disappointment. He hadn't known what to expect, and his expectations had been low. Certainly there was not going to be a key to unlock the chains, thereby allowing him to get the hell out of there.

Only a slightly greater hope would be a handgun, locked away for safety. He might have been able to shoot the chains off, though with his lack of familiarity with guns he knew he might kill himself in the process. Maybe he could have used it to shoot Gallagher if he returned; then they could at least die together.

The third hope, and the most realistic one, was that there was some clue to his location, something that he could use to help Luke find him.

But he was zero for three. All that was in the box were rations, labeled US Army MREs. Bryan had no idea what that meant, but he assumed they were long-lasting rations for soldiers out in the field. Never having been in the army himself, he had no idea if they were any good, but doubted it.

In any event, he had no need to experiment with them; food supply was not his problem, air supply was.

And Bryan had already planned his last meal.

He would dine on the two pills that Gallagher left him.

It was turning into a public relations fiasco for Hanson Oil and Gas.

Of course, Hanson's bottom line did not rely on public relations, so it could fairly easily absorb the damage. But no one wants their company to look bad, especially in a part of the country so close to Wall Street.

Hanson's CEO, Randall Murchison, was kept updated on the calls and e-mails coming from the public. They were overwhelmingly negative, as was to be expected. Also in line with expectations was the fact that very few shareholders were among the complainers. Those who stood to benefit financially from the Brayton natural gas find were inclined to be tolerant of it.

Ironically, the death of Michael Oliver, while a damaging blow to the company, provided a public relations bright spot for Hanson. Through Oliver, they had become the victims of vigilante justice. People didn't countenance water and air pollution, but that was a somewhat less immediate and dramatic danger than bombs blowing up in parking lots.

There was a shareholders meeting coming up, and Murchison wanted it to go as smoothly as previous ones. He didn't want angry townspeople to storm the meeting, yelling their claims that Hanson was going to be poisoning their children. Murchison was known to be a bit of a loose cannon, prone to straight talk that sometimes got him in trouble. But he didn't want to be fighting with a bunch of panicked and angry parents on national television.

So he placed a call to Richard Carlton. The deal hadn't officially closed yet, and the money therefore hadn't been paid, so this was when Murchison would have the most leverage.

"You need to get that situation up there under control," Murchison said. "My people are telling me we don't need this aggravation."

"I'm going to release a statement," Carlton said.

"You're going to release a statement? I got a dead chief engineer, people conducting a goddamn pep rally on the land I'm supposed to be drilling on, half the country sending me nasty e-mails, and you're going to release a statement? Better be a damn good one; that had better be the goddamn statement of the year."

"I will say that we're going to use part of the resources from the sale to expand the auto parts business. It'll mean a thousand more jobs for the locals."

"You're lying through your teeth," Murchison pointed out. "You ain't dumb enough to pour more money into that shit-ass company."

The fact that Carlton was in fact lying through his teeth did not mean that Murchison's accusations didn't make him angry. The truth was that the auto parts company was going to close within a year and the angry people of Brayton would have something else to get angry about.

"My company has been a leader in its field for sixty years."

"Yeah. Until you got hold of it. I'm instructing my people to not make the payment."

"You can't do that."

"Watch me," Murchison said.

"There are plenty other companies that would love to get their hands on that land."

"Right. Every company in America wants to get their people blown up and be accused of poisoning toddlers. It's every CEO's dream."

Carlton was in a panic, and he forced himself to sound conciliatory. "Randall, we don't need to fight like this. What is it you really want?"

"You pay for security for the first year, and you announce it in your statement. Say you're trying to protect innocent people from these vigilantes, and say that Hanson is a responsible corporate citizen who is committed to preserving clean air and water. We'll release the same kind of statement."

"OK. That's fair," Carlton said. "Done."

It was an easy promise to make, because it would be an impossible one to keep.

In a very short time, providing security would be both unnecessary and impossible.

Lucas . . . did I ever tell you I had decided to follow you and Dad and become a cop? In my junior year, I decided to chuck it and I signed up to take the test. But I never took it, I went down there but left before it started. I decided I wouldn't have the courage in dangerous situations. I guess I was right, because right now I'm scared to death, and not handling it well.

I haven't thought about it in ten years. It's amazing how old memories come back when you think you'll never again make new ones.

That's it for now . . . power on the computer is getting low.

Make Gallagher understand. Please.

Chris Gallagher spent almost two hours gauging the level of security.

It wasn't so much that he was concerned that he couldn't handle whatever was presented. He had entered Taliban strongholds undetected; getting into Richard Carlton's house would be a comparative piece of cake, no matter how many guards he employed to protect himself.

What Gallagher learned in two hours he could have learned in ten minutes. There was no outside security in place, other than motion detector floodlights, which he could easily elude.

The wreckage of the guesthouse had been mostly cleared away, and Gallagher could see the foundation with his night vision goggles. It just added to the question that had already formed in Gallagher's mind; why would someone like Carlton, already the victim of violence, not have more security?

It certainly couldn't be financial; just based on the house, and the money Carlton was getting from Hanson, he could have hired an entire army division to protect him. And with his guesthouse destroyed, and a Hanson employee already dead, surely Carlton couldn't be oblivious to the danger.

People like Carlton did not react to physical danger well. Things like that happened to other people, not them. So they overreacted, spending whatever it might take to shield themselves from that world.

Yet Carlton didn't even have his curtains drawn; Gallagher could see him sitting serenely in what looked like his study, on the main floor, reading.

So the question answered itself beyond any doubt in Gallagher's mind. Carlton was not afraid, because Carlton was behind the violence. It was why he knew that he had nothing to be afraid of.

But he was about to find out otherwise.

Gallagher could only see one other person in the house; he looked like he could be a security guard, but there was no way to be sure of that. The challenge was going to be putting him out of commission while not giving Carlton enough warning or time to call 911.

So he walked up to the front door and rang the bell.

Carlton didn't move, showing no concern whatsoever. Through the glass window at the top of the door, Gallagher could see the other man in the house walk towards the front door. As he approached, while his momentum was still going forward, Gallagher kicked in the door. It was a sudden, violent move that he had perfected long ago.

The door smashed the man in the face, probably rendering Gallagher's blow to his head unnecessary. He was not dead, Gallagher saw no reason to go that far, but he would not be waking up for a while.

For Gallagher, it represented the final crossing of a line. His life was essentially over; he recognized that and was comfortable with it. After tonight he would either soon be dead or live on as a fugitive. But he was positive that the answer to Steven's death was in this house, and he wasn't leaving until he had it.

Gallagher raced to the study, just as Carlton was getting

to his feet in response to the crashing noise. When he saw Gallagher coming towards him, he looked towards the phone, but even in his panicked state he knew there was no chance of that.

Gallagher grabbed him at the front of his throat and pushed him against the wall. Choking, Carlton tried to strain upwards and away, but Gallagher just pushed him higher, cutting off his air supply. But Gallagher was not there to kill; he was there to get information.

Maybe fifteen seconds before Carlton would have passed out, Gallagher released his grip and pushed him into a chair. He waited until Carlton could speak his first words: "Who are you?"

"I am Steven Gallagher's brother."

"Who is that?"

"He is the person you framed after you had Judge Brennan killed."

"No, no, no."

"You don't know me, but I am telling you this. Right now I control you, I control your pain, and I control your life. Do not lie to me."

"I swear, I had nothing to do with that."

Gallagher was surprised by the statement. Carlton was petrified; there was no question about that. Gallagher would have guessed he would have caved by then; perhaps the man was tougher than he thought.

So Gallagher tried another approach.

He broke Carlton's arm.

He did it like one would snap a twig, only arms make a louder cracking noise than twigs. Carlton screamed in agony, an appropriate response considering the circumstance, and then started to mix in sobs with the screams.

"Why did you kill Brennan?" asked Gallagher in a calm voice, stepping back.

"NO, NO . . ."

"Why did you frame my brother?"

"NO, PLEASE . . . I DIDN'T . . . I DON'T KNOW ANYTHING ABOUT THAT."

Gallagher started walking back towards him, and saw the total panic in his eyes. The fact that Carlton was not caving was a major surprise to him, and he was not often surprised.

It was a dilemma, in that inflicting more pain would get Carlton to confess to anything; Gallagher could have him admit to killing Kennedy. But Gallagher didn't want a confession that way; he wanted the truth.

"You're lying."

By now Carlton was whimpering. "I swear, I'm telling you the truth. I don't know anything about that."

"Then tell me what you do know."

And Carlton did exactly that.

I should have done it long ago, even though it had little chance of success.

I hadn't wanted to spook Gallagher in the process, but I could no longer worry about that. I hadn't spoken to him in almost thirty-six hours, and in any event I couldn't be confident that I would be able to convince him to give Bryan more time.

I needed Barone's help, and wasn't positive I could get it, at least not on my terms. But I was waiting in his office to make my pitch when he got in.

"Uh-oh," he said, when he saw me. Then, "Let's hear it, fast. Like pulling off a Band-Aid."

"I need your help."

"I thought that's what you've been getting."

I nodded. "And I continue to appreciate it. But we've got to elevate it a notch."

"I'm listening. Reluctantly, but I'm listening."

"We've got to go wide with this." In our parlance, that meant I was saying that so far the investigation had been limited to the officers in our precinct. Going wide would mean bringing in other precincts.

"How would that help?" he asked.

"I believe he's in a bomb shelter in one of three counties. I need every cop that can walk going door-to-door, asking people if they know of bomb shelters in their area, so we can check them out. I also got a list of abandoned missile silos from the Defense Department, which we can do as a follow-up if this doesn't pay off."

"You know what the odds are of this working?"

"Very slim," I said.

"What about Gallagher?"

"I want to leave him out of this, for now. I can't afford to burn that bridge, not while there's a chance of him seeing the light and letting Bryan go. Or at least extending the deadline."

"So I'm going to call in the troops, sending them on a wild-goose chase, and conceal information crucial to the investigation? When the commissioner finds out he'll turn me into a school crossing guard, with a defective whistle."

"It's on me," I said. "If it goes south, you only knew what your people told you, and I withheld the crucial facts. I'll take the bullet."

What I was saying was true to a point, but much was left unsaid. Barone would look bad in the process, and he had to know that.

"This is a big ask," he said.

"Captain, my brother is going to die if we don't do this, and maybe even if we do. I am asking you to do whatever you can to prevent that from happening, whatever the blowback might be."

"You know which precincts we're talking about?"

"I do." I took a piece of paper out of my jacket pocket, and handed it to him.

He looked at it, and said, "This has to go through the chief."

I nodded. "He'll go with your recommendation, as long as you tell him it's life-and-death."

"Which is what you're telling me," he said, pointedly.

I nodded again. "Which is what I'm telling you."

He thought for a moment, then went to his desk and picked up the phone, asking his assistant to get the chief on the phone for him. "If he's not there, find him," Barone said. "This is Grade One."

Within twenty minutes we had the authorization we needed and I was on the way out there to organize the operation, which had almost no chance for success.

I was almost there when my cell phone rang. It showed up as "caller unknown," which gave me hope that it was Gallagher.

It was.

"Stay near this phone," Gallagher said, instead of "hello."

"Of course. Why?"

"I may have information you'll want to hear."

"Good, but when?" I asked. "Time is running out."

"I know the timing better than you," he said. "I just need to confirm something, and maybe save some lives in the process. You'll be a goddamn hero."

"I just want my brother alive," I said. "That's all."

"Then hang tight."

"I will."

He was quiet for a while, and I thought he might have hung up. "Hello?" I said.

"I needed to know that Steven hadn't done anything," he said. Again there was a long period of silence. Then, "I knew, but I needed to *know*."

"Please tell me where Bryan is," I said, but Gallagher ignored my plea.

Instead he said, "Have you ever crossed the line?"

I knew exactly what he meant. "No, I've gone to the edge a few times, but never crossed it."

"Think long and hard before you do," he said. "Because there is no way back."

Bryan . . . we're making great progress. I just had a conversation with Gallagher that was very promising. He said he was soon going to be telling me information that I'd "want to hear."

You would have made a great cop, and it's not too late. All you have to do is give up any hope of ever having a decent house or car, but the upside is that you'll start getting shot at.

You're handling this amazingly well, Bryan, and I'm proud of you. You've always been miscast as the younger brother, because I've always looked up to you.

See you soon . . .

"What the hell happened here?"

It was the question Tommy Rhodes asked as soon as he walked in, but he had a pretty good idea already. He had seen the car leaving, and gotten a look at the driver.

The door to Carlton's house had been ajar when Rhodes came in, and the scene was fairly chaotic. William, who had been assisting Carlton throughout this operation, was bleeding slightly from the mouth, and had obviously come in second place in a two-person encounter.

Carlton was doing quite a bit worse. He was screaming in pain, yelling at William to get the car, and holding his arm at an awkward angle. It was obviously broken, and Rhodes saw it as a good bet that the driver who had just left was the source of the break.

"I've got a broken arm, that's what happened." Then, to William, "Let's go."

"Where are you going?" Rhodes asked.

"The hospital, where do you think?"

"What are you going to tell them?"

"That I fell, that I slipped, what the hell is the difference? If you got here on time, maybe this wouldn't have happened at all."

He started moving towards the door, but Rhodes closed it.

"What are you doing?" Carlton asked.

"I'm trying to find out what that guy wanted, and what you told him."

For a brief instant, Carlton's face reflected some worry along with the pain, but he recovered quickly. "He thought I had Brennan killed."

"What did you say?"

"That I didn't, what do you think I said? Damn idiot, he didn't even know the cops shot the killer."

"Who was he?"

"I don't know," Carlton lied. He wanted Rhodes in the dark as much as possible; he didn't trust him.

"What else did you tell him?"

"Nothing. This hurts like hell, you understand? If they don't operate on it right away, it won't heal right."

"Carlton, you're not in this alone, OK? Tell me what else you told this guy."

"For the last time, Rhodes, I didn't tell the guy anything. Now get the hell out of the way."

But Rhodes was no longer looking at Carlton; he had nothing more to say to him. Instead he turned to William, making eye contact without saying anything.

William understood the unspoken question, and slowly shook his head from side to side. Carlton didn't notice the connection between the two of them; he was already heading for the door.

He got his hand to the doorknob when the three bullets hit him in the back, pushing him into the door, before he slumped to the floor.

"Leave him right here; I want him found," Rhodes said to William.

"He will be."

"Just the latest victim of the outraged citizens of Brayton."

William smiled. "They're out of control."

Barone had done an impressive job.

Whatever he had said to his counterparts in the three northwest New Jersey counties had certainly motivated them. By the time I got to state police headquarters, officers from all three counties had gathered there. There were probably sixty in total, more than I would have expected could have been spared from other work.

"We're looking for someone who has been kidnapped and is being held in what we believe is an underground room. Our assumption is that it is a bomb shelter, though we cannot be absolutely positive about that."

One of the officers asked what made me think it was a bomb shelter, and I said, "The room seems to be soundproof, and fits the design typical of shelters in the sixties. C rations were also found in a metal cabinet, though they have apparently expired.

"We have reason to believe that the shelter has been occupied recently, as there is a satellite television hookup that is operable and in use."

I showed them pictures of Bryan; I didn't mention that he was my brother, but it's likely that some of them made the connection because of the name, and the rather slight resemblance between us.

"There is a complicating factor," I said. "A major complicating factor. There is a limited air supply, scheduled to run out soon. So there is no time to lose."

"What's the plan?" an officer asked.

"The plan is to go door-to-door, asking everyone if they have or, more importantly, know of bomb shelters in their area. We can then cross-check that against our list of homes with satellites.

"Every single possibility must be followed up on immediately, and if we need more manpower, I'll make sure that we get it. I am aware that this is a difficult assignment, but we are one knock on a door away from solving it, and saving Bryan Somers.

"There is no time to lose, ladies and gentlemen. This situation defines 'life-and-death.'"

Lucas . . . I am very, very anxious to hear more about your progress with Gallagher. I don't have to tell you that time is running short.

I keep imagining that I'm having trouble breathing, that the air is running out prematurely. But I'm still alive, so clearly I've been mistaken. So far . . .

Hoping that someone gets me out of here before I run out of air is definitely the textbook definition of "waiting with bated breath."

Hurry . . .

Alex Hutchison was gratified, but not surprised, at the response.

People were scared, and they were frustrated, and they were looking for someone to help them find a solution. Alex was providing, if not a solution, then at least a plan of attack. No one had a better idea, so they followed her.

People had started showing up the day before, bringing their tents and sleeping bags with them. Underneath them was the natural gas that Hanson was planning to bring up, in Alex's mind destroying the environment in the process.

But no one would be able to drill while the land was inhabited by so many people, and it was Alex's intention to keep a good number of protesters there 24/7.

Alex had confidence that the Brayton police would not attempt to evict them; those officers were the friends of the protesters. Their children went to the same schools, breathed the same air, and drank the same water. They would not turn on the protesters and do Hanson's bidding.

Alex spent as much time as she could at the site, keeping morale up, and making sure as best she could that everyone was well behaved. Logical speculation was rampant that the recent violence was committed by protesters, so Alex wanted to keep these demonstrations as peaceful and law-abiding as possible.

But Alex instinctively understood that demonstrations could only be effective if there was someone to demonstrate to. Hanson Oil and Gas had paid a fortune for that land, and they were not about to pack up their drills and go home because there were people camping out on it.

Even if the Brayton police were reluctant to do their bidding, Hanson would undoubtedly get a court order, and then some police organization, local, state, or Federal, would be forced to act on it. Alex needed to make it as painful as possible for Hanson to try and do that.

The only chance to accomplish the goal was to win the public relations battle. That was why she had called a huge rally for Saturday evening. Her hope was to get at least ninety percent of the citizens of Brayton, plus many supporters from nearby towns, to descend on the contested land.

By publicizing the rally as much as possible, she hoped to get the media out in force. Interviews with worried parents, their children by their sides, would send a powerful message.

So Alex made the rounds, talking to the people camped out and offering them words of encouragement. It was not easy for them; these were not wealthy people who could afford to take time out of their lives. Husbands and wives were alternating staying on the property, each arriving as the other went back to their job, earning the money that they needed to pay the bills.

As she walked around, she noticed someone she recognized. She had spoken to the man at her diner; he had asked her a bunch of questions. There was a physicality about him that was intimidating.

But he was minding his own business, talking to no one, and in fact paying attention to no one. He seemed to be pacing the land, as if measuring it out. Then, as she watched, he walked over to one of the areas where test drilling had been done.

He leaned down, and although it was getting dark and hard to see, he seemed to be feeling the dirt. Then he walked over to another, similar place, and did the same thing.

Buttressed by the fact that there were a lot of people around to dissuade the stranger from doing anything to her, Alex walked over to him.

"What are you doing here?" she asked.

"Bothering no one," Gallagher said.

"Do you work for Hanson?"

"Go back to your friends."

He didn't wait for a response, just kept conducting his mysterious examination of the area. She kept following him, not backing down.

"You're not going to drill on this land," she said.

"You got that right," he said. "No one is."

She persisted. "Who are you?"

"Lady, I'm the person that's going to save your life. Don't make me regret it."

"What the hell does that mean?"

"Are you always this big a pain in the ass?" he asked. "When the police tell you to leave this property, don't give them a hard time like you're giving me. Listen to them."

"Our police would never try to throw us out."

"The state police will. Start packing up."

"We're not leaving."

He didn't bother answering her; instead he headed for his car. The decision had been made; he'd call Luke from the car, and tell him what was going on, and where Bryan was.

There was no longer any need for Bryan to die; justice was going to be served in another way. And Luke would help in that process; Gallagher would use him to get the New York State Police to do what they needed to do, one way or the other.

He turned the key, started the ignition, and shared the fate of Michael Oliver.

It wasn't until later, after the fires had been put out and the police and firemen were searching the scene for clues, that they also discovered the body of Tommy Rhodes. He was killed in his car, which was almost a quarter mile down the road from where the explosion took place. It was done execution-style, by a bullet in the back of his head.

This was where I would be for the next thirty-six hours.

I took a room at a Holiday Inn in Morristown, but I'd be spending very little time in it. I was there to find Bryan, and I wasn't going home until he was with me.

And I was going to be out in the field with everyone else. I wouldn't be making door-to-door cold calls, though. We had gathered data from local real estate agents, showing all homes that had been on the market in the last decade that listed a bomb or fallout shelter among their attributes. It was considered a plus in selling a home, albeit a minor one.

So I'd be going to those places that we already knew had such a shelter, after cross-checking it against our list of satellite homes. Unfortunately, this didn't provide proof that there was a satellite hookup in the shelter itself, only in the home.

The officers on the hunt were going out in pairs, because finding the home with Bryan could prove dangerous. Gallagher could have accomplices there that might resist a rescue attempt, and the officers had to be prepared for that.

I also had a partner, the identity of whom was a big surprise. Emmit showed up, looking weak and a little worse for wear, but anxious to be of help. Emmit at half strength was a hell of a lot tougher than I was, and I was happy to have him back. I was also very grateful.

We spent a few hours going over our information, and making sure all the other officers knew their assignments. It was complicated, especially since we were doing it on the fly. We didn't want any duplication of efforts; there just wasn't time to waste.

I was no longer focused on the situation in Brayton. It wasn't that I didn't believe it was connected to the Brennan murder; the fact was that I did. And once Bryan was safe and sound, I would revisit it, and bring in the Feds and anyone else necessary to crack the case.

Brennan wasn't the only victim in that situation. Michael Oliver had also died, and Emmit had been shot. It still seemed illogical to me. Carlton and Hanson Oil and Gas had the most to gain by preventing Brennan's ascension to the court, and therefore had the motive to kill him. But the rest of the violence was meant to hurt those companies. Could there be killers on both sides? It seemed very, very unlikely.

But in the court of Gallagher, I had already milked it for all it was worth. Based on my last conversation with him, I think it had accomplished a lot. But he seemed intent on convincing himself without any more help from me, and I could only hope that he'd do so quickly.

But that was just a hope, and I couldn't begin to rely on it. So Brayton would go on the back burner while we found Bryan.

It was while I was walking through the station that I saw the report on the television. There was another explosion near the site of the property in Brayton. It happened in the parking lot, adjacent to where the residents had set up their protest camp.

One person was believed killed, but either the identity of the victim was unknown or they weren't yet ready to report it. Another person, identified as Tommy Rhodes, was shot in the head and died at the scene. The Mayor, Edward Holland, was again pleading for outside intervention, and railing against those who were not providing it.

The way things were going, I figured that by the time I got back to focusing on Brayton, they would have all killed each other.

We have strong reason to believe you are in a bomb shelter in northwest New Jersey. We have a massive manhunt going on to check every single shelter in three counties. Barone has mobilized a huge number of state police officers, and every one is looking for you.

This is in addition to the Gallagher news I told you about. I'm openly telling you all this because I'm hoping he's reading the e-mails. Gallagher, if you are, please contact me as soon as possible.

We're coming, Brother.

"I have no easy way to tell you this, Jules."

Julie Somers braced herself for what was going to come next. It was going to be bad; Lou Rodriguez was not prone to the dramatic.

"Tell me," she said into the phone, but not really wanting him to.

"Gallagher is dead."

The news hit her in the chest, and pushed her back against the wall. "How?"

"Someone blew up his car in a parking lot in Brayton . . . where the protesters are camping out."

"You're sure it was him?" she asked, knowing the question was a stupid one.

"I'm sure. I'm sorry, Jules."

"Any idea who did it?"

"No, I was watching him while someone must have rigged the car. If it helps, he had gone to Carlton's house, and was in there about twenty minutes. Based on the yelling I heard, it wasn't a fun visit for Carlton. I looked in the window when Gallagher left, and Carlton was holding his arm at a weird angle and still moaning to some other guy who had been there.

"I left to follow Gallagher, and he went to the place he died from there."

"What was he doing there, do you know?" She was trying to get as much information as she could for Lucas; he might have a view of the big picture in a way that whatever Lou saw could be helpful. She doubted it, but had nothing else to hold on to.

"Just walking around, looking at some of the drilling equipment, checking out the dirt, or something. I couldn't tell, really. He spent some time talking to a woman there, the one who was on TV. Then he went to his car and that was it. The explosion took out a bunch of cars around him."

Julie pumped Lou for additional information, but he didn't have anything more of value to offer, and in fact wasn't yet aware that Rhodes was also murdered nearby. And the truth was, she doubted that what he did say could help Bryan in any way.

Gallagher's only value to her was his knowledge of where Bryan was. At the moment, she couldn't care less if he had solved the Brennan murder, or the violence in Brayton, or the Lindbergh kidnapping. He was the only one who had known where Bryan was, and that knowledge had died with him.

And now she had to tell Luke.

We had two chances to find Bryan, and then suddenly we had one.

What Julie had to tell me was even more devastating than that simple math makes it appear, because Gallagher represented by far the greater of the two opportunities. What we were doing in searching for shelters was a long shot at best.

Weird as it may sound, hearing about Gallagher's death made me realize for the first time that Bryan might die as well. Of course I had known that intellectually for quite a while, but I was so wrapped up in the "hunt" that I kept the truth about Bryan's situation tucked in the back of my mind.

Now it was front and center, and it made me so scared that I felt nauseous.

"How bad is it?" Julie asked.

I wasn't going to lie to her. "It's very bad," I said. "And it's my fault."

"How is that?"

"I should have started this search days ago. Instead I focused too much on Brayton, and on convincing Gallagher to let Bryan go. I thought that was our only real shot, so that's where I spent my time."

"It was the logical thing to do," she said.

"No, the logical thing when you have a kidnapping is to look for the victim. I was too intent on convincing Gallagher, and not spooking him."

"Are you going to tell Bryan?"

"I don't know," I said, because I didn't. "I've been getting his hopes up, because mine were up, and because I don't want him taking those pills. I'm afraid if I tell him what happened he might panic and take them. What do you think?"

"I think we need to keep him alive until we can't keep him alive any longer," she said. "Hold off on telling him."

"OK. For now."

"You want to hear the rest of what Lou said, about Gallagher going to see Carlton, and then going to the site of the drilling?"

"Will it help us for me to hear it?" I asked.

"Probably not, but you never know."

She told me the rest of it, and I filed it away to use after Bryan's rescue.

"I'm coming out there," she said. "I want to help search."

"OK. I don't blame you."

I told her where I was staying, and that I'd book a room for her. Unfortunately, I only would need to book it for one night, because that's all we had left.

The media was not yet reporting that Chris Gallagher was the person killed in the blast. Based on what Julie had said, it was unlikely that the body had been ID'd yet or, for that matter, even recovered remotely intact.

If there was enough left of the car they could probably trace it to Gallagher in that way, especially if it was owned or rented by him. If it was borrowed, it would take that much longer. Trying to recover and test DNA would take longer still.

I couldn't stop myself from wondering what the hell Gallagher was doing at Carlton's house, or the disputed land after that. But that was for another day.

Soon Julie would be here, and together we would find Bryan.

Or we wouldn't, and then nothing would ever be the same.

Lucas . . . it's great that you seem so optimistic. I trust that you're telling me the truth.

This afternoon there was no news on, so I watched a movie. It was called The King's Speech; *I doubt that you saw it because it had no explosions or nudity. It was a true story about a relationship between two men, a Royal Prince and the therapist who helped him cure his lifelong stammer.*

The Prince had a brother, who became King and then left the throne for a woman, making the stammering Prince the new King. Though they were brothers, they had no relationship at all, or at least not one worth having.

Maybe facing death is making me sentimental, but it told me that family is not enough, friendship is more important. So if I get out of this, I want to be friends, not just brothers.

And if I don't make it, I want you to know that I forgive you for what you have done, and I forgive Julie as well.

But get me the hell out of here.

Julie arrived ninety minutes later.

She met us in the hotel restaurant, where Emmit and I took her through the progress we had made, and where things stood. As updates go, it wasn't a pleasant one, because we were not getting anywhere.

Of course, in the kind of operation we were conducting you're always getting nowhere, unless and until you have one hundred percent success. We'd certainly eliminated possibilities; officers had filed reports indicating that they had already checked out seventy-one confirmed bomb shelters.

In four of those instances, they were refused admittance until they threatened to bring the owners to the station and make their lives miserable. Failing that, the officers would have gotten search warrants, but it was unnecessary, because in each case there was ultimate compliance.

It was getting late, and we all decided to get four hours' sleep and meet very early in the morning. There was nothing we could do anymore that night, and we needed to be refreshed for the next day. Left unspoken was what we all knew: it was Bryan's last day.

Emmit went upstairs first, leaving Julie and me. We ordered a drink, just one because of that need to be completely alert the next day. It also might help us sleep, although at that point I didn't think a sledgehammer to the head could put me out.

"Have you told Bryan about what happened to Gallagher?" she asked.

"No. Not yet."

She nodded. "Good. Please give it a little time. We're going to get it done tomorrow."

I had strong doubts we would, but saw no need to mention it at that point.

Sitting with her right then was weird but not awkward, if that makes any sense. It was weird because of the awful situation we were facing, and because we were two people who had been in love with each other for six years.

After that one night, we never talked about it or our feelings for each other, and we definitely weren't about to now. But it hung out there over the table like a fairly large-sized watermelon.

Since we couldn't talk about that and we certainly didn't want to discuss Bryan's plight anymore, Julie asked me, "So, at the end of the day, did Steven Gallagher kill Danny Brennan?"

"No way. We can add that to the list of things I'll have to live with."

"He raised the gun, Luke. He was going to shoot either himself, or you. The fact that he didn't kill Brennan didn't make him less dangerous."

"Yeah," I said, with as little enthusiasm as I was feeling. "Did you see *The King's Speech*?"

"Yes. Great movie."

"Bryan saw it the other night; he assumed I hadn't seen it, because it seemed too upscale for my taste."

She laughed and said, "I would assume the same thing."

At least I think that's what she said. I was focusing on the fact that when she said it she put her hand on my arm. It was like a jolt of electricity; she could have been reciting the Gettysburg Address and I wouldn't have noticed.

Finally I said, "I saw it the night it came out."

"Then you had a date that chose the movie."

She had removed her hand, so I was hearing clearly again. "Guilty as charged, counselor. Anyway, Bryan wrote about the relationships that the brothers had, and compared it to the relationship between the Prince and the speech therapist. It showed him that family isn't enough; you need to work at being friends."

She nodded as if she understood; I guess when you live with someone for six years you get a good idea how they view things.

"Funny thing is, that's not what struck me about it at all," I said. "It got me thinking about how we're all programmed from an early age to be what we're going to be. Not because of any royal line of succession like those guys, but by our parents, or our intelligence, or whatever. For a lot of reasons, Bryan was going to be in business and I was going to be a cop."

"I think you both wound up in the right place."

We both realized at the same time the place Bryan was in at the moment, which put an end to the discussion.

"Let's go," I said. I paid the check, and we went upstairs. We walked down the hall to Julie's room; mine was just a few doors past it. When we got to her door, I wanted to go in with her. I'm less in need of comforting than anyone I've ever met, but at that moment we both needed it, and we were uniquely in a position to provide it for each other.

"Good night," I said.

She kissed me lightly on the cheek. "Good night, Luke. Tomorrow is going to be a great day."

"Yes, it is," I said.

She closed the door, and I walked the rest of the way to my room. It seemed like about four miles.

Hang in there, Brother. Big day tomorrow. Julie came up because she wants to be there when you get out; I hope that's OK.

More tomorrow.

I was right about having trouble sleeping.

I lay there for a while, trying to ready myself for what we were facing, and trying to quell the fear.

I think I fell asleep, in fits and starts, and the only reason I say that is because I was having a dream. I don't remember that much of it now, but Bryan was the King of England, or at least King of something, and I was sort of a dope in the castle who nobody paid any attention to. It was the Paterson, New Jersey, version of *The King's Speech*.

I had the dream a little after five in the morning, and the reason I know that is because that's what time it was when I jumped up like someone shoved a hot poker up my ass.

I grabbed the phone and called Julie and Emmit. "Meet me downstairs in fifteen minutes," I said to each of them. They both asked what was going on, and I just repeated, "Meet me downstairs in fifteen minutes."

I was down there in twelve, and Julie was already waiting for me. Emmit was there a few seconds later. There was coffee in the lobby, and we each grabbed a cup and sat down.

"Bryan e-mailed me that he watched *The King's Speech,*" I said. "He's had television service throughout."

They didn't say anything, probably hoping that I was going to offer more than this old news.

I was.

"I read an article a while back, I think it had to do with targeting advertisements to people, but the point of it was that the satellite and cable companies know what you are watching. They keep records of it; they even know what people record."

"I think I read that," Emmit said.

I could see excitement building in Julie's eyes, but it was tempered. "But you know how many people watched *The King's Speech* that night?"

"That's the first thing I thought about," I said. "There's no way we'd be able to narrow it down in time. But it doesn't matter what Bryan watched; what matters is what he's going to watch."

"What do you mean?" she asked.

"You have a friend at the satellite company, right? The guy you got the weather outage info from."

"He was helpful; I wouldn't call him a friend."

"Either he's going to be your friend today or I'm going to strangle him with my bare hands.

"Let's find out where he is and get him up and in his office," I said to Emmit. "And get a court order just in case."

"I'm lost," Emmit said. "What are we asking this guy to do?"

"I'm going to e-mail Bryan and tell him what to watch. We'll do it in a way that stands out. Then we'll get this satellite guy to sit at his computer and find out where the house with that watching pattern is."

Julie opened her purse and took out a notebook. She

turned a few pages, and said, "His name is Daniel Robbins. I think his office is in Morristown."

Emmit stood up, said, "I'll make the calls from the room phone," and walked away, his large frame moving faster than I thought it could walk and showing no ill effects of the shooting. If I were Daniel Robbins, I would do whatever Emmit asked.

"This had better work," I said.

"I think it can," Julie said. "They should have the technology to pull it off."

I didn't take too much comfort in what she said, since she had as little knowledge of technology as I did, which is to say she had none. For the moment there was nothing to do but e-mail Bryan and wait for Emmit.

Ten minutes later my phone rang. I took a quick look and saw that it was a number I didn't recognize, so I figured it was Emmit calling from upstairs. "Emmit?"

"Lieutenant Somers, this is Alex Hutchinson," the caller said, in a female voice that sounded nothing like Emmit's.

It took me a moment to place the name, and when I did I said, "Alex, yes . . . I—"

She interrupted me. "You said I should call you if I knew something important, and I know it's early, but—"

I returned the interruption. "I'm sorry, Alex, I'm in the middle of something. Can I call you back at this number?"

She seemed uncertain. "Yes, I guess so. But I think you'll want to hear it. It's about that man that was killed."

"I definitely want to hear it. I promise I'll call you back soon," I said, though I didn't really plan to. I'd have Emmit call her back when the opportunity presented itself. I knew she was a serious person who would not be wasting my time, but I was going to focus on Bryan, and only Bryan.

Three minutes later, Emmit came into the room. "We're

going to meet him at the tech center. Let's go; it's just ten minutes from here."

"Can he do it?" I asked.

"He's not sure."

Bryan, we're going to want you to do something with the television, probably starting in an hour or so. I'll send the instructions soon, so watch for my e-mail.

Do you have power on the computer?

Do you have a remote control for the television?

Please confirm that you got this e-mail.

❦

Got it.

Down to 9% on the computer, so I can't check that often. I'll try every fifteen minutes, for now.

I have a remote control.

I'll wait for your instructions.

We were at the tech center in fifteen minutes.

Daniel Robbins was waiting for us outside. He was younger than I expected, probably not even thirty, but that was okay. In my experience the younger the person, the better they were with technology. I don't think I've ever met a sixty-year-old computer geek.

He had a serious, intense look on his face; Emmit had obviously impressed him with the urgency of the situation. "Follow me," he said, and we all started walking. "I'm not supposed to do anything like this without authorization."

"Whoever gives you a hard time I will shoot in the face," I said.

He nodded. "That should do the trick."

He led us into an enormous room, the kind you associate with NASA mission control. There were probably a hundred seats at desks, each one with a large monitor. On the wall there were main monitors, with lights and numbers flashing, and maps with display lights. I'm sure it all had meaning to somebody, but not to me.

There were thirty or so people manning the desks, who I assumed were still the night crew. Robbins pointed towards a glass-enclosed office in the back of the room, on the balcony floor. "We're up there."

We followed him up to the room, which looked something like the communication center on the starship *Enterprise*. There were two people already there, a man and woman, both younger than Robbins. "This is Howard Mueller and Sarah Gayda," Robbins said, and everybody nodded. No time for handshakes.

"Howie, you have the floor."

He nodded, and began. "We've never done this; we don't have any interest in what people are watching in the moment; it's always after the fact. That's more than ample for advertising decisions.

"But I think we can set it up for ongoing monitoring; it just might take a little while, because some of the crosschecking will be manual. The computers aren't set up this way, and it might take more time to try and program them than to get things going."

"OK, good," I said. "I need to tell Bryan what he should be doing."

"Sarah?" Howie said, and Sarah took the floor.

"Our computers are designed for fifteen-minute increments. So he should watch something for fifteen minutes, and then go to the very next channel for fifteen, then the one after that for fifteen, and so on."

"Got it. Does it matter which channels?"

"Mmmm," she said, "good question. Tell him to start with 318, then work his way up. Sometimes the number jumps; for instance the one after 319 is 324. But that doesn't matter; he should turn to whichever one is next."

"When should he start?"

Howie again: "It'll take us at least forty minutes to set it up."

I looked at my watch. "OK, he'll start at eight forty-five."

Robbins said, "We'll be back at eight twenty-five," to

Howie and Sarah. Then to us, "I'll show you where the coffee is."

I walked over with Robbins, Julie, and Emmit, but knew that if I sat there and had more coffee my head would explode. I decided to call Alex Hutchinson back. She answered on the first ring.

"Lieutenant?"

"Yes."

"Thanks for calling me back. I'm sure you read about the man that was killed the other day in the explosion; they haven't given his name out."

"I'm aware."

"He was walking around the area where we're protesting just before he died. I thought what he was doing was strange, so I approached him."

"What was he doing?"

"Sort of examining the land, checking out the drilling rigs that were already there, that kind of thing. But that's not why I called you."

"Why did you call?"

"Because I talked to him and he said some strange things that I thought you should know. I figured he was with Hanson, so I told him we wouldn't let him drill on the land, and he said that nobody was going to. Then he told me to leave him alone, that he was saving my life. I may not have the exact words right, but that's basically what he said."

"Anything else?"

"Yes, he said that the state police were going to throw us off this land, and said we should listen to them. Then he said I was a pain in the ass," she said, and then laughed. "Which showed he knew what he was talking about."

There would come a time when all this would be interesting to me, when I would try to bring down everyone involved in the Brayton mess. But that wasn't the time, especially with Emmit across the room signaling to me about something.

"Thanks, Alex. Let me think about this for a while."

"OK," she said. "If you need me, I'll be out here on the land. We're not leaving, and we're not the ones committing the violence, no matter what they say."

I got off the phone and walked over to Emmit, who was reading something on his own cell phone. "What's going on?"

Emmit looked up. "Richard Carlton is dead. Murdered in his own home."

"I guess Gallagher got his justice," I said.

Julie shook her head. "No, he didn't. Carlton was alive when Gallagher left his house. Lou mentioned that he looked in the window and Carlton was holding his arm at a weird angle and yelling at some guy who was there with him."

"William," I said. "He was like Carlton's assistant or something, but he looked more like a something than an assistant."

"Could he have killed him?" Emmit asked.

"I don't know, and right now I don't give a shit. I'd be fine if they dropped a nuclear bomb on Brayton."

I looked over at Howie and Sarah, still hovering over their computers; it was hard to believe that we were depending on them to save Bryan, but that's where we were. Maybe it was to get my mind off that, but I started thinking about Gallagher again. "Carlton must have told Gallagher something. And whatever it was sent him to the drilling site."

"And Carlton knew where he'd be going, and sent someone to kill him, so Gallagher couldn't reveal what Carlton had said," Julie said.

I shook my head. "More likely that somebody, maybe William, killed Carlton for talking and then went after Gallagher. My bet would be that the same person killed Carlton, Gallagher, and Rhodes."

"It would have to be the protesters," Julie said. "Carlton and Hanson have gotten what they wanted. So they killed Carlton for revenge, and they killed Gallagher because they thought he was on Carlton's side."

What she was saying didn't ring true for me, but I shut my credibility bell off entirely, because Robbins was signaling for us to come over. Howie and Sarah were apparently done, and we were about to find out if our last chance was still feasible.

"OK, we've got good news and bad news," Robbins said.

"Let's hear all of it."

"Howie?"

Howie took over. "The short answer is that we can do it. We can tell you who's watching a particular show at a particular time, in the moment. We can't do it in exactly the target area you're talking about, our range is going to be a little wider, but we can do it."

"And the bad news?"

"Two things. One is that a home will be recorded on the list as long as it's on at any moment within the fifteen-minute time frame. So if they scroll through it, it'll be there. That will increase the number of homes and the size of the list."

"What's the other thing?" I asked.

"We have no way of cross-checking the lists by computer; it will have to be manual."

"What exactly does that mean?" Julie asked.

"Well, put it this way. We can print out a list of everyone watching ESPN from eleven to eleven fifteen. Then we can print out a list of everyone watching CNN from eleven fifteen to eleven thirty. But we can't tell you, or at least our computers can't tell you, who is on both lists."

"Can you separate the lists by area?"

He nodded. "Yes, by zip code."

I nodded. "Good. So we'll each take different lists, and

go over it by hand. We'll get it done," I said, though I had no idea if we could, since I had no idea how many lists there would be, what form they would take, or how many names would be on them.

I asked Robbins, "You have people that can help?"

He nodded. "Yes."

"Only those you can trust completely, that you don't think will be careless and miss anything."

"I understand."

"Good," I said. "I'll tell Bryan we're a go."

Bryan,

At eleven o'clock, turn on channel 318, at eleven fifteen, turn on channel 319. At eleven thirty, move to the next channel in order. If it skips numbers, that's fine, just make sure it's the next channel.

Any problem, let me know immediately.

Lucas,

Got your e-mail, and I'll do exactly what you say.

I'll let you know if there's a problem, but please, you do the same. I only have hours left, and I'm not sure how many.

4% on the computer.

Hurry.

Edward Holland was frustrated and angry.

The District Court had declined to provide a court order removing the protesters, choosing to give them more time to respond to Holland's motion. That effectively removed the possibility, for the time being, of state or Federal intervention.

The murder of Richard Carlton was announced after the court issued its ruling, and there was no way they would reconsider before Monday.

Monday wasn't good enough.

It was an uncomfortable position for Holland to be in. He had been the champion of the people he represented, and now he was at least temporarily on the other side. But he was positive that more violence was on the way, and he had to do whatever he could to prevent additional loss of life.

To that end, he again called Brayton's police chief, Tony Brus. "What have you got on the Carlton murder?" he asked.

"He took three bullets in the back from ten feet. No witnesses. Also had a broken arm that happened premortem. Coroner won't know for sure until the autopsy, but his guess is the arm happened within minutes of the shooting. Different gun killed Rhodes."

"Anything that might lead you to the killer?" he asked.

"Hard to say. We took prints, but no results yet. But this was not an amateur job."

"We've got to act," Holland said.

"I'm acting," Brus said, annoyed at the implication. "I've got every officer working fourteen-hour days. You want more action, get me more people."

"I want the protesters removed from the mining site."

Brus was tired of dealing with this asshole, especially since he was more and more inclined to run against him in the next election. "Mayor, I was just there. Everybody is calm; they're barbequing and throwing Frisbees, for Christ sake."

"People are getting blown up and shot in the parking lot."

"I've told you, the violence is being committed by outsiders. I don't know who, but there's no way the people camping out on that land are killing people."

"I don't want anyone killed. By anyone. I want them gone before dark tonight," Holland said.

"You're making a mistake."

"Your point of view is noted. Now I'm the Mayor, and I want them out. Bring tear gas, hoses, whatever the hell you need, but get them out."

Brus was furious, but maintained control. "It will take me a while to put the operation together."

"Do it," Holland said, and hung up.

Brus hung up the phone with one thought on his mind. He would do his job, but there was no way he was teargassing his friends. And whatever he did, he would make Mayor Holland look bad in the process.

The day was already a month long, with no sign of ending any time soon.

At least that's what it felt like, waiting for Howie and Sarah to set up the machines that would start monitoring TV viewership throughout northwest New Jersey.

Of course, at the same time, the clock seemed to be moving at a mile a minute, as it literally wound down the time left in Bryan's life.

All we could do was watch and wait. Every time Howie frowned, I was afraid that he had just discovered something to make the entire project technologically unfeasible. And he never seemed to smile, so there was nothing to provide an upbeat counterbalance to that worry.

Robbins brought three people in, two women and a man. None of them were over twenty-five; retirement age in this company had to be thirty. But they seemed sharp when Robbins downloaded them on what was going to happen, and I further impressed the life-and-death seriousness on them.

I've been present when Julie gave closing arguments to a jury in capital cases, but I've never seen anything

approaching the tenseness in her face and body as I did at
that moment. Bryan was her family, and Bryan was her
friend, and imagining him suffocating to death was completely and totally unacceptable.

I was able to spend the time beating myself up over not
having thought of this earlier. I had known Bryan had television from almost the beginning; all this could have been
accomplished with time to study the data, with more than
four percent power on his computer, and a lot more than a
few hours of air for him to breathe.

"OK," Howie finally said, looking up at us. "We're as
ready as we're going to be. It's ten forty eight; we're set to
go at eleven. We'll have the printout about six minutes after
the time period is up, so we'll get the first one at eleven
twenty-one. That won't do us any good, because we'll have
nothing to cross-check it against. We'll have the second
report at eleven thirty-six. There's no way to tell how many
reports we'll need to eliminate all but one."

He seemed to be a smart and confident guy, which made
me feel better that he knew what he was doing. I liked him,
and if he screwed it up, I was going to kill him.

But the bottom line was that we would not have anything to cross-check for forty-eight minutes. Since each
minute seemed to take about four hours, we were looking
at a long wait.

I didn't want to e-mail Bryan, because I didn't want
him to use up computer power in responding. There was
also no need; he knew what he was supposed to do, and
would do it as long as he could.

I called Barone and told him what was going on, and
asked him to send backup officers and position them in
various areas in the three counties we were looking at. I
wanted us to be able to get to Bryan as fast as possible
once we knew where he was.

And then my mind wandered back to Brayton, again

probably because I didn't want to think about Bryan, counting on us, waiting in that room.

Ordinarily, in a situation like that, I would write down everything I knew. It helps me to think clearly, to make sense out of things that sometimes seem nonsensical. I didn't have time for that now, so I couldn't get my mind around certain questions.

Why would Carlton have been killed? He was no longer a factor in the mining operation; Hanson had already bought the land from him. Was it revenge by the townspeople? That hardly seemed likely. Was it to keep him quiet? Quiet about what?

What could Carlton have told Gallagher, and why did it send him to the drilling site? And what was he doing feeling around in the dirt, and looking at the drilling equipment?

They were questions I would answer, but they would have to wait. It was eleven twenty-one, and the first set of lists was being printed out.

Sarah handed them to us. They were different sizes, and probably averaged about six hundred addresses on each one. We spread them out in front of us on large desks, looking over them, and discussed the best way to go about the cross-checking.

But for the time being we were unable to do anything with the lists.

That would wait for the next list, which would provide something to cross-check them against.

Then it would be showtime.

The situation was way out there beyond the Planet Surreal.

Bryan could see that, even through the haze of fear that was enveloping him.

He was sitting underground, running out of air to breathe, counting on TV programs to save him. On the same table as the remote control was a glass of water and two pills, which he would use to kill himself at the first sign of impending suffocation. And the last person he would probably ever hear speak was on television, trying to sell him a miracle kitchen gadget.

He had a million questions that he wanted to ask Lucas, most of them about Gallagher and the situation in Brayton. For a short while Lucas had been so upbeat about it, and then he stopped mentioning it.

Bryan wondered what had happened, why it had gotten to the point where this thing with the television became what seemed to be his last chance. Had Gallagher refused to intervene, and had Lucas now given up on that?

But Bryan did not want to send an e-mail asking those questions. The computer had long ago told him that it was on reserve power, and he wanted to conserve what little he had left.

He wished he could go online and learn how he would feel when the air started to run out. Would there be a period of time where he felt only short of breath, and slightly dizzy? Would it allow him time to take the pills, and alleviate the suffering? And how long would the pills take to work? All of these questions would go unanswered.

Bryan considered writing a final message to the world, on pencil and paper, a medium that didn't slowly reduce its "percentage of power" remaining. He had thought about it frequently during the previous six days, but didn't know that there was anything special he wanted to say. Or that anyone would ever find the note, or his body.

So all he planned to do was switch the dial at each fifteen-minute interval and wait to be rescued, or to die.

The second set of lists came right on time, six minutes after the time period ended.

Nobody said a word; we all just launched ourselves into the job of cross-checking it with the first lists. It was a tedious, time-consuming job, made even more daunting by the tremendous pressure we were feeling.

My approach was to take the first address on list one and try to find it on list two. If I did, I'd put a checkmark next to it on both lists. If I didn't, I'd put an "x" by it on list one, but I didn't cross it out, in case it was on list two and I had just missed it.

It was so slow that I had the sinking feeling that we were going to fail, even if the process worked. I wanted to speed up the work, but I was haunted by the fear that in doing so I'd miss something. If Bryan's address was on there and we passed over it, just once, then all hope would be lost.

It took me an hour and five minutes to get through my list, and I found thirty-seven addresses common to both lists. I was the first one finished, Julie was second, and the others were all done within fifteen minutes of me. The strain everyone was under was evident in their faces.

While we were working, other lists were being generated, as other fifteen-minute segments concluded. Since we only had to cross-check them against those names that were common to the first two sets of lists, this would go much faster but still take some time.

It was two o'clock in the afternoon before we narrowed it down to a manageable number. At that point we had seventeen addresses in the target area, though I was suddenly flooded with the fear that maybe we weren't looking in the right place at all.

We had only narrowed it down to northwest Jersey because of the weather outages. What if the information we had been given was wrong? What if there had been outages someplace else? Bryan could be in Connecticut, or New York. Or what if Bryan's particular outage wasn't weather related at all? What if it was a local glitch?

But we were where we were, and seventeen was a limited-enough list to get started. I called Barone, and told him to start sending officers to the locations.

I was torn, not sure whether to go out in the field myself or wait for another list that would narrow it down further. I decided to wait, at least for one more list. And then I'd be on the move.

But first I had to make sure that Bryan believed we would save him, so he wouldn't take his own life. If I was wrong, and I knew that could very well be the case, it would be a last, terrible betrayal.

We're coming for you, Bryan . . . it won't be long now.

You can count on it.

The rally was set for 6 PM, and it would be huge.

That became obvious when people started arriving before noon. They joined those already camping out there, and by two o'clock, with four hours still to go, the crowd had swelled to almost six thousand.

Edward Holland and Tony Brus agreed on a plan to clear the land of people. Holland would speak at the beginning of the rally, asking everyone to leave. Neither man had any real hope that his words would be effective, and Brus would have his officers on the scene, ready to move in if it became necessary.

Brus had instructed his officers on procedure. The goal was to get the people out of there and then quickly construct barricades to prevent them from coming back. There was no desire to arrest people; these were not criminals and should not be treated as such.

Brus had originally had the idea to fence off the area before people could arrive, but it was impractical, since so many protesters were already there and others arrived so early. This was going to be a first of its kind for Brayton, and Brus told his second command that it would "permanently change the way we're viewed by the people who live here."

But even a town as small as Brayton has procedures in place for situations like this, and they spent the late morning going over them, and talking about how they would react to various scenarios that could come up.

When they were finished and ready, Brus called Holland. "Mayor, we are as prepared as we will ever be."

"Good. I'll speak to them, and alert them as to what is going to happen. If they don't listen to me, you move your men in."

"You're the boss," Brus said, signaling his reluctant agreement to go along with the plan. He thought this was a serious overreaction, even after the Carlton murder. On the positive side, if it all went the way he expected, Holland wouldn't ever get another vote in Brayton.

"Tony, I know you think I'm overreacting on this," said Holland. "But the downside to doing it is that people will be pissed at us. The downside to not doing it as that people can die."

"OK," Brus said, "I can see that." He knew that Holland did not want any citizens of Brayton to be killed. He also knew that Holland especially did not want them to die on his watch.

The reports coming in from the field were not good.

Barone called to say that officers had already checked out nine of the seventeen matches and come up with nothing. I took down the list of the ones that had been checked out, so that I could check them off our lists.

"What are they doing if the houses seem to be empty?" I asked.

"Hey, Lucas, you think I'd let them leave it at that? Our people are instructed to enter and search the homes, whether people are not home, or not cooperative. We'll deal with the fallout later."

"Thanks, Captain."

"I'll keep you posted as reports come in."

I got off the phone and saw that the next group of lists was coming out. We got started on them, and I didn't eliminate the homes that Barone had reported were already checked out, just in case the officers missed something.

Thirty-five minutes later we had the pared-down list. There were six homes on it, four of which had already been checked by Barone.

Which left two possibilities, one of which was only fifteen minutes from where we were. I called Barone and gave him this new information, and he said that officers were only ten minutes from the other location. He was close to there as well, and would meet up with them.

He would also send some as backup for us, but we were closer than his officers were, so we'd likely get there first.

When I got off the phone, I said, "Let's go. We're covering one of the two; Barone's got the other." I turned to Robbins. "You know how to get to this address?"

"Yes."

"Then come on," I said, and the four of us were off.

The address was in Mount Freedom, a small town northwest of Morristown. Robbins was only partially familiar with it, but told us he thought the address was on the outskirts of town, in mostly undeveloped farmland.

I drove, only because I got in the driver's seat first. Emmit got in the back with Julie, and Robbins sat in the passenger seat. I drove in a way that emulated Emmit's technique, which is to go so fast that the front wheels start to leave the ground. It was all open road, so I turned on the siren and let it rip.

I didn't turn on the GPS, trusting Robbins's assurance that he knew the way. This appeared to be a major mistake when at one point he said, "Turn right here—no, wait." But he soon seemed to get his bearings, and told us he was positive he knew where he was going.

And he did.

We turned off on a small dirt road and pulled up to a farmhouse, small but in good condition. There was a car parked outside, and a pickup truck that looked like it had been a while since it was serviceable.

We got out of the car and ran to the front porch. I rang the bell and no one answered. I rang it again . . . no response.

So I nodded to Emmit, and he kicked down the front door.

The four of us went inside and started looking around. "We're looking for doors in the floor," I said. "Move every piece of furniture; the door might be hidden."

So we searched, with Julie screaming Bryan's name periodically, even though there was no way he could hear us even if he were there. The house was a small one, and we covered every piece of floor at least three times, then went out and looked around the yard.

I could see the satellite dish above the garage, so we went in there and searched just as carefully.

Nothing.

Bryan was not there.

My phone was ringing; it was Barone.

By five o'clock the number of protesters had exceeded ten thousand.

Even though there was no official program, a number of people had gotten up and made impromptu speeches from the stand that had been constructed for the occasion. Everyone knew that Mayor Holland was going to speak at six o'clock and Alex Hutchinson after that.

Holland had not arrived, but Chief Brus had, and was walking among the protesters. The courtesy with which he was greeted, and the almost festive atmosphere, confirmed his conviction that Holland was overreacting to the perceived danger. For God's sake, Brus thought, half the children in town were there with their parents. Would people about to commit violent acts want their children there?

Holland was an idiot.

Brus's strategy was a simple one. He would execute Holland's order and send his men in to clear the place out. If they went peacefully, then that would be the end of it. Holland would take some political grief for having done it, but he could cover himself by claiming to only be concerned with the safety and welfare of the citizens.

If they resisted, Brus would not instruct his men to forcefully remove them. Holland would go nuts, and would demand the use of tear gas or other irresistible force. There would be a public disagreement between the two men, and Brus would not back down.

The net result would be that it would cost Brus his job; Holland had the right to fire him, and would exercise that right. But it would firmly and permanently elevate him well above Holland in the minds of the townspeople, and would be the perfect kickoff for his candidacy for Mayor.

It may not have been a win-win for Brus, but at the very least it was a no lose–win.

So all Brus had to do was sit back and watch Holland dig his own political grave and Brus would move in once he stopped shoveling.

At first, Bryan didn't recognize what was happening.

He sensed that he was breathing slightly faster than normal, but he couldn't tell if that was because he was feeling intense anxiety. He was pretty sure that extreme nervousness caused quickened breathing, but it was hard to remember.

And it was really important that he remember.

But after a few minutes, there could be no denying it. The air he was breathing was less satisfying; he needed more of it. That's why he was inhaling faster and faster, but it wasn't getting the job done.

In full-fledged panic, he turned on the computer, to see if there was a message from Lucas, providing a reason to hold on. There was none, so he quickly typed one of his own. The pills were three feet away, sitting on the desk, next to a glass of water. Waiting.

Then the computer went black and stayed that way. It was obviously out of power; he wasn't even sure if the e-mail he sent went out. The battery had run out, as had Bryan's life.

He picked up the computer and threw it against the

wall, smashing the now useless machine that had been his lifeline. The exertion made him breathe even harder.

It was the moment of truth; if he was to take the pills, now was the time. He had resolved to do so, and felt that he could do it when faced with the certain prospect of death by suffocation.

But in the moment he hesitated. It was death he was afraid of, death in any form, and until he took those pills there was the remote possibility it could be avoided.

So he debated it in his mind, in seconds that felt like hours.

And then he felt strangely peaceful; it's counterintuitive, but a brain deprived of sustenance will create such a feeling.

And with the pills on the desk, he slumped to the floor.

"Negative," Barone said. "It's a goddamn garden apartment."

He was telling me that the other of the two matches that the satellite lists had yielded was a dead end, that there was no underground shelter there.

He was telling me that Bryan was going to die.

There was literally nothing we could do. Either we had been wrong about the general location that he was in or we had missed something in our rush to go through the lists. The latter possibility seemed more likely, but it didn't matter.

There was nothing left to be done.

Julie started to sob softly, and I felt like joining her. I had spent a goddamn week trying to find a killer, and in the process I had killed my own brother.

Emmit, not the crying type, smashed his hand into the car so hard that it made a serious dent. He had given it his all, had even taken a bullet that day by the missile shaft, but it hadn't been enough. At that moment I wished I had taken the bullet and fallen down the shaft and never . . .

And then thinking about that time at the abandoned

missile shaft reminded me of what Willis Granderson of the Morristown police had told us the day he sent us to check out that shaft. He had laughed and said that he knew people who built houses near an abandoned one, set it up as a shelter, and used it as a guesthouse. He laughed and said that he had guests he'd like to put underground like that.

The backup officers Barone had sent were just pulling up, six officers in three cars. I started screaming at them, and at Julie, Emmit, and Robbins, "LOOK FOR AN ABANDONED MISSILE SHAFT! SPREAD OUT AND LOOK FOR A MISSILE SHAFT!"

I saw Emmit's face light up in recognition; he was there when Granderson made his comment, and he remembered it as well. "Come on!" he yelled, and quickly indicated where each of us should look, so as to spread us out to make the search as efficient as possible.

We all took off on the run, trying to cover as much territory as possible without missing anything. Having seen the other abandoned shaft, I knew this one was large enough that someone would realize it if they came upon it.

And Julie did.

"LUCAS! OVER HERE! I THINK I FOUND IT!"

I was the closest to her, so I got there first. She was leaning over, trying futilely to pull on the enormous metal covering. A hundred of her, a hundred Emmits, would not have been able to do it.

But one Emmit proved to be enough. On the other side of the cover from where Julie was standing, he found a small door cut out of it. It was made of metal as well, and as I ran towards him I saw him take out his gun and shoot at the padlock that was on the handle.

He shot four times, and by the time I got there with the other officers he was pulling the door open. He lifted the door and I looked in; there was a long, fairly steep staircase down at least twenty feet.

I headed down; it was so steep that I did it backwards, treating it more like a ladder than a staircase. I was looking down as I did so, but I could hear the others above me, coming down.

The first thing I noticed, even before I got down there, was the sound of the television. When I got to the bottom I could see that it was a small apartment. I was about to call out Bryan's name, and was already panicked that he hadn't called out mine, when I saw him lying next to the table.

Emmit and two officers had made it down, and approached as I leaned over Bryan. One of the officers, who seemed to know what he was doing, felt for a pulse, but didn't say whether or not he detected one. All he said was, "We need to get him to fresh air."

When I stood up, I noticed the two pills sitting next to a glass of water on a table. He hadn't taken them.

I was already feeling light-headed from the lack of air in the room, though some was certainly coming in from the stairwell. Whatever was affecting me didn't seem to bother Emmit, though. This man who had nearly died from a bullet wound, and gotten out of a hospital bed to help, picked Bryan up, and put him over his shoulder.

One of the officers yelled into the shaft, "We're coming up!" and then stepped out of the way for Emmit, who carried Bryan up the stairs with apparent ease. I was feeling so weak that I almost hoped Emmit would come back and carry me, but I followed along.

When I got to the top I saw Bryan lying on his back, with one of the officers over him, doing CPR.

Before I had a chance to ask what his status was, Julie came over to me.

"He's alive," she said, and started to cry.

We sat in the hospital waiting room for three hours.

Dr. Arthur Lansing came out once to talk to us, somewhere around the one-hour mark. Lansing looked to be no more than thirty-five and was tall, at least six foot six. He would have been taller if he had a single hair on his head, but it was shaven clean. I had absolutely no idea what to make of that.

He spoke with authority and confidence, conveying a feeling that he was in control of the situation. "Mr. Somers is in a coma, but his condition has stabilized."

"So that means he'll . . . he'll survive?" Julie asked.

Lansing nodded. "Absent any unforeseen circumstances."

Julie closed her eyes in a silent thanks, and Emmit exhaled about four tanks' worth of carbon dioxide.

I was focused on getting more information. "Why is he in a coma?" I asked.

"His brain was deprived of oxygen for an unspecified period of time. It shut down, partially as a defense mechanism. When it kicks back into full operation, he'll hopefully come out of the coma, and we'll know more about potential damage."

"What's your guess?" I asked.

He smiled patiently. "I'm afraid I don't do guesses very often. If I knew how long he was without sufficient oxygen, I could give you an informed opinion. But I don't, so I won't. Sorry."

"Can we see him?" Julie asked.

"Yes, but give it a little time. He's going to be moved to a private room in Intensive Care; the nurse will come out to get you in a bit."

So we waited. Captain Barone came in to see how things were going. He hugged all three of us, even Emmit. Barone was far more emotionally involved in this than I had realized.

After we had told him what little we knew about Bryan's condition, he said, "So when the hell are you coming back to work?"

"I'm thinking vacation," I said.

"Think again. We've got a murder case to solve."

"Which one?"

"Judge Brennan," he said. "When word gets out that Steven Gallagher didn't do it, the Feds will be all over it. I want to beat them to it."

"Sounds familiar," I said, but the comment stung me. I hadn't thought in a while about Steven Gallagher in that apartment, and the three bullets I pumped into him.

When Barone left, Emmit asked, "If Gallagher didn't do it, who did?"

I was irritated that with all I had learned, I couldn't come close to answering that question with any certainty. "If you're asking who held the knife, my best guess would be Kagan. He possessed the necessary skills. I would have thought Carlton hired him."

"Why?"

"Because he got half the money from Hanson, and Brennan could have been seen as a threat to that."

"But somebody did Carlton, and Rhodes," Emmit said, accurately. "And Rodriguez said Carlton was alive when Gallagher left the house that night."

"Maybe it was William," I said. "The butler did it."

It was a bad joke, and Emmit correctly disregarded it. "Why would he kill his boss? Carlton already had the money; why would William have wanted him dead? Unless it's Carlton's wife; she was dumping him anyway."

I didn't believe that was likely, and said so. She was going to get a fortune in the divorce; it seemed unlikely that she would have engineered something like this, especially the Brennan killing. But anything was possible, and I would certainly investigate it.

We dropped the conversation and resumed staring at the door through which the nurse would allegedly come, inviting us in to see Bryan. I knew she hadn't forgotten us, since I had gone to the desk at least a dozen times to remind them.

There were other things about the Brennan case, especially the situation in Brayton, that still bothered me. There were the items that Gallagher found in Rhodes's hotel room, that he left with me. But even more troubling were the items he didn't find. There were far more explosives missing than had been used, and the timers were not there as well. They could have been set by Rhodes before he died.

There was the Michael Oliver killing. I still couldn't understand why he had been singled out to die; he was no longer a player once he submitted his report, and even before that had labored in anonymity.

But above all, it still made no sense that the violence was coming from different directions. Carlton and his partners had the motive for Brennan to be eliminated, yet all the rest of the violence was directed against Carlton's side.

But sometimes things that don't make sense suddenly do, all at once.

"I'll be damned," I said. "That has to be it."

"Excuse me?"

I looked up, and there was the nurse. Julie and Emmit were already standing, but I had been so lost in thought that I was oblivious.

"Nothing," I said. "Sorry."

"You can see Mr. Somers now," she said.

"You guys go ahead," said Emmit. "I'll wait here."

Julie and I followed the nurse through the double doors, and down a corridor to the intensive-care area. She led us to a room, and opened the door for us. "Just for a few minutes," she said, and we went in.

Bryan was lying in bed, tubes leading into his arm, looking better than I would have guessed. He had his eyes open, but didn't seem to acknowledge us in any way. I reached him first, and gently bent down to give him a slight hug.

"Hey, Brother, it is damn good to see you," I said.

I pulled back slightly, and thought I detected a slight smile, though I couldn't be sure. I looked at him, and then Julie, and felt a tightening in my throat. Humans I have spoken to who are in touch with their emotions have told me that's a precursor to crying, but I can't speak from personal experience. I certainly wasn't going to hang around there and find out.

Fortunately, I had something else to do. "I gotta go to work," I said, and turned and left.

"We have fought the good fight," Edward Holland said as media cameras rolled, "and we are still fighting. We are not going to let the water our children drink, the very air that they breathe, become instruments of harm. Not on my watch."

They cheered him, all ten thousand of them. It was by far the largest crowd ever assembled in Brayton, and Holland had them eating out of his hand. But he knew that was about to change and the cameras would capture that as well.

"But we are going to do it the right way, the Brayton way. Yes, we have lost the battle in the courts, but there are many more to be waged, and we will win more than our share. That I promise you."

The cheers became louder, raining down on him. Alex Hutchinson stood behind him on the podium, smiling and nodding in agreement, though she had no idea what was going to happen next. Holland had debated whether to tell her in advance, but decided she might choose to sabotage it.

"There has been far too much violence, and our side is being blamed for much of it. I know they are false accusations, and you know it as well. But perception is reality, and we must not do anything that feeds that perception.

"I am also concerned for your safety. No, change that. I am *responsible* for your safety. It's a responsibility I will not shirk and I will not delegate. I will do what is necessary, what is consistent with the oath I swore when I took this office, to protect you, the citizens of Brayton."

Holland looked towards the outskirts of the crowd, and saw Chief Brus and his men standing there, waiting. They seemed ludicrously undermanned to get this crowd to do anything, and Holland silently cursed the decision of the Governor not to send in the state police, and the courts to delay issuing the evacuation order.

"We must be law-abiding. We must not trespass on someone else's land, just as we must prevent them from polluting our air and water. We will get our justice, but we will do so lawfully, and safely."

There was a murmuring at that, as the crowd was not sure where he was going but concerned by what they heard.

"To that end, I am directing Chief Tony Brus to help you conduct an organized and peaceful evacuation of this property."

In an instant, the cheers had turned to grumbling and booing. Alex, surprised by what she had heard, was shaking her head no.

"I ask your cooperation in doing this." He motioned to the media cameras. "Let's show the world what Brayton is all about."

Brus and his men slowly advanced into the crowd. They were not wearing riot gear, nor carrying weapons. There would be time to regroup and get all that later, if the situation called for it.

It didn't take long for them to feel the pulse of the crowd, and know that much stronger measures were going to be required.

Holland had lost them, and all hell was going to break loose.

The drive to Brayton should take an hour and a half, so I told Emmit he needed to make it in an hour. Along the way I tried to reach Alex Hutchinson, Edward Holland, and the Brayton Chief of Police, to no avail. They were all at the rally on the disputed land.

If I was right, it was Ground Zero.

When I finally gave up on the phone, Emmit asked, "You want to tell me what the hell is going on?"

"The truth? I don't know, not for sure. But I know what I'm afraid of."

"What's that?"

"The explosives and timers that Gallagher did not find in Rhodes's room. According to Gallagher, it was way more than Rhodes could have needed for blowing up guest-houses or cars.

"And I think there's a good chance that the detonations are going to be tonight. Rhodes was supposed to be on a plane out of here at nine o'clock. I'm thinking that he was waiting to make sure that everything went the way it was supposed to and then he'd leave."

"Then what's the target?"

"The land where the drilling was going to take place."

"Why there?"

"I don't know that, but I do know that there are a hell of a lot of people on that land right now."

Emmit thought for a few moments and shook his head. "It doesn't ring true for me," he said. "What would the companies gain by killing a lot of people? They just want the natural gas."

I nodded. "You're right about that, but just because we don't see the reason doesn't mean it doesn't exist. Very little of this has made sense from the start."

"Then why do you think that's the target?"

"Well, I couldn't understand why Rhodes would have diagrams of the land; there seemed no reason for him to need them. But do you remember when we showed the diagrams to Frank Lassenger?"

"Yeah. What about it?"

"He knew exactly what he was looking at, but one thing didn't seem right. There were markings on the map to show where the drilling should take place, and Lassenger thought they were in the wrong place. That he would never drill where those markings were."

"Damn . . . ," Emmit said, realizing.

"Exactly. If I'm right, those markings weren't showing anyone where to drill. They were showing Rhodes where to place the explosives."

Emmit stepped harder on the gas, and we went faster than I would have thought possible.

As evacuations go, this one was a loser.

With Alex Hutchinson exhorting the people from the podium to disregard Holland's plea, and to resist the police efforts, Brus was having no success in getting the bulk of the people to leave.

After twenty minutes of cajoling by the police, perhaps eighty percent of the crowd remained, and showed no inclination to depart. Most of those who did leave were parents with children, uncomfortable about the turn things had taken.

Holland directed Brus to take stronger measures, but Brus was trying to talk him out of it. "These people are not being violent," he said. "You want me to teargas them?"

"I want you to do whatever is necessary. Once they see we're serious, they'll leave."

"These are not the LA riots, Mayor. We don't have a court order, and there is no reason to risk injury, to the people or to my officers."

"That is your opinion, but mine is the one that matters. I am giving you a direct order," Holland said.

"And I am refusing it. You want to move them out, do it yourself."

With that he turned and walked away. The conversation between them was caught on camera, and not by accident. Brus had orchestrated it; he wanted the voters of Brayton to see exactly what the Mayor wanted to do, and especially his heroic resistance to it.

Brus walked the grounds, ordering his men to the perimeter, an act that was greeted by cheers of triumph from the protesters. It had gone exactly as planned, so well that he didn't even think the Mayor would have the political capital to fire him.

Holland, realizing the police would no longer do his bidding, sought out Alex Hutchinson. "Alex, we need to get these people out of here."

"No, we don't," she said.

"Yes, we do," said Lucas Somers.

It was seven thirty, and Tommy Rhodes had planned to be on a nine o'clock flight.

If I was wrong, we had all the time in the world. If I was right, we could be minutes from disaster.

"Alex, listen to me. I have reason to believe that explosives were planted all over this property, placed on timers. The strong likelihood is that it is programmed to blow at any minute."

"You too?" she asked.

"No, not me too. I have no dog in this fight. It's not my problem, and I basically don't give a shit what happens to this land."

"Thanks," she said.

"But I care what happens to these people, and what happens to you. And right now, standing here, I care what happens to me."

I was waiting to hear her reaction, and trying to figure out what I would do if she wasn't convinced. There was no way Emmit and I could move these people out ourselves.

We could try and bring in the New York State Police,

but the Governor had already refused to act. In any event, it wouldn't be possible to accomplish it on a timely enough basis.

She was honest about it. "I don't know whether to believe you."

I nodded. "I understand that. And if I'm wrong, then the downside is you'll all leave this area for a few hours and then march back in. But if I'm right, then the downside is incalculable."

She didn't answer, just thought about it some more, so I said, "The time to do this is right now. Not in five minutes. Right now."

She turned and walked away, towards the podium. She got up there, took the microphone, and said, "Listen to me, everyone. This is important."

She said it a few more times, and waited while the crowd quieted and turned its attention to her. "The state police have told me that they have reason to believe it is dangerous for us to be here. They've asked that we walk down the road a bit while they check the place out."

There were some shouts of surprise and resistance, as the people tried to decide whether Alex had gone over to the other side. "I believe them," she said. "Once everything has been cleared, we can come back; Lieutenant Lucas Somers has promised that. Come on, my friends, safety is the reason we are here in the first place, so safety comes first."

Some people started to gather their possessions, and Alex said, "You can leave your things here; we'll be back in a little while. This is just a precaution, but it is an important one."

While she was talking, Emmit had gone over to the Brayton Police. He apparently persuaded them to re-engage; Emmit can be a powerful persuader. They walked back among the crowd, helping them to move quickly and orderly from the area, where Alex had gone to lead them down the road.

As they walked off, Emmit and I stayed in the back to round up any slow movers, and in twenty minutes everyone was off the property. It seemed like a lot longer.

I wasn't sure what a safe distance would be, but this wasn't a forced march to Bataan. There were elderly people and children in the group, and there was a limit on how long a walk they would tolerate.

We stopped at about a half mile, and I called Barone, explaining the situation and asking him to pull whatever strings necessary to get the bomb squad out here.

I saw Edward Holland trying to mend fences with the people, but it seemed like he was going to have his work cut out for him. He kept explaining that he was only concerned for their safety.

It was a claim that had far more credibility a few minutes later, when the world exploded.

I'd never seen anything like it.

Well, maybe in the movies. We were half a mile away, and the ground shook so hard I was sure it was going to open and swallow us. The flashes of light, maybe three or four of them, were so bright that for those brief moments it seemed like daylight.

The crowd started to panic and run away from the explosion, though their flight was brief. Within seconds that seemed like months the blasts stopped, and peaceful darkness settled in. Sounds of children crying could be heard; I suspect each of them had some serious therapy sessions ahead of them.

Edward Holland was standing next to me. "My God . . . ," he said, which pretty much summed it up.

Alex Hutchinson came up and asked, "Is it over?"

I nodded. "I think so, but there's no way to know for certain. Make sure nobody goes back there."

"That won't be a problem," she said, and started walking towards the crowd. She stopped, turned, and said, "Thank you." Then she went and started comforting people, trying to calm them. The police were doing that as well, and Holland joined in.

People started leaving, though I assume their cars were destroyed in the blast. In thirty seconds Brayton had become a community of pedestrians.

Emmit and I waited for the bomb squad to arrive, and we told them what we knew, basically the type of explosives that had been used and the fact that they were detonated by timers. Remote detonation seemed unlikely, since Rhodes was no longer around to have done so.

When we got in the car, Emmit said, "I guess you were right."

I shrugged. "It happens."

I called Julie at the hospital, and asked her how Bryan was doing.

"He's drifting in and out of consciousness; at least that's what they're calling it," she said. "I prefer to think of it as sleep. They said it will last awhile."

"Does he know you're there?"

"I don't think so."

"What about the prognosis?" I asked.

"Too soon to know. But the first forty-eight hours are key; at least that's what they're telling me."

"You going back to the hotel?"

"I think so," she said. "The nurse promised she'd call me if he wakes up, and it's only ten minutes away. What about you?"

"I'm staying there until Bryan is Bryan," I said.

"Me too," she said. "How did it go in Brayton?"

"I assume you haven't been near a television?"

"No, I've been in Bryan's room."

"It was fairly eventful," I said. "Turn on the TV when you get back to the room."

I saw Emmit smiling at my characterization of the evening.

"What channel?" she asked.

"Trust me, it won't matter."

We made plans to meet for an early breakfast the next morning at the hotel. We'd go to the hospital together from there.

I got off the phone and Emmit said, "I'm going to head home tonight. I want to see Cindy."

"Emmit, there's nothing I can ever say to you that—"

He interrupted me. "Man, I haven't had this much fun in a long time."

I laughed. "Glad I was able to cheer you up."

As we were getting back to the hotel, Emmit asked, "Who do you think was behind it?"

He was referring to the massive explosions; we both knew that Rhodes was paid help.

"I think I'll let the Feds worry about that," I said. "It's been a pretty long day."

I got back to my room and got undressed. When I emptied my pockets, I saw that there had been an e-mail on my BlackBerry that I never opened. It was from Bryan, and it said:

Good-bye, Lucas . . . take care of Julie.

I love you both.

And then I did something that I hadn't done in many years, probably not since Bryan and I were in grammar school.

I cried.

My cell phone rang seventeen times during the night.

After the third call, I kept it in bed with me, so I could check the call waiting. I didn't answer any; they all seemed to be Manhattan numbers, and I assumed they were trying to get me to do interviews on the events in Brayton. I was only going to answer if it were Julie or Bryan calling, but that didn't happen.

I woke up, showered, and was five minutes away from going to meet Julie when she called. "He's coming out of it," she said.

"I'll be right down."

We drove to the hospital, and that made for probably the only time I've felt things were awkward between Julie and me. I didn't know what she was going to do regarding her marriage, and I wasn't about to ask her. I'm not even sure that she knew.

The truth was that I didn't even know what I wanted her to do. I loved her, and I wanted to be with her. I had been denying that to myself for way too long. But I also wanted Bryan to have whatever it was that Bryan wanted.

I decided not to show Bryan's last e-mail to Julie. He

asked me to take care of Julie when he thought he wasn't going to be around. Now that he was alive and hopefully well, he'd probably feel differently.

I figured it was too much to hope that Bryan met a great woman in the bomb shelter and they were engaged.

We got to the hallway outside his room, and a nurse greeted us with, "Doctor should be here soon, but he's doing very, very well."

At the door, Julie and I looked at each other before going in. I said, "One at a time?" She shook her head and said, "No. Together."

I was shocked at how good Bryan looked. More important, he was alert and smiled when we walked in. It's amazing what access to oxygen can do for somebody.

Julie went to him and hugged him, delicately because he still had tubes attached. She laid her head on his chest and kept it there for a while; she might have been crying, but I couldn't tell for sure.

"Hey, babe," he said, softly.

She lifted her head, and dried her eyes. She laughed a short laugh, and said, "Hey."

I walked over and put my hand on his shoulder. "You made it," he said. His speech seemed a little off but not too bad.

I nodded. "Thanks for hanging in there."

"I knew you'd make it. But I knew you'd be a pain in the ass and wait until the last minute."

"Hey, I've got a lot on my plate. I had to fit you in."

He smiled. "I'm going to want you to tell me everything that happened, OK?"

"I will," I said. "Now I'm going to leave you guys alone; I'll be outside."

It was about forty-five minutes later that Julie came out. I stood up, and she came over and put her head against my shoulder, and hugged me. As always, I didn't have the slightest idea what she was thinking, or what she was going to say.

"Bryan and I are going to try and make it work," she said.

I didn't know how to answer that, so I said nothing.

I'd been saying nothing for a really long time, so I was used to it.

If I had to be doing interviews, I'd have preferred the *Today* show.

Instead, I had two Federal agents at my office when I got in. They had more hair than Matt Lauer but not nearly as much personality.

They were investigating the violence in Brayton. Edward Holland had been calling for Federal or state intervention for days, but it apparently took blowing up half the state to make it happen.

I was a key to their investigation, because I had been the one who realized what might happen that night. It was fairly easy for them to know that, since TV cameras had been at the site and captured everything.

The speeches of both Holland and Alex Hutchinson before the explosion had been playing in what seemed like an endless loop on television, and I had my share of airtime as well. I'm sure that both Holland and Alex were being subjected to the same type of interrogation as I was.

I had no reason to hide anything from them, until I came to a realization midway through. While they were investigating the explosion and murders in Brayton, they had not tied it in to Judge Brennan's murder. They still thought that was solved, and that Steven was guilty.

I'm not sure why I didn't enlighten them; I probably would have if they asked directly. It could be that I was paying back Barone for all he had done for me; I knew that Barone would want a head start in a reopened Brennan investigation, and I was giving him that. I also knew that Barone would want to manage how the information got out to the public that I shot the wrong guy.

I also realized in the moment that I had been through so much that I wanted a shot to get to the bottom of it myself. Bryan went through his terrible ordeal, Emmit was shot, and Chris Gallagher was killed. I wanted to find out who was responsible for all that, and I wanted to do one other thing.

I wanted to get justice for Steven Gallagher.

So I told the agents that I had learned about the Brayton situation while investigating the Brennan murder, but making it sound as if it were peripheral to that. And for a long time I had believed it was, while I was intent on lying to Chris Gallagher, rather than finding the truth.

When the agents left, I went in to see Barone, and told him that, for the time being at least, we had a head start on the renewed investigation into Brennan.

"Now these are the kinds of conversations I like," he said.

"I thought you would."

"So where do we start?"

"In Brayton," I said. "That's where it begins and ends."

"So what is your ass doing here?"

I finally had time to approach the investigation my way.

Without the horrible clock ticking on Bryan's life, I was able to analyze the Brayton system more logically and dispassionately. I did what I always did on a case. I wrote down what I knew, what I didn't know, and why.

And then I went for a drive.

The only people who could be said to have come out of the carnage as winners were Edward Holland and Alex Hutchinson. Holland had constantly tried to protect his citizens, and it was manifested in his constant pleas for outside assistance, and most profoundly in his ordering his police chief to do whatever was necessary to remove them from a dangerous situation.

He risked unpopularity by doing so, but when he was proven right he became a political hero. He was already being talked about as the leading candidate for the open US Senate seat, and he was milking the publicity every chance he got.

Alex Hutchinson was in a similar situation, and her story was even more appealing. She was a mother protecting her children, protecting the children of an entire town, and she stood up to incredibly powerful forces arrayed against her.

Not only that, but she succeeded where Holland and the police had failed; she got the people to move off the land before the explosion. I certainly couldn't have managed it, and neither could the local police.

With Holland moving on to a Senate bid, there was talk of drafting Alex for Mayor. Since there hadn't been a contested mayoral election in Brayton in twenty years, it was hers for the taking. She had also been doing some interviews, but not as much as Holland.

So Alex was my first stop when I got to Brayton. She was at her normal spot behind the cash register at her diner, but that was the only thing that was the same as my last visit. It was so crowded that I had to park down the block, and there was a line stretching out the door of people waiting for a table. Even if Alex did not become the Mayor, she was already parlaying fame into financial success.

I worked my way through the line and went up to the register. She brightened when she saw me, and said, "What brings you back here?"

"My job," I said. "Got a minute?"

She looked around at the madhouse that was the diner, and I thought she was going to ask me to wait. But she called over one of the waitresses and asked her to watch the register.

Alex smiled. "Our regular table seems to be taken. Want to take a walk?"

"Sure."

We went out the back and walked towards a small park, with a children's playground, a couple of tennis courts, and not much else. But it was a nice day, and I liked being around Alex. I figured things could work out between us, if she weren't married, with two kids, and living in Brayton. Oh, well.

"You're pretty famous," I said.

"As are you."

"So are you going to be Mayor, or continue fighting Hanson over the land, or both?"

She seemed surprised. "You didn't hear?"

"Hear what?"

"They're saying that most of the explosives were planted underground, down some of the holes that had already been drilled. It caused like a small earthquake."

"So?"

"So I'm not an expert, but it changed the whole picture. It might have made it too expensive to get to the natural gas in the shale. Either way, it will set them back at least a couple of years before they know for sure."

I hadn't heard that, and I said so. "So you've won, with some help."

She nodded. "Not the way I wanted to win, but I'll take it. That poor guy that was killed that night was right."

She was talking about Chris Gallagher. "What do you mean?"

"He told me that nobody was going to drill on that land, and that we should leave when the police told us to. You think he could have planted the explosives?"

"No, Alex, I don't. I knew him pretty well."

"Oh," she said. "I'm sorry."

We walked some more, and I said, "Alex, I want to ask you a question. But first let's reduce it to simple terms. Your side wanted the drilling stopped, and the other side wanted to drill. OK?"

"OK."

"So it would make sense that someone on your side would have planted the explosives, to stop the drilling."

She shook her head. "Nobody on—"

I interrupted. "Don't get defensive; I'm not making

accusations, I'm just thinking logically. Your side benefited from the explosion; there's really no doubt about that."

"OK . . . ," she said, warily.

"So why would they have been set to go off when there were all those people on the land? It could have been a catastrophe for your side, and the other side certainly gained nothing from people dying."

She thought about it for a while. "On the news they said it was set with timers. So maybe when it was set, they didn't know the people would be there. Maybe they didn't want the people there when it went off."

I didn't say anything, because she had just made me see something I hadn't seen before.

"Does that make sense?" she asked.

"Probably more than you realize. One more question . . . why did you listen to me and ask the people to leave? The Mayor had just said the same thing, yet you didn't listen to him."

"I trust you."

The next stop on my Brayton reunion tour was Edward Holland.

I called him in his office, but he had left early, having done a round of TV interviews that apparently left him too tired to do any Mayor stuff.

I said that I was there on important police business, and they contacted him and I was told I could come to his home.

He lived on a large estate on the outskirts of town. It wasn't ostentatious, but was very comfortable, and certainly nicer than any other homes I had seen in the area.

He greeted me himself, and invited me into the den. If there were any feminine touches in the house, I hadn't seen them, and I asked if he was married.

He shook his head. "Who has the time?" he asked, smiling. Then, "So what is this official police business you're here about?"

"The Daniel Brennan murder."

He smiled. "Haven't we had this meeting already?"

I nodded. "Right. But that's before I knew you were responsible for it."

He almost did a double take. Here we were, talking like buddies, and all of a sudden I was accusing him of murder. "What the hell are you talking about?"

"Here's how I see it. You arranged the sale of town land to Carlton and Tarrant Industries, the secret foreign company that you set up and own, using the tricks you learned in your law practice. Then you paid off Michael Oliver to report that there was a fortune to be made from the shale under the ground, when in reality that wasn't the case."

Holland was smiling, not afraid at all, but nor was he showing any of the outrage an innocent man would be showing.

I continued. "You handled the legal case yourself, going to Federal Court, even though that wasn't the smart way to do it. But you needed Carlton to win, so you paid Brennan off when it seemed he might be on the court. I don't know how you got to him, but you did. And then he probably changed his mind, so you had him killed.

"Then you killed Oliver, and Carlton, and Rhodes, so that no one would be left who could implicate you. Actually, I should say that you had William kill Carlton and Rhodes. And all the time you were committing acts which would logically be blamed on the townspeople."

Holland was not saying anything, just pretending to be amused by it all. He may have been worried that I was wearing a wire, and I wish I were. Because I was one hundred percent certain that I was right.

"Then you arranged for the massive explosion on the land, which would cover up for Oliver's fake report. But you didn't just want money out of this; you also wanted fame and power. So by acting to save the townspeople, you'd become a hero, and shoot up the political ladder. Which is exactly what happened."

"This is all fascinating, but I've had a long day. Is there any chance you can prove any of this?

"Not yet. But I will. All I have to do is find William."

"Let me tell you something, Lieutenant. This is a fantasy which you will never, ever come close to proving." And then he smiled a cold, confident smile. "And you will never find William."

"We'll see about that," I said, but it may have been the most empty words ever spoken. He had obviously disposed of William and he was right; I would never be able to pin any of this on him.

"Be careful, Lieutenant. You've got such a great career ahead of you."

I left; I had no more empty threats to make. Holland was a multiple murderer, and I wasn't even including Steven Gallagher. He was also now wealthy beyond belief, and was very likely to be elected United States Senator.

Not exactly a triumph for justice.

When I got back to town, I went straight to Barone's office.

He had a right to know two things: the identity of the man who had Judge Brennan killed and the fact that we were never going to be able to arrest him.

He believed me on the first part but not on the second. "We can nail the son of a bitch," he said.

I shook my head. "No chance. Everybody with knowledge of it is gone; there is nothing to connect him to it."

"We'll find something."

"No we won't."

"Then let's turn it over to the Feds," he said, surprising the hell out of me. "We'll tell them Steven Gallagher wasn't the perpetrator, and that Holland was behind it."

"Go ahead and do it, but they won't buy it, and won't be able to make the connection. The guy is about to become a major player in national politics; they won't go near it unless the case is clear. And it couldn't be further from clear. Holland played it brilliantly."

"But you're sure?"

"I'm sure. I was sure before I talked to him, and more sure afterwards. He as much as confessed to me."

"I'm bringing in the Feds."

And he did. I wound up doing two more intensive interviews with two different sets of agents. This time I told them everything, and found that all four agents had two things in common: their taste in suits and their obvious skepticism about what I was telling them.

Three weeks later Barone used his contacts to find out where matters stood, and was told that the investigation had been closed for lack of evidence.

Holland was off the hook.

Julie and Bryan seemed to be doing pretty well.

I couldn't be sure of that; it's hard to know what is going on in someone else's marriage. They had me over for dinner one night, and everything seemed comfortable and normal, and I even think I was glad about that.

Physically, Bryan was really coming along, and by all accounts was impressing the hell out of his doctors. His speech was still slightly off, though I think only those who knew him well could tell. And he complained of vision issues in his left eye, though nothing that affected his day-to-day living.

He hadn't gotten back to work yet, but hoped to do that within a month to six weeks. He was already keeping track of goings-on in his office from home, which meant he was getting back to normal.

Julie had taken a couple of weeks off, but was now back full-time, since Bryan didn't need care during the day. We had lunch once, which was also comfortable, at least until they served the coffee.

"We never talked things out," she said.

"No sense starting now."

She laughed. "I knew that's how you'd react, Luke. So I won't make it too painful. I've loved you for six years, I love you now, and I'll always love you. But I also love Bryan, and he's my husband. That counts for a lot."

"I think you did the right thing," I said. "I hope you guys are happy."

She leaned over and kissed me on the cheek. "Thank you."

That was sort of a "moment" for me, and it turned out it triggered other moments. But the immediate effect was to put an end to the mind dance that I had been doing with Julie for years, whether or not she was dancing as well.

It was over, finally and officially. She was my sister-in-law, my brother's wife, and that was going to be OK. I was never again going to let it be anything other than OK.

So I went home and had my other "moments," possibly even large enough to be called epiphanies. It was time for me to get on with my life outside of work, maybe even settle down. Up to that point, settling down had meant a relationship that lasted longer than the NBA play-offs, but I was going after more than that. Maybe even kids. Why not?

I would even give serious thought to moving out of the area. Despite the fact that it seemed like there was a murder every twenty minutes, I liked the feel of a town the size of Brayton. There must be similar towns all over the country, maybe even nicer and more friendly, that could use a Chief of Police.

But the moments were not all upbeat. I couldn't get the Gallagher brothers out of my mind. I thought about Steven for obvious reasons; I was responsible for his death. I couldn't mentally erase the look on his face just before I shot him; the pain he was in was palpable. I believe I was defending myself; I just wish there had been somebody there to defend him.

My feelings towards Chris were more complicated. What he did to Bryan was horrible and inexcusable, but from the first time we talked it irritated me that I understood him. I should have been more angry; I should have wanted to rip him apart.

But I didn't, and on some level I even identified with him. I respected his sense of justice, bizarre as some might find it. And I have to say I envied his connection to his brother. I wish he could have accomplished his goal and gotten real justice for Steven.

I still had the things that Chris had left me, that he found in Rhodes's room. I had forgotten about them, and hadn't turned them over to the FBI. I figured it didn't matter, since they had dropped the ball anyway.

I came to a decision, gradually I guess, and didn't really crystallize it in my mind until close to eight in the morning. I called Julie, and Bryan answered the phone. He sounded better than I had heard him since the rescue.

We talked briefly, and then I told him that I wasn't going to be coming over that night, as we had discussed. I had been planning to bring in dinner, but I said that we'd have to postpone.

"Julie will be disappointed," he said.

"She'll get over it."

"Last time you canceled dinner on us, all hell broke loose."

"I remember."

"You working tonight?" he asked.

"Sort of."

"OK . . . take care of yourself, Brother. Maybe we can spend some time alone one of these days. Maybe fishing, or whatever the hell you real men do."

I laughed. "I'll check my real-men magazines and come up with some ideas."

We got off the phone, and I got dressed.

The Associated Press was the first to report it.

These were the initial words across the wire:

Edward Holland, the Mayor of Brayton, New York, was killed in an explosion in his car in front of his home.

It was the latest in a series of murders that has rocked the small community, and it puts a violent end to a promising political career.

The police have not taken anyone into custody and are asking people with information to call and report it. The explosive used is believed to be the same as in the previous bombings, a very powerful munition called C-245.

Steven Gallagher had gotten his justice.

And I had crossed the line.

Read on for an excerpt from David Rosenfelt's next book

WITHOUT WARNING

Coming soon in hardcover from Minotaur Books

The dam broke at three AM, four hours after the storm hit.

Fortunately, only the North dam was affected, leaving the other two intact. Had they been breached as well, the eighteen thousand residents of Wilton, Maine, would have been former residents of a town that no longer existed. The destruction came as a surprise to everyone, especially the engineers that had certified all three dams as "low risk" just eighteen months before. Certainly Hurricane Nicholas was a powerful storm, but no more so than others that had struck the area in recent times.

But the dam completely came apart from the pressure and flooded the areas in Wilton it had sworn to protect. As the least important dam of the three, this meant that three streets on the outskirts of Wilton were flooded and badly damaged, as was Heritage Park and the town's small, private airport.

The only citizen to lose his life was seventy-three-year-old Warren Williams, who suffered a heart attack during the chaotic evacuation process. He was flown to Bangor Hospital, but was pronounced dead on arrival.

   The people of Wilton were resilient, and there was no doubt they would bounce back from the storm damage. It would cost money, and would take time, but the citizens of the town whose charter had been ratified in 1848 made plans to persevere and overcome.

   Of course, they had no idea what was coming.

I have a lot of anniversaries.

I try not to pay attention to them, but sometimes it's hard. Dates are everywhere, from the TV when you switch channels, to the front of cellphones.

March thirty-first is my birthday. January fourteenth is the day that Jenny and I were married. September seventeenth is the day I joined the force. April first is the day I was promoted and officially became Chief Jake Robbins. My real name is Jason Robbins, but how Jason became Jake is a puzzle my parents have never adequately explained.

August seventh is the day Jenny was murdered; I try not to change channels or look at my cellphone that day.

Of course, there are some events whose anniversaries I don't even know. For instance, I have no idea when my old friend Katie Sanford introduced us to Roger Hagel, the guy she would eventually marry. Nor do I know the date that Jenny and I first went out with them on a double date, although I do remember that we went bowling and then to dinner.

While I know the date Roger murdered Jenny, and even know that it happened at three in the afternoon, I don't know the date he was convicted, nor the one two years later that he was murdered in prison. I do know that I discovered their affair on June nineteenth, but I don't know exactly when it began.

I was tempted to leave Wilton after it happened, but I never took any action towards that end. I had the job I always wanted, more good friends than I could ever need, and was living in a town that I loved.

What I didn't have was Jenny, but no matter where I went, she would never be with me. Roger Hagel saw to that.

Pretty much everything in Wilton reminds me of Jenny, but that's okay. I want to remember her, the good and the bad. Especially the good.

So I stayed here in Wilton, and life went on.

They were heady times for the *Wilton Journal*.

It's a long accepted fact that the media, be it electronic or print, prospers in the face of disaster and tragedy. For example, in the days after 9/11, not too many people were tuned into *I Love Lucy* reruns; they were watching CNN.

So for the *Wilton Journal*, Hurricane Nicholas was quite literally the perfect storm. While it would be a huge event in the life of the town for months, it wasn't much more than a blip on the national scene. The hurricane was only significant national news for forty-eight hours. And Wilton was just one of many areas to be greatly affected.

So if anyone in or around Wilton wanted to know what was going on, the *Journal* was the place to find out. Circulation was up seventy percent in the two weeks following the storm, and the paper's website reported a six hundred percent increase in traffic.

And by all accounts, the *Journal* did a terrific job. Under the leadership of publisher Katie Sanford, it presented the facts accurately and concisely. It also covered the human interest side of the disaster quite well; the reporters stepped up and wrote with a professionalism not usually associated with small town papers.

Each morning at seven AM, there would be a meeting of the ten reporters working the story. The paper actually only employed five full-time reporters, but freelancers were called in and put on what they called "temporary permanent" assignment, at least until the storm story had run its course.

One of the staff reporters, Matt Higgins, also held the title of managing editor under Katie. He chaired the meetings, sometimes with her present, sometimes not. She liked to give him some autonomy, though he always briefed her fully on the sessions that she missed. When Katie was going to attend, she sometimes held the meetings in her home, helping to preserve the family feeling she liked to cultivate among the staff.

Disaster emergency teams will often talk about the gradual move from rescue to recovery, and it was the same for the *Wilton Journal.* As the crisis lessened, the stories naturally gravitated towards the recovery effort, which was going to be a long-term proposition. The damage to the affected areas was severe, and though federal money was sure to be appropriated, it would still take quite a while for Wilton to be whole.

After Katie missed a morning meeting about two weeks after the story, Matt came in with his typically comprehensive update, running down the assignments he had given out. "We're starting to scrape," he said, grinning.

The meaning was clear; they were running out of stories. "What did you come up with?" she asked.

"More human interest stuff, continuing to follow our people." They had focused on a few families particularly hard hit, providing daily updates on how they were coping. "A few more pets have been found; those stories seem to play."

Katie nodded her agreement.

"And someone brought up the capsule," Matt said. "It's right in the flood area; the thought was it might not have been watertight, since no one could have expected it. It's never flooded there before."

There had been a tradition in Wilton, literally since the town was founded, to bury a time capsule every fifty years. It included artifacts from its day, but the main focus was on predictions by prominent townspeople about what life would be like fifty years hence, when it was opened again. The newspaper always supervised the process, and got a bunch of stories out of it. The last capsule had been buried four years earlier.

"Is there any way to test for that?" Katie asked.

Matt shrugged. "I guess just dig it up, and if it's intact, bury it again."

She smiled. "Or let our grandkids open the thing and find it's a soaking mess."

He laughed. "There is that option. Who's going to care either way?"

She thought about it and shrugged. "Might as well dig it up and take a look. You can write about it."

"Me?" he asked, clearly not pleased at the prospect.

She smiled. "I sense a Pulitzer."

For reasons that were mostly contrived, Matt put off the mini-excavation for a few days, until Jenny reminded him that if the capsule were really suffering water damage, delay might only make it worse. He prevailed upon a local construction company, already up to its ears in work, to spare a couple of guys for a few hours to do the deed.

They went out to the scene, along with Matt and a staff photographer, Jimmy Cueto. They brought maps to show them the exact location, but that proved to be unnecessary, as the plaque that had been placed there was still intact. It was near the small airport, but no one would be bothered by any noise from departing or arriving planes. It would be a while before the airport runway was functional again.

The workers had brought heavy equipment with them, but soon decided that the muddiness in the area would make that unnecessary. The capsule was supposed to be buried only five feet deep, and ordinary shovels would make short work of it.

As the two men started to dig, Jimmy positioned himself alongside the hole, so as to get a shot of the capsule when it was first visible.

"I hit something," one of the workmen said, as a signal for Jimmy to get ready.

Matt walked over as well, and the next thing the workman said was, "What the hell is that?" Then the other said, "Oh, my God."

Both men clawed their way out of the hole, leaving a clear view for Matt and Jimmy. But Jimmy didn't take the photograph.

First he dropped his camera.

And then he ran.

I didn't get many calls from Katie Sanford.

We'd had plenty of contact with each other the last few years, both because of our jobs and because Wilton is too small a town to expect otherwise. But our history is such that we weren't likely to be hanging out together very much.

The ironic thing is that Katie and I dated in high school, going so far as to get "pinned." I don't think boys give graduation or fraternity pins to girls anymore, but I can't say for sure. But our being pinned had meant to us that we would always be together, a commitment which lasted until we left Wilton for different colleges.

But her call this time was not to reminisce. "You need to come out here right away," she said. Her voice sounded tense, maybe even frightened.

"Where are you?"

"Out near the airport, where the time capsule is buried."

"What's going on?"

"We found something. You might want to bring some forensics people with you."

We only have one forensics team, and they were out

checking for prints at a robbery scene. There had been some looting in the storm's aftermath, a sorry but seemingly inevitable reflection on the human condition. I left instructions for them to get out to the airport ASAP. Katie wasn't the type to issue false alarms; if she said they needed to be there, it was a good bet that she was right.

I was there within ten minutes, and as I pulled up, I saw three parked cars, one of which I recognized as Katie's. I got out and tiptoed through a still-muddy area to where she was standing. I recognized one of her reporters, Matt Higgins, standing with her. There were two other people there as well, wearing mud-stained work clothes, and another man with a camera. I'd seen all three people around town, but didn't know their names.

They were standing near a hole in the ground, which I assumed was where the capsule was buried. It seemed freshly dug, which explained the two shovels lying on the ground nearby.

Nobody bothered to say hello to me. Katie merely pointed in the hole and said, "Look in there."

So I did, and immediately saw the bones. They were human skeletal remains, though they were broken up somewhat, possibly as a result of the flood waters. "Shit," I said, because I am at my most eloquent in a crisis.

"Tell me that's an animal," Katie said.

"Wish I could. Everybody needs to clear this area, and then we have to talk."

We went back to where the cars were parked. I waited to start questioning until the forensics people showed up, because I didn't want to be interrupted. Katie, of course, had been right to say we'd need them.

I called the department's lead detective, Hank Mickelson, and told him to come out to the airport right away. Basic math said that two people conducting the interrogations would cut the time in half, and since Hank would be very involved in the upcoming investigation, he needed to be there at the beginning. We would be doing the questioning at the station house, but I wanted Hank to get a feel for the crime scene.

The forensics people arrived first, led by Danny Martinez. Danny is sixty-eight years old, three years past retirement age, but in those three years no one has had the guts to point it out to him. The list of cowards includes, among others, the mayor and me.

Danny is six foot four, two hundred and seventy pounds, which makes him more suitable to defensive tackle than forensic scientist. But that's not what intimidates us. Rather it's the fact that he's been doing it for forty-five years, keeping up with every new advance along the way, and is better than any three people we could get to replace him.

And he knows it.

"Talk to me, Chief," he said when he arrived. It's the first thing he always says.

"Human bones in that hole, sitting on the capsule." We were walking towards it as we talked, stopping about twenty feet from the hole.

"Entry and exit?" He was asking me how we'd approached the site. Our footprints would have damaged evidence along the way, so he would want to approach and exit the same way, thereby reducing the contaminated area.

"Doesn't matter," I said, and pointed to Katie and the others near the cars. "A group meeting preceded me."

He frowned and nodded. "Okay. I'm on it."

He was in effect dismissing me, his boss. He was telling me that I could go do whatever it was I do, because the site was now his domain. "Okay, keep me posted," I said, asserting my authority. "And Danny . . . nothing else matters."

We went back to the station to conduct the questioning and get the statements. I had Katie and the two workmen go with Hank, while I took Matt and the photographer with me. We'd reverse it when we got back; I would question the people in his car, and he'd debrief those in mine.

Neither of us would talk about the situation while we were in the car, since each person on the scene would be isolated from the others when the interviews began. I expected that the only ones who'd provide any significant information would be Katie and Matt, but one never knows.

One thing was certain; this was not shaping up as just another day at the office.